The Winter Child

BOOKS BY CARLY SCHABOWSKI

The Ringmaster's Daughter

The Watchmaker of Dachau

The Rainbow

The Note

All the Courage We Have Found

The Secret She Kept

The Postcard

CARLY SCHABOWSKI

The Winter Child

bookouture

Published by Bookouture in 2024

An imprint of Storyfire Ltd.
Carmelite House
50 Victoria Embankment
London EC4Y 0DZ

www.bookouture.com

ISBN: 978-1-83790-898-1
eBook ISBN: 978-1-83790-897-4

I would like to dedicate this book to all my readers who have made it possible for me to be an author! Thank you all so much!

But I would like to mention one reader in particular, Jessi Doerhoff, who told me that one of my books gave her back her love of reading. I am truly honoured that I was able to do that for you – it makes being an author all the more gratifying.

PROLOGUE

4 January 1994

Each year the old man received a letter. And each time it said exactly the same thing – *you are going to die.*

There was no return address. The stamp on the envelope was sometimes from Germany or Poland, sometimes France or England. Always on the same date – 4 January – for the past five years. Why, he never knew. The day meant nothing to him, but in those first years of receiving the letters, he had taken them seriously. He had shown them to the local police, he had looked over his shoulder and avoided dark alleys and strangers.

But, as his birthdays came and went, he found himself taking the letters less seriously. It was the feeling, he supposed, that came with that sort of age, the age when you knew you were already on the downward trajectory towards the grave, such that the threat seemed less ominous and more of a fact. Yes, he knew he would die. And yes, he knew it would most likely be sooner rather than later, especially considering the amount of alcohol he drank and the number of cigarettes he smoked.

Eventually, he found the letters an amusement and desperately wished that he could reply to the sender and explain that he was becoming an old man, and that death was no longer the frightening event it had been in his youth. Now, it was almost welcome.

Yet, as he sat drinking his morning coffee, the latest letter bothered him, despite his best efforts to ignore it.

Who could it be? And why?

Suddenly, from outside, he heard the cry of a child – perhaps in pain, perhaps the normal whimper of a youngster who wants something they cannot have. He did not know the difference. But the cry unlocked something in his mind.

'Please let them go!' The woman's voice was deep within his memory and then began to resurface, surrounding him in that moment. She screamed and cried, then fell to her knees in the snow. The memory was hazy at best as if a grey cloud shrouded most of it, but the smells, the sounds, all of these were visceral.

In this memory he stood on a darkened snow-laden street. His feet were cold, and he could feel the sting of the air on his cheeks.

The woman was still screaming. There was a child in his arms, crying. He could smell the freshness that a snowfall brings; he could hear a car's engine in the background, ticking over, waiting for him and the child.

He did not wish to stay with this memory – a memory that had sat dormant for fifty or more years. He needed it to stay out of focus and locked away. He would not turn it over in his mind again.

Now, outside, all was quiet. The child wasn't crying any more. The memory, too, had dissipated.

He sipped at his coffee, glad that the memory had left him. But then his eyes caught upon the letter once more.

The woman crying.

A child in his arms.

You are going to die.

This time he heard the words – the same words that had been written in the letter. But this time the words were not written. They were said aloud. Spoken in a voice he knew – in his own voice. Words said on a street. In the dark. With the cold of winter deadening the night, leaving no sound to drown out the woman's screams.

You are going to die.

ONE

IRENA

Zakopane, Poland
1 January 1994

The ground in the graveyard was too hard to begin with. The men with spades hacked at the soil with such force that I thought the metal of their shovels was going to break. They took off their thick winter coats, rolled up their sleeves, shoved cigarettes into the sides of their mouths and, with crinkled brows, kept on at it, clearing the top layer of iced grass, then the underlayer of dirt.

Beyond them, the Tatra Mountains were hidden in amongst stodgy grey clouds that swirled menacingly with the promise of more snow. Hidden high up amongst them, the lakes would be covered with a dense layer of ice that made me think that anything trapped within its depths must surely be dead.

The grave should have been dug before the frost arrived, but the priest, Ojciec Paweł, had been in Kraków for a conference with similarly robed priests, their golden crosses shining against the black of their attire as they spoke of the hungry and the poor, and of a new Poland now that the Berlin Wall had fallen and democracy, apparently, had been restored.

I couldn't have given a fig if he hadn't been here to oversee the digging of my husband's grave, but Mateusz had been devout and friends with the hawk-faced priest, so who was I to say how and when his grave should be dug?

There was a rumble from the mountains, and I looked to see if there would be a sudden fall of snow, but there was nothing. I wondered for a moment if one day there would be a huge avalanche that would wipe out the town, perhaps taking me with it before I could finish what I needed to do.

Michal, one of the diggers, stopped working. 'Deep enough, I think.'

Paweł shook his head. 'Do you want the body to come up as spring arrives? Dig deeper.'

Then he turned his attention to me. 'You don't have to stay, Irena. You can go home, get warm. I will make sure everything is in place for tomorrow.'

I shook my head. 'I will stay,' I told him, delighting slightly that the cold was bothering him more than me as he danced from foot to foot to keep warm.

'I don't want to make you ill,' he said. 'You are not much younger than Mateusz.'

'And yet I do not need to dance to keep warm,' I noted.

He pretended not to hear me, as he always did, and began to talk to Michal about the ground, of his meetings in Kraków and his belief that he would soon be promoted within the Church.

The priest's comment annoyed me more than it should have. Of course, I was old, not much younger than the priest, and yet I did not feel it. And I did not want to be spoken to as if I did not know my own body.

It's not easy getting old. I remembered my mother telling me that when I was just forty. She stood at the stove, her hands crooked with arthritis, stirring at a broth for my father, who lay not more than a few feet away, his breathing laboured, his face the colour of a rotting apple – pale yellow, with flecks of brown age-spotted skin.

The broth wouldn't help him – we both knew that – but she continued painfully stirring it, telling me how I would one day feel those same aches and pains as she did, and I would wonder where my youth had disappeared to.

She was right, of course. It sneaks up on you like a stray cat in the night hunting for its prey, finally getting you. I can't remember the day I became old. I am sure it was gradual, but it seems to me that one day Mateusz and I were picnicking at the foot of the mountains in summer, throwing off our clothes and jumping into the lake to cool off, and then, suddenly, he was gone. I was dressed in mourning black, and my knees and legs refused to move as quickly as I wished them to.

And yet, in a strange way, I had been waiting for this day for some time. For years. Nearly fifty of them in fact. And now the day had come, Mateusz was gone, and I could finally do what I had thought about every day and night since my early twenties.

I had worried that Mateusz would outlive me, and I would never get this chance. It is a terrible thought, one that I chastised myself for, and never admitted during confession to Paweł. It was my guilt to bear, I did not need forgiveness. But I needed my husband to die before me, before I grew too old, before my bones stopped working altogether. I was lucky – fate, God or whatever one believes in took him peacefully in his sleep from a heart attack.

It happened just as I was wondering if I would ever get the chance to put things right, before it was my time to be lowered into the cold ground underneath the watchful eye of the mountains.

TWO

IRENA

Zakopane, Poland
2 January 1994

The following day three of us stood in the graveyard, the priest Ojciec Paweł, me and my best friend, Anna.

The snowflakes that fell were so thick that I childishly itched to stick out my tongue and feel one melt in my mouth. Mateusz would have done that, I thought, as the priest mumbled a prayer, shifting from one cold foot to the other. Mateusz would have danced in the snow, would have laughed and delighted in the cold of winter. That was his way his whole life; he loved it – every moment of it, every change in the season, every meal, every drink. He loved life enough for the both of us. He kept my mind busy all these years so that I would not dwell on the past, would not feel the pain that those years had caused.

I felt Anna's hand in mine, her fingers squeezing my skin. The priest had finished and was staring at me.

'You wanted to say something?' he prompted with a hint of irritation in his voice – he was cold and wanted to hurry this along.

'I—' I started, then felt a catch in my throat. Anna squeezed my hand again, giving me the courage I needed to continue. 'I just wanted to say that I loved my husband very much. I could not bear him children, and for that I still feel terrible guilt. But he was a good man – he loved me despite my shortcomings. He loved me and I him.'

The words I spoke were not those that I had rehearsed over and over again. Those carefully practised words, those which I wanted to be able to say, were to tell him how I had delighted in how he brought me flowers from the garden, how those days we spent on our long walks, getting lost, sitting under the cool shade of mountain pines would soothe my soul. I wanted to tell him that he had brought me joy, brought me a semblance of peace that I knew I would never have found without him. And yet, my words in that cold graveyard were hollow, almost formal, and spoke neither to his character nor what he really meant to me.

The priest had already closed his prayer book and was making his way hurriedly out of the graveyard towards the street, where I knew he would seek out refreshment in the Stamary Hotel bar, warming himself up from the inside with strong vodka.

'Come, let's go back.' Anna gently pulled me away from the dark gaping hole in the ground, where the gravediggers were already heaping on the soil they had dug up only the day before. It was a thankless task, I supposed, removing something only to have to put it back again, but I wondered if they thought of what they were covering up – someone, somebody.

My husband.

The walk home took almost twenty minutes. The streets were not quiet; instead, they bustled with tourists, their skiwear too bright for this day of my husband's funeral. We passed a couple, a man wearing a lurid lime all-in-one outfit, his sunglasses covering half his face even though there was no need of them unless you were high up on the slopes. He spoke a language I did not know, and I suddenly itched to yell at him – to tell him that I had just buried my husband and his presence on this street was not welcome.

I didn't, though. Of course I didn't. I kept on towards home, having to walk down Zamoyskiego Street, the small hotels, bars and restaurants lit up inside with a welcoming orange glow, their sloped chalet roofs capped with snow. I tried to remember if it had always been this way – full of strangers, tourists here in the winter for the skiing, then back in the summer for the climb into the mountains and swimming in the lakes. I supposed it had. But it seemed now that there were more new buildings than old, that there were more and more faces that I did not recognise, that even in shops I felt less and less at home. Or maybe this feeling was upon me not because of the popularity of our town, but because I no longer had Mateusz.

Anna and I turned onto the rutted track that led up to my house – a home I had lived in as a child, then once more with Mateusz when my parents died. I still loved this house. Although only set back from the road by a few metres, it felt a little detached from the rest of the street. Pines grew thick and wide, obscuring the front door so that no one really knew that it existed. It was, like many others in the town, built from wood, with sloping slate roofs that hung low over the windows. In the summer I would make sure that hanging baskets full of red and white begonias decorated the porch, and the pink and cream rose bushes that encircled the small patch of lawn in the front were tended to daily.

Looking at it now, though, I felt tired. Would I be able, or would I even want to make sure it looked nice in summer again? Would I still enjoy sitting on the porch, reading a book, listening to the birds as they sang?

'Irena.' Anna had opened the door and was already halfway inside. 'It's cold. Come in.'

As soon as I was inside, the skin on my hands began to scream with pain – the heat was too much for their almost frozen state.

Why had I not worn gloves? Why hadn't Anna? I was about to ask her the question, but she was already pouring us both a tumbler of vodka, and talking about our plans.

'I have the passports ready and the tickets, so you don't have to worry about anything. Just rest today and then get up in the morning, and we are ready to go.'

I thought it ironic that it was Anna giving me instructions for what to do, seeing as though I had planned the whole thing. Indeed, I had planned it for *years*; but now it was finally going to happen.

I sat down in my chair next to the fire that was burning its way to ash, and threw on another log. The predictable crackling and hissing it made as it met the flames comforted me.

Anna sat across from me in what had been Mateusz's chair. We had a matching pair we had bought during our third year of marriage. I could still remember the excitement of that day – how we had finally saved enough money to buy something brand-new for our home, instead of the hand-me-downs that littered our small cottage. We had chosen these chairs specifically for us to sit next to the fire together in the winter evenings – they were both stuffed with horsehair, royal blue with tiny white flowers stitched into the material.

We could not afford for them to be delivered, and I remember how angry I had been, how embarrassed that we had bought the chairs and now would have to save more to get them home.

But it had not deterred Mateusz at all, and he had made it fun. Together, we carried one down the winding streets of Zakopane, summer in full swing, the heat causing trickles of sweat to stream down my back. He had made jokes – 'Ha, look there, Nina,' he had said, using his nickname for me. 'Look at

Piotr! Drunk again, stumbling out of the bar! I saw him last week try and ride home on an old pony that was tied up in a field – you should have seen him!'

The thought of Piotr – a rather large man – trying to heave himself up onto a horse made me laugh, as Mateusz knew it would. And soon we were giggling like schoolchildren as we hefted the chairs one at a time, trying to outdo each other with jokes and gossip.

'Are you all right?' Anna snapped me out of the pleasant memory. 'Do you need to lie down?'

'Of course not,' I retorted. 'I was just thinking, that's all.'

She nodded as if she knew what I had been thinking about. 'Are you nervous about it? Do you think we can still do it?'

I looked at my friend then, properly looked at her, and although lines and creases dug through her skin, although her fingers were swollen and a little bent from arthritis, I could still see the girl from my youth – the girl who had been by my side ever since we were both ten years old, through the war and beyond.

In her youth, she had been a beauty – golden hair, green eyes and a figure I envied. I, on the other hand, was brunette, with dull, almost grey-blue eyes that, in my opinion at least, were far too close together. She had had, and still had, a natural, friendly way about her, drawing anyone and everyone close to her – especially men. I was more reserved, more willing to let her bring people close and only then, once she had completed the hard work, would I open up.

Although, it had to be said, I was the funny one. I was the one who entertained others with silly quips and the random thoughts that would flit through my mind, making people laugh and shake their heads, 'My, my Irena, you are a one-off,' they'd say. I used to take that as a compliment, but now thinking back I was not so sure.

'I'm not nervous,' I eventually told Anna. 'And we can do it. We might be old, but it's time that it happened.'

'But—' Anna began, and I quickly cut her off, knowing she would say what she always had over the years, how we should move on, how we should forget. But I couldn't forget – I wouldn't.

'It's all right,' I told her gently, 'I'll do it all. I always said I would, and I mean it.'

She chewed at her bottom lip and nodded. 'Only if you're sure. Really sure.'

'I am,' I said and leaned back in my chair. 'And I can't wait.'

THREE

IRENA

3 January 1994

The plane heaved its way into the air and there was a brief moment where I thought that the engines had stopped as it seemed to dip slightly towards the criss-cross pattern of the earth below.

Anna was already asleep and did not notice this – the three tumblers of vodka she had drunk at the airport bar would see her gone for the next few hours – so I sat alone, gripping the armrests with such force that my knuckles went from red to white.

But then, my fear suddenly disappeared. I looked at the world below as it became smaller and smaller, soon disappearing behind wisps of clouds. I felt utterly at peace. Seeing from this height the world that I inhabited spread out below me, it made me realise how insignificant I was. If I said this to Anna, she would say that we are all significant and that she was worried about my maudlin brain, perhaps thinking that I was more grief-stricken than I was about my husband's death.

But what I wouldn't be able to explain to her was how that

feeling of being insignificant made me realise that, whatever happened in the coming weeks, it would not matter – not in the slightest. The world would keep turning, and I would be gone from it. But at least I would have done what I had been put on this earth to do before my departure.

A child in the seat in front wedged their head into the small gap between the window and the seat to look at me. I could not tell if it was a boy or girl; all I saw was a squished face and a cheeky grin. I smiled back, glad that the child was having a good time.

The child tried to reach one of their hands round and wiggled their fingers. I yearned to reach out and tickle their skin, to feel what it would be like on my own. Did children at this age still have that lovely soft skin that babies had? I wondered. Or did their skin change? I didn't know, and it would be a strange thing to ask Anna – or anyone in fact.

I sat back and did not touch the child's hand, and they soon tired of the game and disappeared into their seat as we hit a small pocket of turbulence.

I did think about how I would have reacted when I was a child. Would I have loved the experience of flying or would I have been scared? I set my head back against the seat and closed my eyes as the clouds outside thickened, trying to think of who I had once been.

The memories did not come easy – they had been buried for so long, I suppose, under layer upon layer of trauma, of pain and worry. But there, *just there!* I caught a glimpse of a girl, plaits in her hair, wearing a yellow sundress, playing in the barn with a litter of black and white puppies, ignoring the shouts of my mother as she called for me.

But as soon as the scene came to me, it disappeared under a thick layer of grey smoke and a new memory – one that haunted my dreams – appeared.

I opened my eyes and looked around me at all the people on

the plane – some eating, some talking but many, like Anna, already asleep. Although I could hear the whirr of the engines, although my eyes could see that I was no longer in that fraught memory, it would not leave me. I could hear the clatter of plates, the shout from a man, and before I could stop my brain, I was back there, back on that day that had decided my fate.

FOUR

IRENA

Hotel Grand Stamary, Zakopane, Poland
May 1941

In the spring of 1941, Zakopane was no longer the home that we had all known – not the one I had grown up with.

Gone were the days of giggling with Anna on the banks of the Morskie Oko lake, the Tatra Mountains reflected in its glassy surface, weaving daisy chains and imagining what our future might look like. Gone were the days when the streets were busy with folk simply going about their days, with perhaps the most pressing thought being what they would eat for dinner that night. Gone were the throngs of tourists that descended upon us for skiing and spending time on little wooden boats on the smooth waters, perhaps fishing, perhaps watching as their children jumped into the ice-cold depths.

Now, all joy seemed to have disappeared.

German soldiers, Gestapo mainly, had made our town their playground. They descended upon us, filling the bars and restaurants and making us feel constantly on edge, questioning us as they walked past, leaning into our faces with their sour alcohol-laden breath.

'Wer sind Sie?' 'Zeig mir deine Kennkarten!' 'Schnell! Schnell!' they would bark at us as we fumbled, trying to find our ID cards, asking who we were. Then they would walk away, laughing, leaving us standing pale-faced and shaking on the pavement. It was sport to them, I knew, to see how scared they could make us as we simply went to work, or to the shop. And as much as I knew this, and as much as I told myself it was just a game, that I didn't need to be so scared when it happened again, I fell to pieces each time they shouted in my face.

They had also commandeered our two largest hotels – the Palace, recently nicknamed Death's Head Resort, now the Gestapo headquarters, where Jews and dissidents were taken to be interrogated and were never seen again. And then there was the Grand Stamary, a hotel I had recently started working at – a building set back in parklands, a building that I used to look at and admire. I did not any more. It was now where the Standortkommandantur and various other Gestapo personnel were billeted. Not only that, but they had also started to use the basements in the hotel to train Ukrainian soldiers in Gestapo interrogation methods. It was talked about by the staff, but I always turned my ear away. I could not bear to think about what they were being taught, or what was happening at Death's Head, just a few streets away.

I did not want to work at the hotel, and yet I had had little choice in the matter. When my father has said he could get me a job there, I had wanted to vomit. The nerves had chewed their way through my insides so much so that I was sure it was going to kill me. My father had been, until recently, a professor of literature at Kraków University, and since losing his job, the little money that he and my mother had saved over the years had dwindled to nothing.

Yet, I was angry with my parents – although loving, they

had been frivolous with money, and had also treated life as a big game. As a child it had made me nervous when they would suddenly declare that we would be going on a holiday, spur of the moment, with little planning involved. It had been I who had acted like the parent – warning them when money was low, advising them not to spend on yet another holiday when our roof had a leak. It was exhausting. And now, I had to be the parent again.

But I had been lucky so far – as much as one could be lucky in the situation I now found myself in. I hadn't had to interact with the Germans much as they drank the hotel bar dry, singing songs and demanding more food. I just had to help in the kitchen, wash pots and pans and stay out of the way. It was the new girl, Karina, who I felt more anxiety for – a girl who had just recently arrived to serve in the dining room, and whose hands trembled on her first day.

She was petite, with a frailness about her that reminded me of my long-gone grandmother. She barely looked at me, her eyes firmly staring at her shoes, her nerves betraying her before she had even started. I didn't blame her. After two months, I still found it hard to look at the officers we served – their uniforms were unwelcome here, and yet we had no choice.

I tried to keep my voice light as I explained the dinner and lunch times, who she would serve in the main dining room, and if she had to take any meals up to individual rooms.

She nodded along as I spoke, but I wasn't sure she was listening.

'But *you* don't serve in the dining room,' she squeaked at me. 'Can I not stay with you and deliver the room service or just help set up the dining hall before the meals?'

'How old are you, Karina?' I asked, placing my hand on her shoulder. Perhaps I had misjudged her, perhaps she was still a child.

'Eighteen,' she murmured.

'It will be all right, I promise you. And you need the money, don't you?'

She nodded.

'We all do. My father hasn't worked for a year, and my mother can't, so we have to help if we can, don't we?' I suggested to her.

Again, she nodded.

'It will be fine,' I told her and plastered a fake smile on my face. 'You'll get used to it. Just pretend they are not who we know them to be. Pretend they are just customers.'

'How is that even possible?' she whispered. 'How is it possible to pretend? And be kind to them?'

I opened my mouth to tell her, but nothing came out. There was no way to pretend, was there?

For the past year, I had been learning German to appease our captors – pretending for *them*. I hated the language – it felt like marbles in my mouth, all jostling about, taking up the space of my native tongue. Every time I spoke it, even though I knew what I was saying, it felt alien to me, and in my brain Polish words fought to get out instead.

'You speak German, yes?' I asked Karina.

She nodded.

'Well then. That's enough of a pretence. That's all you need.'

My words meant nothing to her, and to be honest they meant little to me too.

There was little time to talk, little time for me to really offer the support to Karina that she so obviously needed, as I was to help Bartok, the chef, with the food deliveries and accounts. I left her to try on her new uniform – a light-grey smock with white lapels. It did not suit her, just made her pale face even more drawn and scared than it was.

Bartok had quickly become a close friend. He was in his

fifties, a large man in both height and width, and no matter the season, his face was always a deep shade of pink.

I loved Bartok. He made me feel at ease in the otherwise strange world that we all now found ourselves living in. It was almost as though he had taken it upon himself to keep the jokes flowing; his face would crease with delight as soon as our laughter reached his ears. I suppose it was what helped him to keep going, keep moving.

'*Irena!*' he called for me, bent double over a wooden crate. 'More vegetables have arrived.'

I went to help him, once more marvelling at the amount the Germans ate. At first, we had provided locally grown vegetables and meat reared from local farms, but we could never keep up with their demands. Now produce was shipped to us, sometimes sent from Germany, but more often than not simply appeared at the rear doors of the kitchen, delivered by a wiry nervous man who smoked so hard on his cigarette that he would burn his fingers.

I did not need to ask whether these goods were from the black market – that was fairly obvious. But what I had asked Bartok the first time I had encountered this thin man and his large wooden crates was why Bartok was going so far out of his way, doing something illegal to help our unwanted guests fill their bellies every night.

'A German is bad enough,' he had explained. 'But one with an empty stomach and an empty wine glass means trouble. They don't care where I get my produce from as long as there is a full menu each night, and their glasses are topped off.'

I could see what he meant, but it did not help the fact that they ate like kings whilst the rest of us in town were constantly scrounging for food, using our ration tickets with care, bartering anything we had for just an extra loaf of bread, or pound of flour.

As I reached Bartok, I saw that the wiry man had been

replaced by someone much younger, with a crop of sandy brown hair that was just a little too long, and a clean-shaven jaw. As soon as he saw me, this someone broke out into a grin, making him even more handsome than I had first thought he was.

Oddly, I felt my face heat up under his stare, and busied myself unpacking the crate.

'Who's this then?' I heard him say with a hint of humour in his voice.

'This is Irena,' Bartok proudly announced. 'She is my right hand. Could not do without her.'

I knew that if I lifted up my gaze, I would find both men looking at me, and I knew I couldn't do it without turning red again at Bartok's compliment and this *someone's* wide smile.

'Does she speak?' the man asked.

'She never shuts up normally,' Bartok lamented. 'Irena, get your nose out of there and say hello to Mateusz.'

Mateusz. That was his name. This man with a smile that had sent me silly in the head.

I stood up and bit the inside of my cheek to make myself think of the pain and not how stupidly embarrassed I suddenly was.

'Irena,' he said, stretching out his arm, his hand seeking mine to shake.

I took it, briefly, barely touching his skin.

He seemed to notice my reluctance and laughed. 'I shall call you Nina. Does anyone call you that?'

'No,' I managed to say.

'Well then, Nina it is. My special name for you.' He laughed again, and I wasn't sure whether he was laughing at me or not, so I grabbed an armful of potatoes and scurried away into the safety of the kitchen.

I could still hear the men talking, and Bartok said something that made Mateusz laugh loudly. I itched to go back and look at his face again, to look properly at it and try to find out why the way he had looked at me had sent me into an embarrassing mess.

'More than usual,' Bartok said as he dragged the full crate into the kitchen with his strong arms.

Mateusz was gone.

'Who is he?' I asked, trying not to sound too excited, organising the potatoes into a row for some reason.

Bartok saw what I was doing. 'They need *peeling*, Irena,' he grumbled. And then, 'or should I call you Nina as well?'

My hands immediately dropped to my sides as I scanned the kitchen for the potato knife even though I knew very well where it was kept.

'Ah no. That's *his* name for you,' Bartok teased, perhaps delighting in how uncomfortable and nervous the brief encounter had made me. 'He'll be back.' He winked at me, then patted my arm. 'Peel those.' He nodded at the potatoes.

As we prepared the food for that evening, my thoughts were not on the task at hand, and although I was enjoying myself with snippets of daydreams – wondering who Mateusz was, when he would be back – and hummed tunes, I irked Bartok as I dropped a slab of butter on the floor and then managed to burn the onions.

As we worked, Anna came to the kitchen door, her face flushed, her smile wide.

'Irena!'

'Anna.' I went to her, a potato still in my hands. 'What are you doing here?'

'I escaped the clutches of my parents.' She grinned at me. 'I can't sit in that house any longer, Irena. It's driving me insane. All they do is sit and talk, then go to the window to look outside as if at any moment they are expecting soldiers to walk up to our door.'

'You never know...' I started.

'I know, I know. Not you too. Please,' she lamented. 'Can I come in? Will Bartok mind?'

'I will mind.' His voice carried towards us. 'Lunch is being served in thirty minutes. Irena hasn't the time to chatter.'

Anna rolled her eyes. 'Fine. Can you see me afterwards?'

I nodded. 'I have something to tell you,' I said, thinking of Mateusz and knowing how Anna would delight in a bit of gossip.

'Good or bad?' She wrinkled her nose.

'Good, I think.'

'Wonderful! Meet me by the pond when you're done. We'll talk.'

I went back to my daydreaming, and it was only when a yell came from the dining room and a terrified and tearful Karina raced through the doors that my thoughts slipped away.

She stood in the kitchen, her eyes red, tears dripping down her face.

'What happened?' I asked her.

'I dropped it,' she stammered, 'I dropped the plate on his lap and now...'

Her words became quickly muddled as the sobs took over her, and no matter how many times I asked who she was talking about, she could not tell me.

'You'll have to go out there.' Bartok was by my side, peeling a shaking Karina out of my arms and towards the pantry, where he sat her down on a stool next to bags of flour.

'Stay here,' he told her, then turned to me. 'You need to go out there, Irena. Find out what happened. Make sure they are happy and take over for a while.'

'But can't one of the others do it?' I asked. I had no desire to serve those men, and my clumsiness was well known – if Karina had dropped a plate in someone's lap, then surely, I would fare no better.

'There's no one – we're short today. You need to go and see.'

Bartok was busy fussing over Karina, whose sobs would not be calmed, and I knew that I had to do it. Just this once.

I entered the dining room to find Hauptsturmführer Christoph Richter standing next to his chair, wiping at his trousers with a linen napkin. I shuddered. I had only seen him a few times – he had been pointed out to me by Bartok as one of the Gestapo heads who had taken up residence in the hotel. His face seemed always to be pointy – *flinty* would be the word. His jaw, his nose, everything seemed to have an edge to it.

'*You!*' He suddenly looked at me and pointed a finger in my direction. I felt a pit form in my stomach as my hands began sweating.

'You! Come here!' he demanded.

I walked over to him, trying not to look at his face, which was puce with anger.

'Do you see what your girl did?' He gestured towards his thighs.

'She's... she's not my girl,' I stammered.

'You're not a manager? Then who the hell are you?'

His voice was so commanding, so guttural, that the chatter from the other officers in the room immediately ceased and I could feel all eyes on me.

'Irena,' I said stupidly, wishing that I had something else I could say – wishing that the ground would open up and swallow me whole.

Suddenly, he laughed. At first, he was the only one, and then the others, taking his lead, began to laugh too.

'Irena!' he guffawed. 'I ask her who she is, and she says, "*Irena*",' he mocked, putting on a falsetto.

I did not know what to do. I knew I wasn't to laugh, but was I just to stand there as they mocked me?

'Fine. Irena.' He stopped laughing and his face was perilously close to mine, so much so that I could smell his stale breath. 'You'll serve me. Just you, and if you make one.

Wrong. Move' – he jabbed a finger into my chest – 'then I can simply make you disappear – just like I might do with that useless bitch that was here before you. Do you understand?'

My legs were shaking, my eyes on his shoes the whole time, stupidly marvelling at how shiny they were, my mind trying desperately not to think about what he was saying, or how close he was to me.

'I understand,' I told his shoes.

'Look at me.' He placed his index finger under my chin and raised my head to meet his gaze. His eyes had no colour. Of that I was sure. Just darkness.

'I understand,' I told him again, and as soon as I did, he began to laugh loudly in my face, spittle landing on my skin, the rest of the officers joining in with the 'joke' once more.

I don't know how I got back to the kitchens. I don't know how I managed to take the plate from Bartok that he had replenished with mutton, potatoes and vegetables. It was as though I was in a dream, and before I knew it, I was back in the dining room, my legs walking towards Hauptsturmführer Richter.

He stood still as a statue. He did not sit at the table, did not wait for me to wait on him. Instead, he stood. Watching me. Waiting for me to fail.

He smiled.

He waited.

I stepped forward. I felt as though my whole body was not my own any more. I could not stop it from shaking. I could feel sweat collecting under my armpits and on my top lip. The closer I got to him, the more I was sure that at any moment the plate would suddenly slip from my grasp, and I would dissolve into a heap on the floor.

'Here she is. *Irena*,' he said and grinned at me, baring his teeth like a wolf waiting for its prey. 'Place it right there, on the table,' he commanded. 'And. Don't spill it.'

As soon as he said those words, laughter rose once more from the other officers, all of them delighting in this game.

'You remember what I said about making people disappear – you don't want to disappear, do you?'

All at once, I thought of all the people from the town who had disappeared – taken away in the middle of the night – and the stories that my father told me of packed train wagons, people made to stand in cattle cars that took them to God knows where.

Bile rose from my stomach and caught in my throat.

I watched my hands as they placed the plate, the meat swimming in gravy, on the table, the liquid threatening to spill over the side.

It was done. I had done it. I stepped back, still staring at the plate of food on the table, relief that I hadn't upset him washing over me.

He seemed almost perturbed that I had mastered this task, and he stood for a moment, looking at me, and then back at his meal.

'Very good,' he said, then sat down.

I made to leave, but he called out my name. 'Come here, Irena, stand by my side for a moment.'

I did as he requested, standing as he shovelled food into his mouth. I can't say how long I stood there, perhaps a minute or more, but time seemed to stretch endlessly on.

He suddenly dropped his knife and fork onto the plate with a clatter, leaned back in his seat and wiped his mouth with the napkin. Then, his arm reached out until his hand was on my behind. He patted it, then finally looked at me.

'Irena, you will serve me every day from now on, is that clear?'

His hand stayed on my bottom, his eyes boring into mine.

I nodded.

'Good, good girl,' he said and patted me again before withdrawing his hand and waving for me to finally take my leave of him.

Back in the kitchen, Bartok asked me how it had gone.

I couldn't answer him. I couldn't answer because suddenly my stomach, which had been twisted with nerves, sent me running to the sink to vomit.

'That bad?' he asked.

'Worse,' I finally managed to say. 'Much worse.'

FIVE

IRENA

Hotel Grand Stamary, Zakopane, Poland
May 1941

I met Anna at the pond after work. Her skin was goosepimpled, her bare arms wrapped around herself. It was our spot – a place where we came to talk or to swim in the summer months when we could not be bothered to make the trek to the greater lakes in the mountains.

It was not as beautiful as those glassy lakes, surrounded by pines and the awe of the mountains. Instead, this pond was surrounded by thick clumps of trees, making the area seem, sometimes, dark and ominous. But it was not far from home and offered us a quiet spot where we could, for a short while at least, disappear.

'How long have you been here?' I asked her.

'I didn't want to go home. If I did, getting out again would have been a nightmare!' She patted the dry grass next to her for me to sit as a dragonfly skimmed the surface of the greening water.

As soon as I did, she rested her head on my shoulder and let out a tired sigh. 'I hate all this, Irena. I mean, here we are in our early twenties, and we are supposed to be getting married, having babies, just living our lives. And instead, I'm like a prisoner in my own home!'

'At least you don't have to work,' I said, immediately thinking of Richter, his hand, the way he had looked at me. I shuddered.

'I'd much rather be working. Do you think Bartok could get me a job?'

I was going to tell her no, absolutely not, and even tell her why, but she was already talking again. 'Doesn't matter. My parents won't let me anyway.' She let out another sigh. Then she lifted her head and shook it, her eyes wide.

'I'm so selfish!' she half yelled at me. 'I am. I mean people are disappearing, beaten and taken from their homes. Those damned planes fly over every day, dropping their bombs all over the country. People are dying, Irena, and I am moaning about being bored!'

'It's still normal to think about yourself, even when everything has gone mad. It's still okay to think like that.'

'You think so?' she asked desperately. 'I don't want to be like those people we know – like the Nowaks, who pretend nothing is happening and still have dinner parties and invite the Germans to them.'

'You're not. We're not,' I said. And again, Richter came into my mind. I hadn't invited him to touch me, but he had. Did that make me just as bad as the Nowaks?

'So, tell me, how was your day? You looked all happy earlier when I saw you, but now your face has fallen.'

I didn't answer. I wanted to tell her about Mateusz, about how I'd had this weird feeling when I had looked at him and I thought that it was attraction. I had never been attracted to anyone before and I knew Anna had, so I wanted to hear what she thought the feeling was. But the whole thing at lunch,

Karina, Richter, had doused any joy I had felt earlier, any flutter of excitement.

'You all right?' I could feel Anna looking at me. 'Something's wrong, isn't it?'

I wanted to tell her that, yes, something was very wrong. But I was afraid that voicing my fears, turning them into words and letting them escape my mouth, would make it all too real. I mean, it was real. But I don't know – I just couldn't bear Anna's worry on top of my own – I couldn't face that this was all really happening to me. Anyway, what would I say? That a high-ranking Nazi had touched me. That I had done nothing about it. And now I was scared that he would do it again.

No. Keep it inside. Make it like it's not really happening. *Say something funny instead, Irena.*

So, I did.

'Bartok told me a joke yesterday; do you want to hear it?' I asked her.

'Yes, but—'

'So,' I cut her off. 'Hitler visits a lunatic asylum. The patients give the Hitler salute. As he passes down the line, he comes across a man who isn't saluting.

"Why aren't you saluting like the others?" Hitler barks.

"Mein Führer, I'm the nurse," comes the answer. "I'm not crazy!"'

It took Anna a moment, but then she burst into fits of laughter. 'I'm not crazy!' she yelled over and over again.

Although I had not found the joke that amusing when Bartok had told it earlier, I now found myself smiling and, within seconds, laughing along with my friend, enjoying a few seconds of pure joy.

The following day Emeryk, the manager, came to see me in the kitchen and told me that I was now to serve in the main dining room – specifically serving Hauptsturmführer Richter.

'I don't know what you did, but he has taken a shine to you,' Emeryk told me. 'Well done. Do what he asks. Keep him happy.'

'But I—'

Emeryk held his hand up to silence me. 'Keep him *happy*, you understand?'

I nodded, and turned to Bartok as soon as Emeryk had disappeared through the doors. 'I don't want to,' I said, a ball of anger, frustration and, yes, fear all intermingling in my brain, all vying for attention.

'I know.' Bartok wrapped his arms around me. 'But that snivelling manager of ours cares more for them than us. He likes the little extra money they throw his way. A traitor in the making, I would say.'

I pulled away from Bartok's embrace. 'He's hardly a *traitor*.'

Bartok shrugged. 'Anyone who is kind to those monsters for their own gain is a traitor in my book.'

'So, I am?'

'No! You don't *want* to do it. And you gain nothing from it. Emeryk – he loves it. I see him grinning and bowing as soon as he sees them. "Can I help you, sir?"' Bartok put on a high-pitched voice. '"Can I take you to the toilet and wipe your Nazi arse?"'

The more Bartok pretended to be Emeryk, the more I felt my mood lighten, and soon joined in.

'"But please,"' I added in my 'Emeryk' voice, '"Please can I read you a story before bed? Perhaps I can wash your back as you bathe?"'

The thought of our wiry manager, with his glasses steamed up, washing the back of one of the Germans soon had us both laughing.

'You see,' Bartok said once we had both calmed ourselves. 'You'll be fine. You're strong like me. You'll be fine.'

The closer it got to lunchtime, the more my nerves came rumbling back, and no matter how much I tried to amuse myself with thoughts of Emeryk doing silly things for the Germans, the anxiety took over completely.

By the time I had to take Hauptsturmführer Richter his soup, my hands were shaking so much that I almost cried.

He sat at the head of a table filled with men all wearing the same grey-green uniforms, their hats removed and placed next to their plates as if they might have to don them at any moment and rush from the hotel, their black long leather coats hung off the backs of their chairs.

I did as I had the day before. I stared at my hands holding the bowl, told my feet to walk slowly, told my lungs to stop breathing so heavily.

Within seconds, I was there, at the table. I placed the bowl in front of him and once more felt relief that I hadn't spilled anything.

'Ah! Here she is. Irena, wasn't it?' He laughed. 'You did well.' His hand immediately began to roam my lower back, tracking down further until it had found its resting place.

I didn't thank him for the compliment. I wasn't sure I was supposed to. I just stood there dumbly whilst his hand stayed on my backside.

'You know, I hear your father was once a professor,' he said, staring up at me.

I nodded.

'And now you are the only one who works. It cannot be easy for you all?'

He asked the question with such gentleness that for a moment I was thrown off guard. 'It isn't,' I admitted.

'Well. You keep this up. You take care of me, and I will take care of *you*.' He squeezed my bottom. 'How does that sound?'

He didn't wait for me to answer – not that I could – and just slapped my backside, indicating that it was time for me to leave.

Back in the kitchen, I didn't tell Bartok what he had said. I knew what he had meant. I had seen the women of the town accompanying our occupiers to dinner, accepting gifts. I wasn't so naive that I didn't know what they did for these men in return for a few extra ration tickets, or a new dress.

All I did know was that I did not want to be one of those women, and yet how was I to tell a Hauptsturmführer no? And what would happen if I did?

I didn't have long to wait until I found out the answer to my own question. Just before dinner service, I had to go to the foyer to ask Emeryk to come and talk to Bartok about supplies.

I walked across the tiled floor, passing the two sofas that were positioned next to the fireplace. I had never sat on them and sometimes wanted to, sinking into the cream cushions, looking like one of the elegant women who would sometimes wait there as their husbands paid, smoking a cigarette and looking as though they had no care in the world.

The reception desk sat close to the double-door entrance, polished to a high sheen, the brass bell on the counter almost glowing with the care and attention that Emeryk gave to it each morning.

Hauptsturmführer Richter walked through the doors as soon as I reached the reception desk, his face lighting up when he saw me. I immediately wanted to run back to the kitchen, but I was stuck there, frozen to the spot.

'Irena!' he greeted me and broke away from the other man he had walked in with.

As soon as he reached me, he placed himself so close to me that I could smell him – the slight musty odour of his body mixed with cigarette smoke and something else that I could not place, something tangy, something that shouldn't be there.

He traced a finger down my cheek. 'I am so glad to see you again. Tell me, are you glad to see me?'

This time, he waited for my answer.

I could see Emeryk glaring at me from behind the desk, his eyebrows raised in encouragement.

'I-I-' I stumbled over my words.

'Ah, so *sweet*! I make you nervous, don't I?'

I nodded.

'Good,' he said, then leaned into my face, his breath hot on my skin, and whispered, 'I like it when I make you nervous. It's so much more exciting.'

I wanted to push him away from me. I wanted to run and run and just keep going. But I stood there as he whispered, as he pushed his body uncomfortably close to my own, and did nothing.

It was only when he finally took a step away from me that I identified what the unusual smell had been. There, on his shirt that peeked out from his jacket was a shade of crimson that I knew to be blood.

'Well. I've had a busy day,' he said to me. Then he turned to Emeryk, who immediately asked him if he would like a drink in the bar before dinner. 'I'll change first,' he told him. Then he looked at me. 'I'll see you shortly, little one. My little Irena. All *mine*.' He winked at me, then left me standing in the marbled foyer.

I had no choice.

I could not say no.

No didn't matter.

I was his.

SIX

IRENA

4 January 1994

The plane began its descent. A small ping rang out and the seatbelt light lit up above me.

'Are we there?' Anna turned to me and yawned. 'I think I slept most of the way. Did you manage to?'

After changing planes in London, I had grabbed a few hours of uncomfortable sleep – that kind where you can still hear everything going on around you, whilst your dreams mingle in with reality. All my memories of what had happened with Richter during those first few days had haunted me as I slept; that absolute sickness that fear brings, the way that I had no idea what to do – how to stop him from touching me, from seeking me out had made the sleep I had had more tiring than energising. As I woke up, at first, I thought I was back in the past, stuck there in time, waiting for the inevitable to happen – he had wanted me, and as much as I didn't want him, he would eventually get his way.

Anna didn't wait for me to answer but leaned over to look out at the criss-cross of fields below. At first, it was just green and brown, but as we got lower, houses began to emerge, then roads and cars. I thought of the people living their lives; scurrying about, eating dinner, sitting at home. Then my thoughts travelled to the specific people below I had come here to see. One did not know I was coming and the other – well, she did, but she had not responded to my letter.

In just one moment I had forgotten her name. Her father's I knew: Carlos. But he had unfortunately retired and left his daughter in charge. Who was she again?

I reached down to my handbag, wedged under the seat in front. As my hands rummaged inside, I felt the tickle of wool on my skin and thought about drawing out what I had hidden inside, then thought better of it. It wasn't the time to think about that now. Indeed, it would bring me a memory that was so visceral, so haunting, that I rarely allowed myself to think of it. I had to banish it away. I had to leave it locked somewhere deep in my mind, otherwise it would have been impossible for me to survive.

My hands finally found what I was looking for. I drew out the piece of paper I had written her name on.

Sara Martinez

Why hadn't she replied to me? Her father had been somewhat helpful, and I had hoped that his daughter would have taken up the reins of his work in the same way. Yet she had been silent.

'Is that her?' Anna leaned over to look at the names and addresses on the paper on my lap. 'Sara? When will we see her?'

'Tomorrow,' I reminded her.

'And this one?' She pointed to the other name. 'Peter Smith.' She sounded out the name. 'When will we see him?'

'Tomorrow too,' I said. 'He said he'll meet us at the hotel.'

She patted my arm. 'I'm glad you've kept it all straight. I tried to, you know, after Mateusz died. I thought that I could be the brains for once.' She shook her head. 'But you know, it won't keep the information like it used to. Or maybe it never did!' She chuckled. 'You know me. My mind, it just wanders.'

I nodded. Yes, I knew about Anna and the way her mind worked and had taken care to keep track of every piece of information, every name, every address. It was seared into my mind.

'So, they'll help, these two?' she said. 'You think they will? I mean, do we tell them everything or just keep it that we're on holiday?'

'Holiday, for now,' I said. 'Let's see what they're like before we trust them with anything else.'

'Right you are, Captain,' she joked. 'Mum's the word,' she said in English. She had learned the expression years ago. 'No, sorry.' She stopped. 'Not Mum. You know. Just keep it zipped and all that.'

I nodded again. Silence, at least for now.

Although, I thought to myself, as the plane's wheels found the tarmacked runway and we bounced along in an undignified fashion, I couldn't stay silent forever. Nor could Sara. And nor could the other name on the list – the one name scribbled there underneath Sara, Carlos, and Peter. The one name that Anna would not, could not, say out loud, not even after all these years.

I was finally here, and, at some point, we would all have to break our silences. It was time. And the first person I needed to see, the person who would help me find the others, was a man called Peter.

SEVEN

PETER

Pinamar, Buenos Aires, Argentina
4 January 1994

Santiago's bar was not a place that many went after dark.

The bar was in a winding back alley, boarded on both sides by three- and four-storey houses that had been converted into apartments. During the day, their balconies heaved with life, full of potted plants and drying laundry, a barking dog, a child playing, an old couple simply watching the world go by. But by night it became quiet – too quiet, not even an echo of a voice from the apartments, not even the sound of TVs blaring out some God-awful soap opera. It was as though the inhabitants of the street simply disappeared by night and let the stray dogs and cats bump about in the shadows, knocking over steel bins scrounging for food.

It would make most people nervous to walk down such a street, especially the gaggles of tourists that had recently descended on the area, and it was no different for Peter either.

Although he had lived in Pinamar now for over ten years, he

still felt a slight unease at times – his 'otherness' was still in stark contrast to the locals who surrounded him.

His height of six feet five and his crop of blond hair and blue eyes made him stand out as the foreigner, and no matter how much time he spent speaking Spanish, or making friends, he still never felt quite at home as he should.

Sara, his girlfriend of the past five years, had given him some anchor here, and he was sure that one day he would propose and really, truly settle down. But, as he walked down the quiet blackened street, he could not shake the feeling of not truly belonging anywhere.

Even growing up in England he had known he was different. Adopted by a wealthy politician and his wife, he was rescued as a German orphan just after the war, which set him apart from his family. He was never quite right – nothing quite fitted.

But Sara – ah, Sara. She had made things different for a while. The way she cajoled him – even though she was thirty-seven and he fifty-one, she was more of an adult than he ever was, or ever could be. He liked that she cared about him in that way; neither of his adopted parents had ever really cared enough to even yell at him. Even when he had got into that trouble in England – selling stolen goods, not that he had known they were stolen – they didn't yell. His 'father', whom he called Maurice, never Dad, never even Father, had arranged for him to start a new life here with the help of his friend Ricardo.

Peter would have been grateful for the help, but it wasn't really help, was it? He had wanted to come here. He had needed to come—

Suddenly, a cat ran past him, so close that he felt its light paws brush his feet. Startled, he looked about as if more cats would suddenly appear, then laughed at himself. What had he been thinking about? Sara? Yes, Sara.

He needed to do more, tell her more about him. But whenever he tried to tell her about his past, about who he was, the words clogged in his mouth. He would look at her, her wide, open honest face. A woman who knew right from wrong, whose moral code could quite frankly be etched in stone; he felt he couldn't tell her the truth. It would sully her, just as it sullied him.

Besides, if he told her everything, would she still look at him in the same way? Would she still love him? Would she get used to him – the real him – and could they still have a life together?

Irritated by these thoughts, Peter reached up to his neck as a mosquito pricked at his skin. He could not get used to the insects, that was for sure.

As he grew closer to the bar, he could finally hear some sounds of life. A radio played a Spanish song that he did not know, filling the still air with a festival feel, as guttural laughter and the odd shout came from deep inside. They had obviously started without him.

Inside he saw Ricardo, his father's friend, a man he had never heard of until he had organised for him to leave England behind and come to Argentina to start afresh. The old man was as leathery as they come – many hours over many years spent sitting in the sun, drinking and doing little else had left him looking much older than his seventy-nine years.

Ricardo grinned at him, showing nicotine-stained teeth, his skin crinkling into millions of tiny lines as he smiled.

'Come, come sit, Peter!' Ricardo yelled, and Peter knew that he was already half-drunk, his usual daytime quiet demeanour taken over by the effects of his night-time alcohol.

Peter sat at the round plastic table, cards and red, white, green and blue chips scattered on its surface.

Santiago plonked an ice-cold bottle of beer in front of him, then sat next to him and toasted to his arrival.

'Welcome!' Santiago said, then gestured towards the other two players, both laughing and barely looking at their cards.

Although this was what it was always like – less playing the game and more drinking.

Peter raised his bottle in greeting at the two men and then took a deep swig of the beer, letting the icy coolness slip down his throat and the alcohol take its effect on his brain.

'You have had a good day?' Ricardo slapped him on the back and leaned towards him, his smoky breath pungent in his nostrils. 'You are seeing Sara this evening, yes?'

'In an hour, so I can't stay long,' Peter told him.

'You can't be a slave to what women want!' Ricardo responded, then poured a shot of Fernet-Branca into a glass and handed it to Peter. 'You're a man – take control! Do what you want to do.'

A part of Peter wanted to refuse the drink and leave. He wanted to be with Sara. But all the men's eyes were on him now, and he did not want to have to argue with them.

So he drank.

By the time the poker game ended, Peter could not tell the time – every time he looked at his watch, the numbers seemed to shift and move – but he was sure that it was well past eleven.

'Did I tell you,' Ricardo slurred as they walked down Av. Arquitecto Jorge Bunge. 'Did I tell you who I meet all the time at that pool I go to? You know when I go swimming? I see this man and he's worse than me. At least I think so. Worse than me. Accepts my money...'

'Money for what?' Peter asked, his words coated with alcohol.

'Ah you know – my secrets!' Ricardo winked at him. 'Stay with me tonight. We're close to my house. You can't walk all the way back to the beach. Stay with me, and I'll tell you my secrets and I'll tell you his too,' Ricardo continued.

'I can't – Sara,' was all Peter could say.

Ricardo suddenly stopped walking. Peter turned to see him standing under the garish orange glow of a street lamp, and in that moment, the way Ricardo was looking at him, Peter felt something sinister creep over him, but he could not place exactly what the feeling was.

'Go. Go to your woman,' Ricardo spat. 'See if I care. You'll never know my secrets then!'

He watched as Ricardo retreated back towards Santiago's bar. He knew he should go after him and make sure that he got home all right, but he was in no real state to do what he needed to.

Instead, he walked on and thought of secrets – both his and those of Ricardo's.

And for a brief moment, in his addled brain, he truly hoped that was the case.

EIGHT

IRENA

Pinamar, Buenos Aires, Argentina
5 January 1994

The dawn was just breaking as I reached the seafront. I had left Anna asleep in our hotel – a ramshackle affair that sat between more luxurious hotels, and which Anna had lamented over, asking why we hadn't booked into something newer. Cost was one thing, I had reminded her, and of course the fact that we were not here on holiday. Besides, I liked the charm of it; run by a husband, Marco, and his wife, Carmen, for thirty years, it was an old home converted into ten bedrooms that gave us a bed, a shower and a fan, which I had left Anna snoring in front of, tired as she was from our long flight and exhausted from the heat that comes to this part of the world in January.

I was not opposed to the heat and was quite glad of it. I had left behind my home, frozen in winter, and was now standing in a country where summer was in full swing. I did not mind it at all.

I, too, was tired, but I could not sleep – I did not want to miss a moment of this. Standing, watching the sun gently peek up from the curvature of the earth, lightening the sea from a cloudy grey to a deep blue, patterned with pure white of the tips of waves, I felt a calm come over me.

I had been waiting years. I had been patient. And now it was finally here – I was finally *here*.

In that moment, I was not old any more. I closed my eyes and felt the breeze lift strands of hair from my face. I stretched out my arms wide and lifted my head until it found the warmth of the rising sun. I imagined myself young again, with skin that had no mottled brown spots, nor wrinkles and crevices. I was young. I was strong.

A cacophony of caws from a colony of gulls made me open my eyes, and there I saw the morning in all its glory – the burned orange of the sun wakening this country from its deep slumber, the gulls dive-bombing the sea, the waves gently lapping at the shore, dragging themselves away again, leaving soft, wet sand behind.

The thoughts of my days at the Stamary Hotel had not left me, and snippets of memories of Hauptsturmführer Richter kept sneaking their way into my mind. I had tried hard all these years not to think of him –not to think of what had happened – but I supposed it was inevitable that, at some point, I would have to relive those days.

His face sometimes woke me in the night. Sometimes, I thought he was in my room, watching me, waiting for me. The way he would smile at me, touch me, single me out and mock me – all of it made my skin prickle with anger and shame.

I shook my head, trying not to think of the worst that had happened to me. I walked to the shore and let my feet sink into the sand, wriggling my toes, feeling the squelch of it, and it was then that I felt a memory from long ago tug at my brain. I had never been to the beach before today. I had no memories of it, so why did I feel so forcefully that I had?

It was then that it came to me. I had been standing on the

bank, my feet in the water, a thinner silt of sand nestling between my toes. Only it had been mine and Anna's pond. I had stood there trying to think of how I could get out of working at the hotel. Everything had changed – I had changed – and it was then that Mateusz came to me, appearing much like a magician from thin air to stand by my side, letting the cool water soothe us both.

NINE

IRENA

Zakopane, Poland
July 1941

I stood at the water's edge. All around me the thick scent of pines tickled at my nostrils, the warm sun beat a drum on my back, and yet I did not care for any of it. I looked into the water, at the tiny fish that I did not know the name of, swimming and circling the half-buried pebbles and stones, marvelling at how quickly they could swim without once ever bumping into each other.

Very unlike me. If I were a fish, I would be the clumsiest fish. I would knock myself about against rocks, other fish, and probably tangle myself in a throng of reeds. The past few months had, paradoxically, made me more clumsy and more careful all at once. In the dining room, I would sweat profusely, watching my still-nervous hands carry plates, glasses and bowls to the soldiers and officers, and as soon as I had successfully done my job, I would return to the kitchen only to immediately walk into the chopping block, the thick wood knocking and bruising my hip bone. Then it would only be a matter of time until I spilled soup, or chopped my finger as well as the vegetables, leaving a smear of blood behind.

My life within the hotel had become a game – a game that I had no desire to play, and yet I had little choice. I was the mouse, Richter the cat. He toyed with me, played with me, always being sweet, placing his hand on my behind, my arm, sometimes lifting a strand of hair from my face. And my role in this game was to stay away from him as much as I could. I knew he wanted me – he wanted it to go further than this forced flirtation on his part. Perhaps he thought I would warm to him, but every time he touched me or spoke to me, I felt as though I wanted to recoil with revulsion, and I would flinch at his touch. Oddly, this made him more enthusiastic, and I wasn't sure how long I could keep it up – could I really not give him what he wanted? Was I allowed to say no?

I did not hear him approach me. My mind was so consumed with the hotel, Hauptsturmführer Richter and the constant barrage of news about the war that only when he placed his hand gently on my shoulder did I realise that I was not alone.

'You scared me!' I yelled, jumping away from his touch and realising who it was all at once.

Mateusz.

He laughed and bowed his head with apology. 'I didn't want to disturb you – you looked so serene looking out at the water, so I watched you for a while, wondering what my little Nina is thinking about.'

Although I had not seen him since that one day – that one day when Karina had dropped the plate on Hauptsturmführer Richter's lap – the fact that he called me 'his little Nina' sent my heart racing.

'You don't mind that I disturbed you, do you?' His jovial face had taken on a look of concern at my lack of response, and I realised I was standing there simply staring at him. I was sure, too, that my mouth was open like the fish I had just been watching. 'Only I was taking a walk, and I had found this spot before, and I wondered if I could find it again. Secluded, quiet, you know? You don't mind?'

'No – not at all,' I said, trying to inject some enthusiasm into my voice, but instead it came out too formal.

Thankfully, Mateusz did not seem to mind, and smiled at me. 'So, what had you so deep in thought?'

I shrugged. How could I tell Mateusz what I had been thinking about? How I was scared to go to work each day – how Hauptsturmführer Richter would always place his hand on my lower back, sliding it down and making me want to slap him in the face. How I spent so much time hiding from him, never leaving the kitchen, and having Bartok walk me home so that I would never be alone with him so that he could not continue his game with me.

I didn't know Mateusz – there was no way I could tell him my deepest thoughts.

'I just like looking at the water,' I said and wished that it didn't sound so stupid and childish.

He nodded as if he understood, then pointed at the Tatras. 'I prefer the mountains to the water,' he said. 'I like to be up high, looking down on the world. It all looks so different when you are up there – almost like there isn't a war happening – like you are safe from it all.'

I watched him as he spoke, how his face had gone from humour to some kind of wistfulness, how his green eyes scrunched up as he thought about what it was he wanted to say.

He caught me looking at him and winked. 'But then, I am a bit of a dreamer,' he added. 'My *tata* used to say that about me – that I was a dreamer – my *matka,* though, she would say that I was like a wild stallion; couldn't be tamed and wanted to constantly be on the move. Perhaps I'm both?' He shrugged.

I was oddly uncomfortable and intrigued at the same time by the openness with which he spoke. I wanted to offer some part of me – something eloquent to match his words to me – but I found nothing in my head, nor in my mouth, other than, 'I have to go home.'

'Well then,' he replied, 'I shall accompany you.'

As we walked side by side back towards the town, Mateusz kept up a flow of conversation, pointing out Sanktuarium Najświętszej Rodziny, an old Catholic church that I had never been inside, giving some piece of history about it that he said he had picked up somewhere once, but had no recollection of whence it came.

We stopped for a moment outside of the Palace Hotel – a newer building than the Stamary, where I worked. It was concrete, mostly, and did not offer any sort of warmth nor welcome. The smooth grey and white walls and wrought-iron balconies, whilst modern, did not have any charm. In fact, it stood out in the town as something alien – and indeed it was.

'Death's Head Resort,' Mateusz said.

I nodded. I knew the name. I had heard the tales of what happened in there. How people went in but never came out.

I said as much to Mateusz, and then remembered that Jedrzej *had* returned. Physically at least, but perhaps not mentally.

He had been found to be hiding one of his Jewish neighbours in his attic and had been taken – all of this was relayed to us by his wife, Alicja, who had clutched at her husband's hat.

'He doesn't go anywhere without it! He must have it. He must. I have to go there and give it to him,' she had wailed.

My mother had stopped her. Grabbed her by her arms so that she could not move.

'But I have to give him his hat. I *have* to!'

I couldn't understand at the time, why this hat was taking up her thoughts, but later that night my father had told me that in a moment of terror, of complete and utter fear, our thoughts become rambling torrents.

'Imagine a waterfall, Irena,' he had said. 'Imagine all that water gushing from a precipice, tumbling, rambling down, each drop bashing into the next. That's what her thoughts are like now. She cannot distinguish one drop from the other.'

As much as I was glad that he had given me this analogy, I was also annoyed – I would never be able to look at a waterfall again without thinking of Alicja screaming for her husband and wanting to give him back his hat.

The days that he was gone, no one spoke of it. No one dared. It was as though if we voiced our fears, our presumptions of what could have happened might come true.

Yet none of us knew the complete terror that Jedrzej had gone through – we could only guess when he was released after a week, his face a swollen, purple, blue-and-black bloodied mess. Even his hands were swollen with bruises. Once a tall man, he seemed to have shrunk – he was bent almost double as he and his wife shuffled home – and I could not help but notice the dark stain on the back of his trousers; not just wet, but stained crimson.

I must have shuddered with the memory, as I felt Mateusz gently take my upper arm and pull me away. 'It's best not to think about it,' he murmured as we walked. 'I have heard what happens there. It will give you nightmares.'

We walked in silence for a minute or two, then wishing to break away from the thoughts of Death's Head, I tried to act normal – act as though we were simply two people going for a walk, and there was nothing to be afraid of.

'I don't remember seeing you around before,' I said, trying to inject some lightness into my voice. 'Where do you live?'

He shook his head. 'I'm not from here. I came from Kraków.'

'To work?' I asked, wanting him to tell me more about who he really was before he disappeared for a time again, only to perhaps return at the kitchen doorway with more supplies for Bartok.

'Have you been to Kraków?' he asked, instead of giving me the reply I so wanted.

'Never,' I told him. 'I've hardly been anywhere. My parents are from here. I like it here.' As soon as I said those last words, a black car with the tiny flags of the Reich flapping on its bonnet drove past. 'I *liked* it here,' I corrected myself.

I saw him look to the car and, for a brief second, almost imperceptibly freeze to the spot. 'Come, let's get you home,' he then said, and began striding ahead of me as if he knew where I lived.

When we reached my parents' home, I found out that he did know where I lived. In fact, he knew much more about me and my family than I had thought possible.

Before I even had the chance to open it, my father must have seen us approaching the door and it swung open, revealing him in his tatty brown jacket that he so loved and which my mother hated.

'*Mateusz!*' my father greeted him, with an outstretched hand, and guided him into the house, leaving me bemused on the doorstep. How did my father know Mateusz? What was going on?

I followed them inside and found them both already in the sitting room, my father in his wing-backed chair, which he had brought back from his teaching days in Kraków, and Mateusz perched on the edge of the mustard-coloured sofa.

'Has it been decided?' my father was asking him, then, realising I was in the room, made a downward motion with his hand as if telling Mateusz not to answer him.

'Irena, you have already met Mateusz? My former student!'

I looked to Mateusz then back to my father, and before I

could ask what was going on, my father instructed me to go to the kitchen to get some refreshments.

I didn't argue with him – there was no need to. I knew my mother would be in the kitchen and I also knew that she would tell me everything that was going on without hesitation.

I found her shelling peas at the sink, her sleeves rolled up to reveal her thin forearms. She was a tiny woman, delicate, a dancer in her youth; she had managed to cast a spell over an older university lecturer, my father, who had got her pregnant as soon as the wedding was over.

'To keep her close to me,' he had said to me once. I understood what he meant – she was a beauty and he was a slightly overweight balding man, and the thought of her in Kraków, dancing at night as he waited for her at the stage door, had obviously been too much for him to bear.

Not that it had bothered my mother at all. She had delighted in moving permanently to my father's holiday cottage in Zakopane and relished the thought of bringing up hordes of children in the countryside. But alas for her, only I arrived – those other babies simply did not want to come into this world. In this moment in time, I oddly envied their decision.

'Matka,' I said to her back, making her turn round. She immediately grinned at me and dropped the remaining peas, unshelled, into the sink.

'You met him? Mateusz? I met him before your father was fired a year or so ago. A nice boy, isn't he? Handsome?'

Her words tumbled excitedly one after another out of her mouth – she got like this whenever something new happened; almost a childlike response, just like her childlike frame.

'Matka, what is happening?' I asked, trying to get her to stop babbling about how handsome Mateusz was. 'I met him at the hotel, and then again today. He brings food to Bartok, so why is he here? Visiting Father?' I suggested.

'Oh no! Much more than that, much more!' she almost

shouted, then, containing her excitement, stepped close to me and whispered: 'Your father and I are going to help.'

'Help what?'

'The resistance of course!' She raised her voice once more, then went back to shelling peas as if what she had just said was an everyday occurrence.

I shook my head, realising that once more I had to be my parents' parent, the voice of reason. The pair of them could so easily get carried away with things – once they had bought a horse because they had read a poem one evening that had spoken of horses' beauty; neither of them knew a jot about how to care for a horse. And yet it came, and with my twelve-year-old's voice, I explained to them that they couldn't just leave it in the garden and that it needed much more than they could give it. Within a day, the horse was gone.

'Matka.' I tried to cut through the tune she was now humming. I knew of the resistance, I wasn't stupid, and I knew of what Mateusz might be involved in, but this was not a romantic notion – it was not one of the stories from Father's books that he would talk about to his students, this was real life, and neither of them had any real clue of the danger.

She ignored me and continued her tune. '*Matka*,' I said more harshly, making her turn, looking at me with a sad expression.

'You're going to say we are being stupid, aren't you?' she asked. 'Well, we're not.' She tried to draw herself as tall as she could, stretching her neck so that I could see the throb of her pulse below her skin. 'We've thought about it and talked about it. The couriers need help – all sort of things. Education is one, and your father has offered to help teach some former students, and Mateusz says that they are starting to move people across the mountains now, not just food and weapons, so it seems right that we help too.' She finished her speech, and I couldn't help but feel that it had been rehearsed in order to placate me.

'So, you are going to trek across the mountains, are you?' I half laughed.

Her face reddened. 'No. If you must know, we are going to have some guests stay with us,' she countered. Then her eyes went to the floor. 'Well. They have to stay in the basement, but I can make it comfortable for them.'

I realised then what she meant. That she and Father were offering to hide people in the basement until Mateusz or some other person came to help them escape across the mountains. It had been done before – a family we all knew had hidden an old Jewish man in their home, a man who hadn't been able to leave before the Germans threw out all the Jews; and now the family were gone, as was the old man.

'Are you *mad*?' I shouted at her. All the frustration that I had felt with my parents over the years was finally being expressed. 'You both live in a *dream world*! I had to get a job because neither of you had any money left as neither of you saved anything over the years – always buying things, always going to the theatre – and now look! Do you have any idea what it's like, Matka? Any idea at all? Just because the soldiers here treat this place as their own holiday camp, it doesn't mean that life here is shielded from what is happening. Don't you remember what happened to Jedrzej? Do you want that to happen to you and Father?' I thought of telling her then about Richter, about the risk I took each day going into that hotel, but I stopped myself. I had run out of steam.

I sat at the kitchen table staring at the wood grain, trying to figure everything out in my mind. I was sure other parents were not like this. I knew from Anna that her parents were so scared by everything that they barely left their home and would not let Anna go out unaccompanied. But my parents – it was like they lived in an entirely different reality.

Suddenly, my father appeared in the doorway and, sensing that the rehearsed speech had not been to my taste, patted me absently on the back. 'We're doing something good, Irena. Can't you see that? This is something we can do...'

I didn't want to hear his reasonings – as sound as they might be – I just wanted for life not to be like this any more. I didn't want to be groped at the hotel each day, I didn't want to hear the stories about what was happening in the cities, I did not want to see soldiers every time I walked down the street, I did not want to see the shadows of planes in the sky. I just didn't want it. None of it.

'You're tired from working so much,' my father insisted. 'That's all it is. Once you get some rest, you'll see that what we are doing is a good thing and no harm will come to us. You'll see.' He patted me on the back again and retreated from the kitchen.

'He's right,' my mother agreed. 'I'll make you supper and then you need to get some rest. It's your day off and you need to sleep and then we will talk again tomorrow.'

Wearily, I pushed myself up to stand. Instead of making my way upstairs to my tiny bedroom, I headed for the front door and stepped out into the sunlight, hoping that the fresh air would take away my fears and worries.

TEN

IRENA

Zakopane, Poland
July 1941

It was noble of my parents to want to do something – I, too, wanted to do something, had wanted to for a long time. Ever since neighbours began to disappear, and the Palace Hotel became known as 'Death's Head Resort', there had been a stirring inside me that we couldn't just sit here and do nothing. Yet, the swarms of soldiers that patrolled the streets, the Gestapo officers, the trucks, the guns – it made everyone, including me, lose their nerve. What could we do? How could we stop this? I couldn't even stop Hauptsturmführer Richter from touching me.

'Lost in your thoughts again?' Mateusz asked, appearing once more.

'You're like a ghost, you know.' I turned to look at him. 'You walk so softly I never hear you.'

He seemed to like the compliment and flashed me a wide smile. 'I practise,' he said. 'You're not happy,' he continued. 'You don't want to help?'

I shook my head. 'It's not that, it's just my parents – well – they just do things without thinking and—'

'They'll be all right,' he interrupted. 'I know your father, and I know what he can be like. But he has a good heart. So does your mother. That's all that matters.'

I had never heard a man speak the way he did – so open, so honest – and for a moment I wasn't sure how to respond.

Mateusz did not seem to notice my hesitancy and pulled out a packet of cigarettes, offered me one and, when I refused, lit one and dragged on the tip. 'I was a great skier,' he said. 'Still am. In the winter I worked on the slopes with the tourists, you know, showing them how to ski.'

He waved his hand with the cigarette in the direction of the mountains, and I could see how his eyes had taken on the kind of light that Father's got when he saw a new book.

'You love it,' I said.

'I do.' He blew out a plume of smoke. 'That's one of the reasons I do what I do now – there's a few of us who know how to navigate the mountains and get things in and out.'

'And people,' I added.

He nodded. 'And people.'

'Are you not scared?' I asked.

He shrugged. 'I was at first. But then my mother and father were taken, so...' he trailed off and shrugged again as if that explained everything.

'Where were they taken?'

'You know. When you're up high and you look down on it all, it doesn't seem so bad. Maybe that's why I like it,' he answered as if he had not heard my question.

I didn't ask again. I knew that so many people had been arrested and never returned home. I knew about the ghettos for Jews. I knew that no matter if you were Polish, Jew or gypsy, no one was completely safe.

'It must be nice. Seeing the world like that, as if nothing is happening.'

'It is.' He flicked his cigarette, and we both watched the orange tip burn out.

'I have to tell you something,' he added. His face was a sudden blank page, and I felt a churn in my stomach that something was wrong.

'It's about Karina – the girl who worked with you at the hotel?'

'She's gone,' I told him.

'I know. The thing is, she was last seen going into Death's Head.'

As soon as he said the words, it was as though my stomach dropped to my feet. I felt cold all over, and yet I had started to sweat.

He took a step towards me and placed his hand on my shoulder. 'It was her father first – he was working with the Gestapo, finding the jewellery and money some of his Jewish neighbours had hidden. But he tried to stop, tried to get out of it, so they took him. And then a few days later, they took Karina.'

'It was Richter, wasn't it?'

He narrowed his eyes with confusion. 'Richter?'

'He's at the hotel – lives there. Karina spilled something on him, and he told me if I didn't do well, I could simply disappear. He said it, that he could make people disappear.'

My breathing was coming faster, my heart pounding in my chest. What had they done to Karina? How had they tortured her, had she got free? What had happened?

'Breathe, just breathe.' Mateusz's grip on my shoulder tightened. 'Listen to my voice and just breathe.'

I tried to listen to his words, I tried to let them soothe me, but my thoughts were coming too quickly, all merging together, imagining what could have happened to Karina and wondering if it could happen to me too.

'I-I-' I tried to talk, but my breathing was too fast. I felt cold and sweaty at the same time and knew that if I didn't calm down, I would pass out.

'Listen to me,' he said, sterner now. 'Watch me. In, out, in out.' He placed a hand on his chest and emphasised his breathing so that I would follow suit.

After a few minutes, my heart returned to a somewhat normal beat.

'How are you feeling? Are you all right?' he asked.

'I think so...'

We stood staring at each other, neither of us speaking, just breathing, in and out, in and out. Just looking at his face made me calm, made me feel as though I were completely safe. It was such an odd feeling to have when I barely knew him that my face betrayed my thoughts and I blushed.

He grinned at me as if he knew what I was thinking, then took a step back and broke the spell. He lit up another cigarette and dragged deeply on it. 'I don't know about Richter,' he told me. 'I'll find out, though. You see him there every day?'

'Most days. I have to serve him his meals. Me. No one else.'

'You need to be careful—' he started.

'I can just quit – I can just leave,' I interrupted him. 'I'll just not go back.'

He shook his head sadly. 'Nina, there's no way out for any of us. If you're right and this Richter wants you and only you, he won't let you go.'

ELEVEN

IRENA

Pinamar, Buenos Aires, Argentina
5 January 1994

He won't let you go.

Those were Mateusz's words. If I had known then what I know now, I would have been braver – I would have at least tried to get away from Richter's grasp in those early days. Because, of course, Mateusz had been right – Richter would not, and did not, let me go.

Thinking back now to that life seems absurd in itself. The normality of eating breakfast, cleaning the house, working, as at the same time all around us there was danger on every corner, in every aspect of our lives, and yet we carried on.

I remember that not so long ago, Anna had made me go to the cinema with her to watch some sort of American horror film. Throughout the film, Anna had gasped and grabbed at my arm, scared, as someone with a knife and a mask terrorised pretty young women. Afterwards, as we walked home, she had asked me if I had been scared.

'How could I be?' I had asked her. 'That wasn't horror.

Horror is the constant unknowing in a life that seems normal but isn't.'

She hadn't understood me, so I had tried to explain my thoughts to her. 'Think about it, Anna. The only thing that was scary in that film was the not knowing – the constant worry, the constant anxiety of what *might* happen or what *might* be behind the closed door. As soon as you see the monster, it becomes less scary, because he is ridiculous.'

'But Richter,' she had reminded me. 'He was our monster, and we were afraid of him – even when we saw him, we were still afraid.'

I didn't have an answer to that. She was right. But at the same time, I still thought it was the not knowing what he would do next, what would happen, that made me more scared of the eventual things that he did to us both.

The sun had firmly set its place in the sky, and I left my maudlin thoughts on the beach and headed to the hotel for breakfast. Anna had finally risen and had secured us a nice table on the terrace so that we could look out at the scenery and enjoy the warmth of the summer heat as we ate.

'Did you see they have eggs?' She immediately asked as I sat down and perused the menu. 'I think it says eggs – does it say eggs, Irena?' she babbled. Before I could answer, she had turned her attention to a couple at another table and began to posit who they were and where they were from. Anna still had a childlike way about her – still excited by things and with the same short attention span. I smiled as she rambled on.

'It's good to see you smile, Irena,' she said and gave me a grin in return. 'I know Mateusz has gone, but you can still smile, you know. You used to be so funny – remember? You used to tell jokes and make everyone smile and feel comfortable even when things were bad.'

I did remember. But that Irena was long gone. She had been that way before the war, and forced a sense of humour during it, but afterwards, I had become a sort of half-person. Sometimes, I could laugh and smile with my husband and friends, and then other times, I became this silent shadow that wanted solitude. Who was I now that Mateusz was gone? I wondered. Would I revert to being the young girl before the war? Would I just become sullen? Who was I now?

'Irena?' Anna's hand sought mine across the table. 'I didn't mean to upset you.'

'You didn't,' I told her. 'I just got lost in a thought, is all.'

A waiter thankfully interrupted us and took our orders – eggs and fruit for Anna and a sweet pastry that he assured her she would like, and toast and black coffee for me.

'It's beautiful, isn't it?' Anna swept her hand out towards the ocean. 'I could live here, I think. But in a nicer place. Did you see the hotel down the way? All glass and a swimming pool too. I could live there.'

'You couldn't. You'd get lost *constantly*. Remember when you went to Kraków on your own that time? You were lost within minutes.'

Anna nodded in agreement. 'Never been good with directions – streets all look the same to me – and then I see something in a shop window and completely forget what I was supposed to be doing or where I was supposed to be going!' She laughed. 'Not like Mateusz. He was so good, wasn't he, with directions and such like – going over those mountains – I mean, can you imagine if it had been *me*?'

I chuckled. No, I couldn't imagine Anna doing what Mateusz had done during the war.

For a while, Anna and I talked of him, delighting in memories – like how he would always pick fresh flowers for me in the spring and summer, how he would insist on cooking as he thought himself a great chef, even though most of the time he would either burn or undercook the food.

'You were so lucky, Irena,' Anna murmured.

'I was. He was a good man.'

It was true, what she had said. Mateusz and I had only ever had each other, and we had to be everything to each other – friend, lover, spouse. That's not to say that it was picture perfect, but sitting here now, with the morning sun warming my neck, my friend excitedly nibbling at a sweet pastry, I could not think of any one argument that we had ever had. All I could think was how lucky I had been with him.

I just hoped that my luck would hold out a little longer and that the two people I so desperately needed assistance from, Sara and Peter, would be as good as I needed them to be. They had to be. There was no other choice, not now.

I was here, and it was literally now or never.

TWELVE

SARA

Pinamar, Buenos Aires, Argentina
5 January 1994

She rolled onto her side and her arm immediately searched for the body that should be next to her. Upon finding the rest of the bed empty, she woke with a jerk, a sickening feeling in her stomach. How long had he been gone?

Sara swung her legs off the bed, found her white robe still crumpled on the floor where she had left it the night before, wrapped herself in it and padded to the living room, knowing what she would find when she arrived.

And there he was. Peter. Asleep on the sofa, his long legs in an awkward position that left him half on and half off the furniture, his hands curled under his head to make a makeshift pillow.

She wanted to wake him, to shout at him and ask how much money he had lost – to ask him how drunk he had been with Ricardo and Santiago – but something stopped her. As she stood staring at his prone body, she could not help but see him as a small child – a baby, even – someone who needed to be cared for. He was a man, that was for certain, a man who was almost fourteen years older than herself. And yet, he exuded this quiet air of someone who was not yet sure of his place in the world and desperately needed a compass.

And it was Sara – at least she thought so – who could be that for him.

She went into his kitchen and began to noisily clear away the mess that he had left – pots and pans that still held the remnants of whatever food he had managed to make were banished to the sink, where she ran the hot tap, letting it fill each one. It was only when she put her hand inside to scrub at them that she realised the water was cold.

She quickly abandoned her task and made a cortado instead, pouring it into an espresso cup, glad at least that Peter had managed to buy milk for her knowing she would be coming over.

Taking her coffee, she went outside and sat on the love seat that Peter had made with odds and ends of driftwood. It had been a gift to her, but as she lived in an apartment in the city, it had stayed with him; he had explained that when she was ready to move in with him, then it would already be here.

The problem was, even though she didn't act like it, she was a traditional woman at heart. She loved Peter dearly and wanted to live with him, wanted them to make a life together. But first she wanted him to propose, to ask her father for her hand, to get down on one knee and make it official.

As she watched the morning break over the ocean, she realised that, after all this time together, Peter may not ever propose. He had mentioned once or twice their age difference, and suggested to her that she should find a younger man. At times, this niggled at her, and she, too, had contemplated whether she was doing the right thing or not, being with a man who was so much older than her, with no real job to speak of, and who lived in a house on the beach that was falling down around her ears.

If she lived with him, she would have to be the breadwinner – her law practice was flourishing now that her father had retired and she was able to bring in new, fresh clients instead of the dusty old businessmen he had dealt with for years; she had even been able to hire a few more associates.

She was pleased that she had taken it upon herself to learn languages too – English, German, French and Italian were complemented by Luis, her legal partner's, Russian and – oddly enough – Finnish. She hoped that one day she would possibly be able to move back to the capital, where she could make herself a name competing against the bigger law firms; her father had once had an office in the capital too, but now his empire had crumbled somewhat and the office in Pinamar, almost four hours away from where all the action was, was all that was left.

Sara's father, Carlos, had gifted the firm to her almost three years ago now when his problems with bribes, money and a lawsuit against him had forced him to quit. He had raised her singlehandedly after her mother died when she was four, and had tried to teach her the law as he saw it.

'It's a murky place,' he had said to her. 'There is right and wrong, of course, but there's also this grey area – this place where you have to be the judge and jury.'

At first, she had listened to him, and perhaps even agreed a little with his philosophy, but after law school, and as she grew up, she realised that she didn't want to be the kind of lawyer her father was.

His backhanders, bribes and working with people already on the fringes of the law had made her uneasy to say the least. And in the last three years, she had transformed the firm into a reputable practice.

But there was one client she had inherited from her father,

an anonymous client whose file her father had yet to give her. And there was now a problem with it.

About two weeks ago, she had received a letter requesting a face-to-face meeting, and she had been blindsided by it. She had asked her father who the client was, but her father would not, or could not, say.

She had called her father about this client when she had received the letter, but he had purported not to know what she was talking about.

'I'm retired,' he had told her. She could hear laughter and the clinking of glasses in the background. 'I'm busy enjoying my life. Leave it be.'

She knew he was lying to her. His voice had been a little stilted, and he had rushed her off the phone as soon as she had agreed that she would not bother with this client. But there was something there – something that she couldn't let lie. Who was this client and who were they looking for? Perhaps, she supposed, she was her father's daughter, after all.

'All they asked me to do,' he told her, 'was find someone who they said was family. And I did.'

'Why do they want to meet now, if you found them?'

'I never said that I had *definitively* found them.' Her father laughed. 'Who can find someone anyway? Did you see that film I told you about? You need to see it,' he went on, not so subtly changing the subject.

She had not persisted with the questioning; there was no point. If he wanted to tell her something, he would, and if not, then even God himself would not be able to drag it from him. He had spent three months in prison once for not revealing something to a judge – Sara was therefore no match for him.

Sara was reluctant to deal with a client who not only did she have no knowledge of, but who had been her father's client for years. It wasn't that she didn't trust her father, but it wasn't like she could trust him completely either.

She thought now of the request – to meet, to talk about finding this missing relative of theirs. But it bothered her – why someone would want to remain anonymous if they were searching for a missing family member made no sense to her, and it made even less sense that they had asked for legal help in the first place.

'You're awake?'

She looked up and saw a dishevelled Peter standing in the doorway, yawning and scratching at three-day-old stubble.

'Are you?' she quipped.

He plonked down beside her and looked at the demitasse she held in her hand.

'There's more inside, make it yourself.'

'Someone woke up on the wrong side of the bed today.' He grinned and threw an arm over her shoulder.

'And you woke up on the couch. *Again*.'

He didn't respond; she could see that his eyes were already scanning the sea, perhaps looking for somewhere new to go.

She felt that old niggle again in her stomach. He hadn't proposed. Perhaps he never would – maybe he was going to leave her and go somewhere else.

Despite her anger at him, her insecurities got the better of her and she leaned into his body, smelling his familiar natural scent that always held a salty and sweet mix that she so loved.

She knew that he loved her, but there was always something about him that made her feel uneasy – almost as if he never felt truly at home here. She supposed he didn't, but he spoke so little of his life in England, always shutting down conversations before they really got started.

His last few months in England, she knew, had been filled with court cases. He had got into some trouble with the police over selling stolen goods and once more, whenever probed, had talked about it very little.

Now, though, she felt at least that she had provided some

sort of grounding for him – an anchor to this place, this life. He had never got in trouble with the police here – in fact, he was so quiet, so content that she still could not ever imagine that he had been a wild, untameable man in his past.

'How much?' she finally asked him.

She heard him exhale loudly. He didn't want to tell her, but he knew, as she did, that he had to.

'How much?' she prompted again.

'Not a lot. A hundred.'

'Dollars. A hundred dollars?' She moved away from him and stared at him. 'The same amount you were paid yesterday for taking that businessman out on a fishing trip?'

He didn't look at her, merely shrugged, his eyes now squinting as he sought out the horizon.

'It doesn't matter,' he said. 'I've got that tour job from Marco at the hotel' – he absently pointed towards the González Hotel on the shore only a few hundred metres away – 'taking some old women about the city.'

'It does matter, Peter!' she exclaimed. She stood and stalked back inside to the bedroom and sought out her clothes for the day.

How could he be so careless all the time? How could he not see that wasting your money on a poker game with that Ricardo was not what he should do with the little money he earned fishing and acting as a tour guide?

Ricardo. The thought of that leathery old man made her grind her teeth. She did not like him and found it hard to be around him. She understood that he had been a friend of Peter's father and had got him out here when he had found himself in trouble. But there was something not right about him – perhaps the way he spoke, or the way he could not stop staring at her when she saw him – perhaps—

'Your jacket is on inside out.' Peter's voice cut through her thoughts, and she shrugged herself out of it and put it on the right way round.

'I'm sorry,' he said, his giant frame closing in on her. Before she knew it, she was wrapped in a tight embrace as he whispered self-recriminations into her hair and promised he would never do it again.

Tired and frustrated, she pulled away from him. 'You always say that,' she told him sadly.

'But this time I mean it. I do. I promise I won't let Ricardo convince me again. I promise. Cross my heart and hope to die,' he added in English.

Despite herself, Sara smiled and kissed him briefly on the lips before walking out of the bedroom.

'If you do, I will kill you myself.' She half laughed as she left.

Outside, the sun was already battering its heat on the roads, a shimmering mirage as the heat hit the tarmac. She climbed into her car and was glad to feel that the steering wheel was not yet boiling as she knew it would be by lunchtime.

As she pulled away, her thoughts went to the day ahead – the meetings, the phone calls – and then landed on the same thought she had had earlier. The letter requesting a meeting.

She knew the date that they had asked for, and even though she had not responded, she wondered whether her father had perhaps gone behind her back and done so on her behalf. And if not, would they simply show up anyway?

She knew the date, and perhaps that was why she had thought of them this morning. Because by 2 p.m. today, she may or may not have a surprise visitor.

THIRTEEN

PETER

Pinamar, Buenos Aires, Argentina
5 January 1994

He stood on the shore as the waves crashed noisily against the rocks, and watched as the foam burst, leaving trails of white, spotted spit on the grey stones. He breathed in and out, one after the other, feeling the salted air hit his lungs and awaken him to the day. His head was still fuzzy from the night before, and the dispute with Sara had made him more confused, more unsure of himself than usual. Here he was, he mused, a fifty-one-year-old man who still felt, deep inside, like a little boy.

He looked out at the sea that endlessly continued to the horizon and beyond, and wondered what shore the waves would meet next and whether they would be the same waves that he had just witnessed kissing the shore.

There was a part of him that wished to simply disappear in amongst the noisy violence of the sea.

'Peter?' a voice sang out, almost consumed by the sound of the waves. 'Peter?' the voice sang again.

He looked to his right to see two old women who had

booked a few days sightseeing with him, insisting that a German speaker be available. And so they had found him, an Englishman but one whose parents had insisted he speak fluent German, amongst other things. A fisherman, a gambler, a man without a real home – apart from Sara, that was – and now a tour guide.

He automatically rubbed at his face with his palm, trying to rid himself of the thoughts that plagued him, and of the hangover that he knew would not dissipate until later that evening.

'Peter? You *are* Peter?' One of the old women stepped forward, and he immediately saw that she was not as old as her companion. This woman stood straight, tall, her greying brown hair scraped back into a bun, her blue-grey eyes free from the wrinkles that her friend had.

'I am,' he answered in German, and the woman smiled at him, revealing neat white teeth, not at all like the false teeth he had encountered in other elderly people like Ricardo.

'Irena.' She held out her hand. 'Irena Zaleska.'

He took her hand in his. 'Peter Smith,' he replied, and she nodded, seemingly satisfied she had found her guide.

'We went to the fishing shop you told us to meet you at, but the man there said that you would probably be here. He said you had a late night, and this is where you would go?'

He nodded, feeling the pain in his head as he did. 'I'm sorry. It was a late night.' He shrugged and grinned, hoping that she would not be too angry. He had to pull it together, he really did. Just like Sara had said – what on earth was he playing at, at his age?

'We've all been there. I'm just so glad I found you. There are not too many tour guides that speak German, and we were so thankful to have found you.' Irena nodded towards her friend, who was looking out to sea, lost in some own thought of hers.

'Well, I'm glad to be of assistance to you,' he said. 'What is it that you would like to see? I mean, there's not much here. It's just a beach town. If you want to go to the capital, we can. It's about a four-hour drive, but there's more to see there—'

Before he could continue, the old woman waved her hand at him, signalling him to stop. 'I have a list of places I want to see,' she said, and handed him a creased piece of paper.

He read some of the street names that were written in a neat hand.

De las Gaviotas, Marco Polo, De las Ondinas

None of these were near the seafront, where most people wanted to go, nor even near the town centre – in fact, most were residential streets.

She must have noticed his confused expression because she added, 'I'm retracing the steps of someone I used to know.'

He looked at her and wanted to ask what that meant, but she had turned her face away from him to speak to the other woman. When she turned back to him, he simply nodded his agreement – who was he to question what she wanted to do? As long as she paid, that was all that mattered.

'Shall we get going?' the other woman asked, then added, 'I'm Anna.'

The pleasantries over, he led them to his beaten-up minibus, won from a friend of Santiago's on one of the rare occasions that he had had a good hand at one of their poker games.

Neither of the women spoke to him as he drove; the pair chattered to each other in their native tongue – Polish, was it? Or Russian? Or Hungarian? He had no real idea and yet he found the patter of their language soothing.

As he turned towards the city centre, his headache began to subside, and he now felt almost in a good mood – buoyed perhaps by the idea of spending an easy morning strolling the streets and getting paid for it.

He pulled into a tight parking spot on Av. Arquitecto Jorge Bunge, the irony not lost on him that only a few hours earlier he had stumbled down this same road with Ricardo.

He opened the door for them, and each took his arm for assistance as they stepped out onto the pavement. Irena stood for a moment, looking up and down the road at the simple cafés and office blocks, as the other woman fussed in her handbag for something.

'It's not what I thought it would look like,' Irena told him.

He shrugged. 'It's just a small city. I mean, there's really not much here. Most come for the beach. But I like it – it's better than all those big cities around the world. I prefer nature – being close to the sea, if I can.'

'You're a world traveller?' she asked.

'I was, once,' he conceded.

They began walking, at a pace that was much slower than he was used to. 'Can I ask why you want to see these particular streets?' he asked the pair.

The other woman, Anna, offered him a boiled sweet from a paper bag that she held in her hand – that was what she had been looking for, he thought.

He took one and rolled it round in his mouth, tasting strawberry.

'You need sugar,' Anna said. 'I love it. Whenever I see sweets, chocolate, anything, it goes right in here!' She pointed at her mouth. 'But you asked about the streets, didn't you?' she asked.

He nodded.

'Sorry. I have no attention span – one minute you could be saying something to me and the next I forget. It's not old age, you understand, I've been this way forever, haven't I, Irena?' she asked her companion, who barely nodded, her eyes moving from building to building as if she were expecting to see someone or something that she knew.

'Anyway, yes, streets,' Anna continued. 'You see' – she moved closer to Peter and lowered her voice a little – 'we're retracing steps. Steps someone we both knew took once. We just want to see what they saw.'

Irena shot a glance over her shoulder that told Peter that Anna was not supposed to have revealed what she had. But Anna had already lost interest in that conversation, and turned her attention to Peter.

'You're German?' she enquired.

'No. English, brought up in Kent,' he told her.

'But you know German. Do you speak other languages?'

'Spanish, of course,' he told her. 'My parents spoke multiple languages and made me learn.'

'A good skill to have I suppose,' she said, the sweet in her mouth knocking against her teeth as she spoke. 'I don't like languages much – never really had much use for them – but I had to learn German. Had no choice in the matter.'

She threaded her arm through his companionably, and Peter found that he was quite enjoying their company – this woman with her endless chatter and natural friendliness and the other, her eyes darting here and there, her face set in concentration as she obviously tried to imagine whomever it was walking this same route once upon a time.

He did want to pry more and ask who this person they knew was, and yet, a private person himself, he realised how Irena may not appreciate the line of questioning. He was dearly hoping that they would perhaps need him for another day of roaming the streets. He had to make money somehow, and he knew that, if he didn't pull himself together soon, Sara wouldn't keep putting up with him.

They walked for over an hour, meandering down streets, neither woman ever stopping or remarking on anything. He wondered whose steps they were retracing and why, and, not for the first time, thought that maybe they had mistaken

Pinamar for somewhere else – surely, they meant to be in the capital? Surely, there was no one here they had once known.

They soon reached the coast and passed Brisa Marina – a restaurant sat on stilts in the ocean, the tables on the terrace all bedecked with white linen tablecloths that flapped in the sea breeze. It was where he and Sara went often, sitting long into the night, listening to the ocean, drinking wine. It was the place where he was at his happiest.

'Ooh, this is lovely, isn't it, Irena?' Anna said. 'Can we sit, maybe get a coffee?'

Peter smiled as Anna spoke – it was as though she were a child asking her parent for permission. But Irena seemed not to hear her friend and kept walking.

'Please. My feet are still swollen from the flight. Just a minute, Irena, please...'

Finally, Irena stopped and turned, and gave a wry smile. 'Fine. One coffee and then we keep going.'

'And a pastry, maybe cake?' Anna asked, already pulling Peter towards the door.

'*Peter! ¿Cómo está?*' Alvaro, the manager, greeted him as soon as he walked in, then raised his eyebrows at his companions.

'*El trabajo*,' Peter explained. Work.

'I'm Anna.' Anna pushed Peter aside and held out her hand to Alvaro. Then, seeing his confusion with her German, she said it again in English.

'Ah! Beautiful ladies.' Alvaro rose to the occasion, plastering on his grin that he saved for tourists. Peter couldn't help but smile too, delighting in Alvaro's pronunciation. 'This way, just for you. Sit outside and hear the waves, yes?' He almost bowed as he led the way to the terrace, pulling out chairs for each of them, even Peter.

They sat at a table close to the railing, Anna leaning over it to look into the water as Irena told her to be careful.

He ordered for them – three cafés con leche, and *medi-alunas* for Anna.

'Where are you from?' Peter asked Irena as Anna dug into the pastry, scattering soft, flaky crumbs over the tabletop.

'Poland,' she said and offered no more.

'I've never been to Poland,' he tried.

'It's nice.'

'It is? Maybe I will have to go one day,' he said.

'You know, for years it wasn't great, but now it's better.'

Once more she did not elaborate and it caused Peter, a man who rarely became intrigued by anyone or anything, to question more.

'You mean the war?'

'What else could I mean?' she scoffed. 'The war, after the war, the Russians. It was always something – someone else trying to tell us what to do. Only now is it like it should be.'

'I'm sorry,' Peter said. 'I shouldn't have asked.'

She waved his apology away with a flick of her wrist. 'I understand that you want to know what it was like. All the time now, younger people ask me what it was like. You see, they've seen those movies – the ones that make it glamorous. Fighting the Nazis, the soldiers brave and fearless, the whole thing reduced to some action movie. But it wasn't glamorous – there is nothing entertaining about war. Every day was a battle for survival – not just the Jews, but all of us. You wanted to keep your family safe? You wanted more food? Well, you had to pay those brutes or work for them. And what do you do if you cannot? Well, you have to make a deal with the devil.'

The old woman suddenly seemed exhausted by her speech, and she slouched in her chair and batted a hand in front of her face.

Anna, not liking the silence – or perhaps not really listening when Irena spoke – said, 'You should tell him about Zakopane,' her mouth full, her hand already raised to wave the waiter over to order something else.

'There's not really anything to tell. It is a nice place – mountains, lakes and lots of tourists,' Irena said.

'Remember what Abel said?' Anna asked. 'Remember – how he said Zakopane was like a slice of heaven?'

Whoever Abel was he obviously meant something to Irena, whose face suddenly became animated with the memory. 'He said a lot of things. I don't think he ever stopped talking the whole time he was there!'

Peter was relieved to see that a smile had now appeared on Irena's face.

'I wonder still about Henryk,' Anna mused, then took a large bite of her pastry, scattering crumbs once more. 'You should tell him about Henryk and Abel,' she continued as she chewed. 'The bit where you helped them – the start – he'd like that, wouldn't you, Peter?' Anna directed her attention to him.

He wasn't sure whether he would or wouldn't but nodded anyway. 'You should know something about the war, not just those movies that Irena was talking about. That's not real life.'

'I don't think this is the best time,' Irena told her friend. 'It's not a completely happy tale, and I am not sure that this young man really wants to hear it.' Then, Irena broke away from her German and spoke in rapid Polish to Anna, who seemed to argue back with just as much vigour.

The pair then settled into silence, and Peter saw Irena look over his shoulder at the ocean, her eyes scanning the vastness as if she would find something there.

He knew she was thinking of the men her friend had mentioned. And as much as he wished she would talk, he let her sit in silence, remembering someone from long ago.

FOURTEEN

IRENA

Zakopane, Poland
August 1941

Abel and Henryk Eisenbach arrived at our home on 24 August 1941, in the dead of night, carrying nothing but a battered leather bag each.

To me, Abel seemed older than his sixty-two years – his face was sunken, deep lines etched in his forehead, and every single hair on his head was pure white. Henryk, his grandson, seemed the opposite – he was, he said, nineteen years old, and yet he looked like he was only fifteen. Although tall, his body was so slight that I felt as though just a breeze would blow him over. His face, too, was shrunken, but rather than revealing heavy wrinkles like his grandfather, the skin was taut across his skull, and he had large black rings under his eyes.

Mateusz came with them. It was the first time I had seen him since he had arranged with my parents that they would help with his cause.

I had not been forewarned that this was happening – my parents had busied themselves getting the basement ready, and

I had been at work in the hotel almost every day – so it came as a surprise to find the trio in our living room with only two candles lit so as not to alert any German eyes that our house might be awake at this hour.

On seeing Mateusz, I wanted to immediately tell him the fortunate news that Richter had barely been at the hotel recently, and I felt that perhaps I was now safe. I wanted to tell him so much as I hated the thought that he might have been worrying about me, but then again, I sort of still hoped he had been thinking of me.

'Sorry for the hour,' Mateusz said as my father wrapped his dressing gown cord round his waist and tied it into a thick knot. 'But it is the best time.'

My father seemed not to hear him and went straight to the old man, Abel, and the young man, Henryk, and shook each of their hands, assuring them that they would be safe here.

'Please sit, sit.' My mother indicated the couches. 'I'll get you a drink and some food.' She scuttled off to the kitchen before anyone could agree or thank her, leaving me standing next to my father as the three men sat on the couches. I was suddenly very aware that I was in my nightgown and dressing gown. Normally, my father would have told me to change, but in the circumstances, he seemed not to notice nor care about our normal practices.

Abel looked uncomfortable. He barely sat on the couch, and rather seemed to be perching in case he had to leap up at any moment. His eyes could not settle on one particular spot, and even though Father and Mateusz talked to him, he did not respond with anything but a gentle nod.

Henryk looked as though he was going to fall asleep at any moment. His lanky frame leaned into the thick cushions and his slim, pale neck seemed unable to hold the weight of his head.

Suddenly, Abel's eyes landed on me, and a look of surprise came over him as if he had only just realised I was there.

'I am so sorry.' He stood and held out a hand that was shaking slightly. I took it and felt his cold skin under the warmth of my own. 'I did not see a young lady here. I am sorry to come to your home at this hour.'

He was so sincere, so serious, that I immediately wanted to take him in an embrace so that he felt a little more at ease. Instead, I joked, 'This is what we normally do in the night! You should see us – people arriving all the time – you'd think we were running a brothel!'

I knew it was the wrong thing to say. It had fallen out of my head and my mouth with little thought. My father's face reddened, and I could see he was readying himself to admonish me. But Henryk saved me by letting out a brief bark of a laugh, and Mateusz followed suit, both dispelling the awkwardness I now felt.

'Even so,' Abel said with a grin, 'I apologise for the way we have arrived – and indeed the way we *look*.' He nodded towards his clothes, stained and muddied.

'No matter about that!' My father stood and wrapped and arm round the old man's shoulders. 'We'll soon sort you out with some clean clothes.'

The pair of them then sat down once more, allowing for a moment for Mateusz to explain what had happened and what was going to happen. I perched myself on the edge of a side table, taking in this strange scene and watching the faces of our new guests as Mateusz spoke for them.

'You know Abel, I think,' he began, nodding towards my father. 'He worked at the university in the science department.'

My father scrutinised the old man's face, seemingly not remembering him, and then suddenly his eyes widened. '*Yes*! Of course. We have met on several occasions. I am sorry not to have recognised you.'

'It can't be helped,' Abel said. 'I hardly look like I did two years ago.'

'I got a letter from another academic who told me that Abel and his family were in the ghetto in Kraków and needed to get out – so I did what I could,' Mateusz said.

'And you did well,' my father said.

Mateusz shook his head. 'Not as well as I had hoped...'

'My wife,' Abel started and then stopped as though something had suddenly become lodged in his throat. He coughed, once, twice, then tried again. 'My wife, and my daughter, Henryk's mother, could not come. Maybe a month ago they could have. But not now. Now they have gone somewhere better.'

'But—' my father started, and then stopped when he realised what Abel was saying. They could not come because they were dead.

A silence hung in the room. There were no words. I had heard of the ghettos and could only imagine what it was like for them there. To know that this man's wife and daughter had died there sent a chill down my spine, and, at the same time, morbidly made me want to ask what had happened. But I did not. Now was certainly not the time.

My mother broke through the quiet, bustling in with sweet cookies, bread, left-over chicken from the night before and coffee, which I knew would be weak as our rations were depleting quickly.

Abel and Henryk became animated with the arrival of both my mother and the food and, for a moment, the reason why these two people were sitting in our living room was forgotten. Mother entertained with her ramblings about being a dancer, questioning them over what they liked to eat, and her general good humour.

It was Mateusz who drew us back into reality, warning that both Abel and Henryk needed to be in the basement sooner rather than later and that was where they should stay until Mateusz returned to take Henryk with him.

'With you where?' my mother asked, oddly surprised. Had she thought that they would live with us forever? I wondered.

'Henryk, when he is fit enough, wants to join the partisans – us – and we will take him. He's young, strong and has skied before. That's all we need.'

'And Abel?' my mother asked.

'Abel will get across the mountains as soon as he is well enough,' Mateusz said.

'I hope it will be soon, madam,' Abel said to my mother. 'I have a bad leg' – he indicated his left – 'and it may take a little time for it to heal.'

My mother did not ask to see his leg but instead threw herself onto the floor and ruffled up his trouser leg, revealing blue, purple and red bruises, so raised and ugly that it was as though something under his skin was trying to get free.

'Please, please...' Abel tried to stop her; she who was already commenting on the state of his leg and how she might be able to fix it.

'Let her help, Grandfather.' Henryk finally spoke, his voice calm and measured. 'He's not very good at letting people help him,' he told the rest of us. 'He wants to help everyone else – in the ghetto that's all he did – try and help others, and this is what he got for trying.'

'They beat you?' My mother looked up at him, tears shining in her eyes.

'They did,' was all Abel said.

'Beat him? They had him in a cell for three days because he tried to stop a guard from hurting a small child. I am still surprised he survived.'

It was then that I heard a steely determination in the young man's voice – he wanted to help Mateusz, help others, do anything to fight back. And it was in that moment that I finally became a little braver.

If this boy could do it, so could I.

FIFTEEN

IRENA

Zakopane, Poland
August 1941

Over the coming days, as soon as I finished work, I would arrive home and immediately make my way to the basement to talk with Abel and Henryk. To my parents' credit, they had made the basement as homely as possible, including beds, a desk and chair, rugs on the floor and a makeshift toilet that unfortunately had to be emptied each day, but had been partitioned behind a makeshift wall so at least they had some privacy.

Father had also covered the basement hatch with carpet and a heavy bookcase.

'Rugs, yes,' he told me as he laid the carpet. 'You see a rug, you think there might be something underneath, but carpet, no.'

It was an oddity to have carpeting in the study, where the hatch was located – until then, our house had been all floorboards and rugs – but Father's office in Kraków had once had wall-to-wall carpeting and he had become fond of it. 'I like the feel under my feet,' he said, probably happy that finally he was getting what he wanted, even if it was just a ruse to hide the hatch.

It was an effort to get down to the basement and required two people to move the bookcase, then peel the carpet back, letting the person go down as the other laid the carpet back on top. We were very careful, methodical in how we did it each time, all of us keenly aware that searches could happen at any time, and that Death's Head Resort was just five minutes from our house. Any or all of us could end up there at any time.

I enjoyed Abel and Henryk's company, and brought Anna to meet them, trusting that she would be able to keep the secret. It had buoyed Henryk's mood to meet her – he liked her gentleness, her prettiness and made him smile and talk more than usual.

Abel had still not elaborated on his life prior to coming to us, and I knew that the pain that he must have experienced, both physically and emotionally, must be too hard to put into words. He had told me, however, how brave Mateusz had been, and how he owed him his life.

'Some others managed to escape,' Abel told me one evening, his voice low, as gentle snoring came from Henryk.

I sat on the one chair in the basement and Abel sat on his bed, his left leg wrapped in linen that contained a poultice that my mother had assured him would cure the bruises and whatever other damage lay beneath the skin.

'I never thought that we would be able to escape,' he continued. 'There was talk of it, of course. Every day we talked with our friends and wondered how it could be done. But one had to be careful about talking too much – you didn't know which of your friends might tell the guards.'

'They would do that to you?' I gasped.

'Indeed. But it wasn't done lightly, my dear. Those who told the guards things did so because of fear for their own family, or because they were so hungry and they thought that they might get a little more food.'

He stopped and I wanted to ask more about what it was like for him, but he moved on.

'A letter came to me from a man I did not know. He was a Polish man who delivered food into the ghetto a few times a week. How he found me I do not know. Why he took the risk for me, again I do not know. But I remember holding that letter in my hand, reading it, then rereading it again and again. It had come from a colleague of mine at the university who told me that in two nights' time Henryk and I were to sneak out of the apartment we lived in and hide behind a bakery. It would be there, early in the morning, when flour was delivered, that we were to get into a truck that would be driven out. There was no other instruction. No talk of being caught. It sounded simple – and doable. And yet, I knew of the myriad of dangers that awaited us. It wouldn't be so easy to get into a van when the boots of guards and soldiers patrolled the streets, when the razor-topped wire had men with guns perched in towers all along it. But then, what choice did Henryk and I have?'

'You were very brave,' I told him.

He gave a weak smile, then waved my compliment away. 'Not bravery, my dear. It was desperation. My wife and daughter were dead. And I knew death would come for me and Henryk soon enough.'

'And his father?' I nodded towards the sleeping Henryk. 'What happened to him?'

Abel ran a hand over his tired face. 'He died when Henryk was a boy. It had just been the four of us for years. And what wonderful years they had been!' As he thought of his past life, it was as though the years and worry and stress fell away from his face.

'We had a lovely home in Kazimierz,' he said. 'Do you know

it? It is a bustling part of the city – well, it was. Shops, a wonderful bookshop, restaurants – we could just step out of our home and within moments be entertained with life! It was everywhere. Henryk, he went to school, and I taught at the university. My wife was a great cook and so was my daughter, and they spent much of their time not just keeping our home in order, but seeking out the right ingredients for the wonderful meals they would make for not only us but our friends and neighbours.

'In the summer, we would picnic in the parks, in the winter, we would sit by the fire and tell stories, read and play on the piano. It was perfect. I just didn't realise how perfect it was until I didn't have it any more.'

His face then took on the same air it usually had; tired, worn out, despondent.

'But you have some hope now?' I tried, wanting to see again the expression from when he had talked about his old life.

'What hope?' he asked. 'I have to hide. My grandson will leave to fight. I want him to. But I will lose him too. So there isn't much hope for me, I'm afraid.'

'But Mateusz said that when you're well enough, you will leave?' I countered.

'To where? Hungary? Slovakia? My old bones won't get me very far. I doubt I will see the end of this war.'

His statement was said with such an air of finality that I believed him. He didn't want to survive, because, as he had said, what would he be surviving for?

'But young Mateusz' – he reached across and patted my hand. 'I still thank him every day for what he did for us. He was there that night, you know, when we escaped. In the passenger seat of that bread van delivering flour. It was simpler than I had thought it would be – there seemed to be fewer guards about, fewer people, and I think, although I am not sure, some money must have changed hands. Others who had escaped had managed to get through the fence or had seen a moment when guards were not looking and taken their chance. But this was different from what I had heard about – this was planned with such precision.

'The moment we got into the van, both of us still scared that we would be caught, it was Mateusz who told us that everything would be fine, that he would keep us safe, and he said it with such conviction that I have to tell you – I *never* doubted him.'

I must have smiled, or perhaps blushed, as Abel spoke of Mateusz, so that he grinned at me and said, 'He's a good man. You couldn't have picked a better man.' He then patted my hand, and this time, I knew I was blushing; my face flamed with such heat that I was sure I was going to explode.

My reaction made Abel laugh loudly. 'It's all right, my dear. It is nice to see some happiness, some joy in the world still. Look at how much they have taken from us and look at how we still feel, still want things in our lives. *Enjoy* it. Don't feel guilty about it.'

I squirmed. It was as though Abel was reading my mind. I knew I felt something for Mateusz – I had done from the moment I met him – but yes, I had pushed any feeling aside because there were bigger things to worry about – bigger things that were affecting me.

'Enjoy it,' he repeated. 'You still have a life to lead. After all this you will still have a life.'

'And so will you,' I said and stood, leaning down to kiss him on his papery cheek. 'You should still hope, Abel. Something good will happen for you too, I am sure of it.'

He bade me goodnight, and I climbed the stairs and rapped three times on the hatch so that my father would peel the carpet away and set me free.

I just hoped that, one day, Abel and Henryk would be free too. Maybe we all would.

But one thing I didn't know then was that we were in the calm before the storm. We thought we had endured everything that could possibly happen, but we had no idea of the struggles yet to come.

SIXTEEN

IRENA

Pinamar, Buenos Aires, Argentina
5 January 1994

I did not know how long we had been sitting on that terrace next to the ocean, with me and my thoughts of Abel and Henryk, Anna with her pastries and Peter, who seemed to enjoy the quiet, his eyes on a seagull that pecked at the deck.

'I'm sorry,' I told Peter. 'I disappeared for a moment there.'

He smiled at me. 'Not a problem. I like to be with my own thoughts too.'

'Not a great talker either, eh?' I joked.

He shook his head, and a serious expression replaced the smile. I had struck a nerve, it seemed.

'Sometimes people speak, but they don't really say anything, you know?' he said. 'And then sometimes when you have something you should say, it's hard to say it.' He shook his head again and then laughed. 'And now I'm sorry – I am not sure what I am trying to say!'

'I always know what to say,' Anna said. 'I just say whatever is in my head at whatever time it comes to me. It's pretty easy, I find.'

'Shall we get going?' Peter asked, already pushing his chair back.

I checked the time: midday. Just two more hours to go. 'We need to look at some of the other streets and addresses,' I said and stood. 'We still have some time.'

Anna was unhappy that we were walking the streets once more. The heat was becoming a bit much for me too, but I wasn't going to stop.

We passed an old man – a beggar, I assumed – who, as soon as he saw us, stepped out of the shadow of the doorway he stood in and began to ask for money. His beard was matted, his face dirty, and I stepped back and held my bag to my chest.

Peter, though, was not scared. He talked briefly to the man and handed him a crumpled-up note, which the beggar took with a nod of the head before retreating into the coolness of the doorway.

'It's okay,' Peter told us. 'He's harmless.'

Anna did not seem to think so and gripped my upper arm as we walked.

'You were kind to him,' I noted.

Peter shrugged. '*There but for the grace of God go I*,' he said. 'I heard that somewhere once. It wouldn't take much for any of us to be in his situation.'

I thought then once more of Abel and Henryk. If they had not been taken in by my parents, they, too, would have been hiding on the street. In fact, it could have just as easily been me, my parents, or even Anna.

'You're a good man,' I told him.

'I try. But I'm not always successful.'

We walked down a narrow street. A few shops sat underneath what I assumed were apartments. Someone on one balcony that overlooked us was playing a tune on a harmonica.

Both Anna and I stopped for a moment to listen, then I saw Peter step away and talk to a large man who sat sweating underneath a yellow umbrella.

He nodded to the man, then came back to us.

'Just talking to a friend,' he said. 'Do you want to continue? Is there a specific place that you want to see?'

I could hear a tinge of frustration in his voice. He wanted to know why we were randomly walking residential streets and not wanting to sit on the beach all day.

'Nothing specific,' I told him. 'Just a few more streets to look at.'

Peter nodded, and we continued on. As we passed the large man under the umbrella, I noted the name scrawled in green paint above the doorway – *Santiago's Bar*.

'The man you were talking with,' I asked, my heartbeat rising in my chest.

'Santiago,' Peter confirmed. 'He's a friend of mine.'

'You go to his bar often?' I asked.

'Sometimes.' He shrugged. 'It's not the best place to go to. Especially at night.'

'But you know him – you know Santiago well?' I was sure there was a wobble in my voice as I spoke, and I saw him raise his eyebrows as he heard the question.

'I do...'

Anna grabbed my arm and squeezed it tight, then leaned in and spoke in Polish. 'Now isn't the time.'

I wanted to ignore her. I wanted to go back to the bar that was only a few feet away. I wanted to look more closely at Santiago.

But of course Anna was right. Now was not the time.

SEVENTEEN

SARA

Pinamar, Buenos Aires, Argentina
5 January 1994

Sara arrived at the office much later than she had planned. The supposed quick appointment had turned into two hours, and the news she had received had made her so confused that she had ended up sitting at a café, watching as pigeons pecked at nothing on the ground.

'You're late!' Luis said as Sara entered. Immediately, he stood, and waved a manila folder in her general direction.

'Not now, Luis.' She waved her hand at him.

'Everything okay?'

'Fine. Just tired. Just give me a few minutes to settle in,' she told him and made her way to her own office that sat at the rear of the building. It was the largest office – it had once belonged to her father – and she had loved visiting him when she was a child. He would sit behind the large mahogany desk, a cigarette always burning away in the ashtray, the sash windows open, letting in a breeze and sounds of life from outside.

She had always thought that her father was a very important man. He had his own office, a big desk and a brown leather armchair that he would let her sit in and do her homework whilst he worked. He had offices in the capital, and in some other parts of the country too, and sometimes he would take her to see them, and all of his employees would shake his hand and smile at him. Yes, he had been important back then.

'Sara.' Camila, her secretary, stopped her from turning the brass doorknob. 'You've got a client. I let her wait inside, because, well, you know...' She spread her arms at the tiny space that was called a room, barely big enough for the secretary's desk, let alone a seating area for waiting clients.

Sara nodded her thanks, and it was then that she realised the time was 2 p.m. How could she have forgotten?

The morning's disruptive appointment pushed aside for now, she opened the door, not knowing who to expect.

'Ms Martinez,' an old woman, tall with her hair scraped back into a stern bun, greeted her, and – oddly – made Sara jump.

'I am so sorry,' the woman said, taking a step towards her.

Had she just been standing in the middle of the room, waiting for her?

'I'm Irena Zaleska. I was your father's client, but I think I now belong to you?'

Sara composed herself and took a step towards the mysterious client, and shook her hand, noting that the woman's German accent was not quite right – at least Sara did not think so; but then who was she to say?

'I'm happy to meet you,' Sara said and indicated the brown leather armchair for the old woman to settle into.

She, in turn, sat behind her desk and noted how warm it was in the office, then stood and opened the window, possibly letting more warmth in than out.

The woman watched her every move – she could feel her eyes on her – yet she did not speak, and Sara realised that she was waiting for her to begin.

'Mrs Zaleska,' Sara began.

The woman held up her hand to stop her. 'Irena, please. Call me Irena.'

Sara nodded. 'Irena. I received your letter, but I am not sure what it is you want nor how I can help you. You see, we deal mostly with corporate work. I'm not entirely sure how my father has been helping you nor what it is you would now like from me.'

All the while Sara was speaking, Irena nodded gently in agreement as if she had been expecting this exact response.

'Your father did not tell you about me?' she asked.

'Only the basics. After I received your letter saying that you were going to visit, I asked him about you. He said that he was just doing a favour – finding someone for you. My father is retired,' she told the other woman. 'He can't take on anything now. It wouldn't be possible.'

She wanted to add that her father wasn't allowed to. His licence had been taken away from him – a fact that Sara did not wish to think about, nor admit to anyone else, let alone herself.

'I understand,' Irena said. 'But please let me explain it to *you* then. You see, I hired your father to find someone for me. A friend of mine recommended him and said he could help. And, true to his word, he did. But he couldn't find the person; he only knew that they were here – that there had been sightings, that they had settled here. But he was sure – absolutely sure that they were here, and I said I would come to visit as soon as I could so that I could conduct my own search, as it were.' She smiled at Sara, and in that moment, her face completely changed.

Sara had thought her stern when she had entered her office.

But as soon as she smiled, she almost transformed into someone younger, someone who you knew would make you laugh, someone you knew you could trust.

Sara smiled back; she couldn't help it – all at once she wanted the woman to like her and to keep talking, stay a while and drink coffee.

'But you see,' Irena continued, 'it took a while until I could get here. But now I am, and I would like your help as I continue my search.'

Before Sara could protest and tell her that they were not the police nor some detective agency, Irena pulled some papers from her handbag. 'I have everything here,' she said. 'Last known address, places he had visited. I went there today – roamed the streets thinking that perhaps fate would allow me to see him, but it did not—'

'So, it is a *him*?' Sara interrupted.

Irena stopped looking at her papers and stared at her. 'Your father really never explained what it was that I wanted? What this was all about?'

'No. Like I said, he said it was all solved, that there was no more to be done.'

The old woman licked her bottom lip, then her eyes darted to the window, where they rested for a moment, watching the birds fly, watching the blind catch a breath of air and bump against the window frame. Then she turned back.

'You strike me as a very intelligent woman,' Irena said.

'Thank you.'

'Also earnest. Trustworthy. Moral.'

'I would hope so,' Sara responded, wondering where on earth this conversation was going.

Irena smiled, then nodded gently again. 'I thought so. Your father, he is a little different from you, isn't he?'

Sara wasn't sure what to say. What was happening? What

was the old woman trying to say to her? Irena stared at her, waiting for an answer, and Sara knew that she had to respond.

'He is – well, he *was*,' she admitted. Of course he was. He had done deals with people that Sara would never have done. He had handshakes with politicians, the police. He manoeuvred in the grey area, whereas Sara only saw black and white – that was what he would say to her – *there is always a grey area, Sara, remember that!*

But, for her part, she didn't feel comfortable operating the same way; she felt that the law was the law, and that was that.

'He... Well, he saw things in a different way to me,' Sara said.

Irena began to place the papers back into her handbag, and Sara felt a slight wave of relief. The meeting was obviously over – Sara was not her father, and this woman needed someone who would be happy to work in the shadows.

She saw that Irena had dropped something and went to help. When she bent down, she saw that it was a knitted cream baby mitten. She picked it up and handed it back.

As soon as the old woman saw the mitten, her eyes widened.

'You dropped this,' Sara said.

'Thank you.' She snatched it from her, shoving it deep into her handbag.

Normally, Sara wouldn't have thought anything of it. Perhaps she was knitting things for a baby, perhaps she had just bought it. But the way in which Irena had reacted, the way her hand had snatched it back as if Sara had been trying to steal it, made her wonder what it was all about.

'Please pass on my best to you father,' Irena said, composed now.

Sara offered her hand, but then dropped it. 'Can you tell me who the man is? Who is it that you are looking for at least?'

Irena seemed to be busying herself with closing the gold clasp on her handbag as the papers threatened to spill out.

'Well, my dear' – she stopped fussing and looked at her – 'I'm looking for my husband.'

EIGHTEEN

IRENA

Pinamar, Buenos Aires, Argentina
5 January 1994

Why had I told her that? I shouldn't have. She was not her father – that much was clear – and I needed someone who would be willing to understand the situation as a whole and to understand why I had to do what I had to do.

But her question as I was about to leave caught me off guard a little, and I don't mind admitting it: I liked her and wanted to give her something; just a tiny bit of information that would perhaps satiate her curiosity enough – just enough.

I do not know what happened. As soon as I told her who I was looking for, she sat down heavily in her chair and asked me why I didn't know where my husband was, and hadn't I just told her that my husband had been sick?

I noticed that her face was pale, a little sweaty even, and I sort of remembered that look, but I couldn't quite place where I had seen it before.

I told her as much as I could – as much as I dared. I did not trust that she could cope with the whole truth, and told her that my husband – rather, ex-husband – had moved here some years before and I could not find him. I gave her a sob story – one I made up on the spot and one that to be honest I was very proud of. Anna is always saying that I don't have much of an imagination, but there I was, almost in tears telling this lady a story I had just concocted.

Twice she drank water; I noted that – I notice everything these days. I have to be ready – I have been preparing for it.

Then she asked me my ex-husband's name. I didn't want to say it out loud, so I wrote it down – Christoph Richter. But her father had found out that he went by a different name now and yet was not registered with any official body. His last known name was Santiago Lopez. I thought of the man underneath the yellow umbrella, wondering again if it was him. My heart quickened with the thought.

'He changed his name?' Sara asked me. 'But why?'

I shrugged and told her it was about money – about something that had happened in his youth. But God, I yearned to tell her the real reason; but I knew I couldn't.

I found myself out on the street, walking aimlessly, the years, the past shrouding my brain and the harsh truth that Sara and her father did not know where Richter was now. But could it be Santiago – Peter's friend? Was it a common name in Argentina? Was it a simple coincidence that we were walking down a street that Carlos had said Richter had been seen on, and his name was Santiago? Was I hoping too much that it could be... him?

I mean, he could be that street vendor, I thought, that old man bent over a grill. But was he too young, too old?

Or was he the man who had just passed me in a flamboyant pink shirt and green hat tipped at a jaunty angle? I doubted that the old Richter would ever have dared to wear such a thing, but time had moved on, and he was sure to be a different man now.

I was supposed to meet Anna and Peter at a church just a

street away from Sara's office. Peter had asked me where I was going, but I had not told him the truth. I just told him I needed an hour alone and he was to keep Anna company. He didn't ask anything else, and I was glad of his silence.

I knew I should turn left to go back to the church, but my brain was not working, and I turned right instead, soon finding myself in a small park, the edges of the grass browning from the summer heat, a red and rusted swing set in the middle with no children in sight.

I found a bench and sat down. I scrunched my eyes closed for a moment and tried to remember what Peter's friend Santiago had looked like. Fat, a lot of facial hair, brown skin. Could Richter have changed that much? Would I recognise him now, even if I bumped into him?

I could simply ask Peter to take me back to the bar and introduce me to his friend, but I needed to be careful – I needed to do this on my own.

I would go back this evening, alone, or maybe with Anna. I would ask for Santiago and look him in the eye. I felt sure that no one could change their eyes. And I would know Richter's – I knew I would.

I opened my eyes and let them drift around the park. For a brief moment, my thoughts disappeared and I simply saw the grass, a car pass, a bird hop from branch to branch. It was a blessed relief to have no thoughts – like being dead, I mused. At peace.

Suddenly, my hand went to my handbag as if my body was not matching my mind – it could not be at peace, I could never rest, not really. For a few seconds, my heart raced with panic – it was gone. I scrabbled about until finally my fingers found something soft. I pulled it out – a cream knitted baby mitten. As soon as I held it, I felt calm again. My fingers stroked each stitch, remembering the day that they had happily held the knitting needles over my large belly, click-clacking them, making something for my unborn child. A child that was gone. A child that had died. A child taken from me, by one man. Richter.

I only had the one mitten – its mirror had gone, and I did not want to think about the day that it had happened. I did not want to remember that day and wished it would disappear from my memory. But it was the reason that I was here. I had to find Richter. I had to confront him. I had to make him feel the fear he had made me feel. I had to make him feel the same pain I had felt, and I had to do to him what he had done to my child.

But there were more memories that told the story that led up to that day, all jumbled together like a knotted, twisted ball of wool. As soon as I pulled at the string, it would snag and lead me on to a different thought. Was it my age, perhaps? Or was this how everyone remembered their lives, in a fragmented and hazy way?

Behind me, there was a blare of music, something new to me – perhaps Spanish? I turned to see that a bar had opened up and a young man danced with a broom in his hands as he swept the pavement; another man, younger and smaller, carried crates inside.

I felt a small leap of joy at the scene; of two people enjoying music, getting ready for a night of fun.

But then, my stomach dropped as one of those fragmented memories assaulted me. Music. Dancing. Laughter.

Me.

Anna.

Richter.

NINETEEN

IRENA

Zakopane, Poland
August 1941

It was a Saturday when things changed once more. An irreversible change that would set us all on a new path, even ones we had no desire to travel on.

The Grand Stamary Hotel seemed ominous that morning as I arrived. A sudden change in weather that brought grey, heavy clouds sunk low, so low that the tips of the roof had disappeared. Usually, the hotel was elegant; its brick and stone walls, its peaked roofs and acres of parkland made it look, at least to me, like a fairytale castle. But today there was something different – perhaps the red bricks were duller, perhaps the balustrades were dirty and worn – either way, I did not want to go inside.

The air beneath the clouds was as thick and hot as soup. It felt as though we were even more trapped than we already were and, even before I reached the kitchen entrance, my back was soaked with sweat.

I could not help but feel nervous as I walked through the

kitchen doors, like perhaps someone would immediately look at me and say that they knew who was hiding in our house and the Gestapo were on their way.

They are safe. We are safe. I kept telling myself this as I donned my apron and entered the kitchen.

We are fine. They are fine.

Bartok was in no mood to talk to me – his face was redder than usual, his sleeves rolled up over his thick forearms as he stirred at steaming pots that bubbled on the stove.

'What's wrong?' I asked as I placed an apron over my clothes. 'This is a lot for lunch.'

'It's for this evening,' he gruffly responded. 'They're having a dance in the main hall.'

It was strange to think that once upon a time, perhaps not that long ago, the thought of a dance in the main hall of the Stamary would send me running to Anna's in excitement, hoping that we would be invited. But now the thought of all those Gestapo men, their green-grey uniforms, their leather coats and black shining boots, their laughter, their language, even, made me nervous.

It was different when they came and went for lunch, for dinner. But to have them all in one place, *all* of them, felt as though we were not so much feeding the lions from a distance any more but were in the den with them.

I didn't voice my fears to Bartok; instead, I simply did what I always did – told him that it would be fine. That we could manage the enormous amount of cooking for the evening. I plastered a smile on my face, joked around and pretend that everything was fine.

I always did this – always wanted to make other people feel comfortable, less worried. I suppose I could blame my parents for this. I was always the anxious one, the one who had to be responsible even if I felt like I was crumbling inside. So, I pretended that I was fine, and, in a strange way, I felt that by going through the motions, my feelings would catch up and I would be fine.

Fine.

Good.

Those words – I think I must have said them a thousand times that day in the kitchen. 'Everything will be *fine*, Bartok.'

'I'm *good*, Bartok.'

'No. I'm not worried. I'm *fine*. You're *fine*! We're all *fine*!'

By late afternoon, the words had lost all meaning and my fake smile had dropped from my face as I stirred at a cream sauce, the steam burning my face and sending my hair into disarray. Had my smile dropped in there? I wondered as I stirred. Would some guest this evening reach for a canapé and instead find my smile stuck to the top of it?

'Your friend is here.' Bartok shook me out of my strange thought, and for a moment, I thought he meant Mateusz was back and a sudden lightness overcame me.

When I turned to look, it wasn't Mateusz but Anna.

'Irena!' She came to me and wrapped me in a hug. I could smell soap on her skin, a freshness that I yearned for in this hot kitchen.

'What are you doing here?' I asked, pulling myself out of her embrace, noticing how her cheeks were flushed, her blue eyes brighter than normal.

'I heard there is to be a dance,' she said, her eyes roving about the kitchen as if she had expected to see a band, or ladies dressed in gowns. 'I just wanted to look,' she added.

I remembered our conversation at the pond months ago. I shouldn't have been surprised that she had found out and managed to get down here away from her parents, who had kept her locked away inside so much that we had barely had a chance to see each other. She had said that day that we were young, we were meant to be going to dances, meeting men and thinking of marriage. But this wasn't the time nor the place for her.

'It's a dance, but not for us,' I said. 'It's not going to be what you think it will be like. It will be full of... *them*,' I emphasised.

'I know, I know. I don't want to go or anything. I was just – I don't know – am I being selfish again?'

I could see the excitement had drained from her face, and I felt a shred of guilt that I had taken that tiny bit of delight that she felt away from her.

'Look. If you come back at seven, then I'll let you peek through the door,' I suggested to her. But her attention had been taken by something else – her eyes were now lingering on the cake that Bartok was icing.

'Here, taste.' Bartok proffered the bowl, and she dipped her finger in, bringing out a clod of icing.

I couldn't help but smile as I watched her suck her finger, her eyes growing wide with the taste of sugar, a commodity we rarely had any more.

'What would you wear, Irena?' she asked, her lips still slapping together as she tried to get the thick icing from the roof of her mouth.

'I wouldn't go even if I was invited,' I told her.

'No! I mean let's say that it's just a dance, that the people there will just be us and our friends. What would you wear? Come on, Irena, play along,' she cajoled.

I could see Bartok rolling his eyes at us – he had no patience for this kind of talk – so I told Bartok I would be back shortly and took Anna out into the kitchen courtyard.

We sat on empty wooden crates, and for a moment, neither of us spoke, both perhaps delighting in the quietness that the courtyard offered us. It did not present a picturesque scene, rather a grey concrete wasteground full of broken chairs, a mattress from one of the rooms propped up against a wall, covered with mildew. And yet, I had found myself trying to take advantage of any calmness, any quiet that life now offered, whether it be sitting in a courtyard with my closest friend or standing by the lake. Either way, it offered some respite from the constant churn of anxiety that liked to spend its time in both my stomach and brain.

Finally, Anna could take it no more and broke the stillness that surrounded us.

'How are Abel and Henryk?' she whispered.

'Hush. Not here,' I told her, quickly looking about even though I knew no one was there.

I heard her harumph, then saw her cross her arms.

'Fine. If I were invited to the dance, I would wear Mother's old cream dress – the one she would wear when she'd go out dancing with Father. Not that it would fit me.'

'It is *divine*,' Anna said dreamily, seemingly cheered now I was engaging with her. 'But a little out of date. Me, I'd wear that red dress we saw in Lewandowski's shop. The one pinned in at the waist. That's what I'd wear.'

'And you'd look beautiful in it.'

'I would, wouldn't I?'

I looked at her, but she was staring up at the sky in a little dream world where she was going to a dance wearing a new red dress with some beau on her arm.

I wished that the world was different, that Anna could dance, that Abel and Henryk would be free, that the many uniformed men would simply disappear and let the rest of us live our lives.

'I should go back in,' I told Anna. 'Come back later and I'll let you sneak a look.'

I bent down and kissed the top of my friend's head and left her sitting on an upturned crate, staring at her dreams in the sky.

Later that evening, I had completely forgotten about Anna. The kitchen was a hive of activity; pots and pans were continually being scraped, stirred and washed, Bartok was redder than usual, and steam heated up the kitchen along with the humid air of the evening, causing all of us to become slick with sweat.

I was thankful, though, that the evening did not require my presence in the hall. As it was not a sit-down meal, canapés, sorbets and tiny cakes were ferried out to a long table covered with a white tablecloth. Not that many cared about the food. Each time I had managed to pop my head through the door, the dance floor was in full swing, a myriad of blue, red and yellow dresses being twirled about by men in their dark uniforms.

I could barely make out who the women were. They must have been from the town, and yet the lighting was so low, the dancing so fast that their faces all seemed to blend into each other.

'*Irena!* It's boiling over!' Bartok yelled at me to rescue a cheese sauce.

I raced to it and burned my arm as I lifted it off the stovetop. 'I've done it again,' I said to no one in particular. As I placed my arm under the tap, I noted the number of tiny silvery burn marks that I had acquired since working here. I wondered if when I was old and grey they would still be there, reminding me of this very moment.

'Lost in a thought?' Bartok came to my side. 'Wasn't Anna supposed to come?'

I looked at the clock – 8 p.m. We had almost finished in the kitchen and soon I would make my way home. Where was she? She had been so enthused by the thought of taking a peek at the festivities that I couldn't imagine she wouldn't have sneaked out.

'One last tray and you can go home.' Bartok had moved away and picked up a silver tray bearing tiny *pączki* that I knew he had filled with cream.

I picked up the tray, but before I could leave, Bartok

instructed me to open my mouth and popped one of the sweet doughnuts into it.

Oh, the *joy*! I had not eaten sweet things in such a long time that the cream inside tasted almost new to me. I watched how Bartok grinned at me, delighting in the simple moment of happiness it had provided.

Swallowing and with a smile on my face, I left the kitchen ready to place the last tray down and then return home, possibly stopping by Anna's house to check she was okay.

I stepped into the hall. The lights had been turned down low, but I could see the tables with their bright white linen cloths positioned around the room. Candles flickered on table-tops, illuminating faces, some smiling, some laughing, some deep in concentration as they watched dancers being whisked about to the tunes from the band.

The music was something I had heard before, and yet I did not know the name. I knew it was American, and this surprised me as most radio stations now only played music that had been approved by the Reich.

But here, soldiers and officers danced with women they did not know in front of a band that played furiously, sweat dripping from their brows. I knew the man who played the double bass – his name was Jan and he had one leg shorter than the other, which made him walk lopsided. This sometimes proved a form of an amusement for others in the town. However, Jan always made fun of himself first, cutting off any mean comments that came his way. Plus, he was a musical genius and could be relied upon to play at local dances, weddings and parties, so no one wanted to upset him. I tried to give him a small wave, but he didn't see me –his eyes were busy flickering nervously as they looked at the Gestapo dancing in front of them. He was scared. Even now. He knew that his luck could change within a second – one wrong note, perhaps a song chosen that they disapproved of, would be met with punishment.

It was then that any interest or excitement I had had at the prospect of seeing this dance, of hearing music, of perhaps feeling normal for just a moment, drained from me.

I looked to the dance floor, to the lipsticked smiles of the women, the slicked-back hair of the Gestapo, their boots shining, their smiles just a little too wide, a little too confident, and I felt I was in hell. It was hot, loud. It was too much.

I turned to leave. I had to get home, I had to breathe.

It was then that I caught sight of someone I knew, and my breath was nowhere to be found.

Anna.

She stood at the opposite end of the room, a glass in her hand, a man talking to her, his back to me. She smiled at the man, but it was tight and not quite right. She wore a red dress, but not the one from the shop that we had been discussing. This was one of her mother's I was sure, and Anna had wrapped a belt round her waist, trying to draw it in, trying to look like she belonged here.

How had she got in here? Why would she want to come with a Gestapo officer? Was she mad? Her parents would kill her. I itched to push my way through the swirling bodies and get to her, drag her away and keep her safe, but I knew I couldn't.

I tried to catch her eye, tried a wave, but she could not see me through the dimmed light. Then suddenly, the man she was talking to grabbed her arm. I saw her look to it, then back at the man's face, and shake her head. He must have said something to her because she shook her head again, her eyes wide with unmistakeable fear.

Then the man started to walk away, still holding on to Anna, dragging her towards a darkened doorway to the left of the hall's doors. I knew that was a cupboard, and I had a feeling I knew what he was going to do in there.

What should I do? Should I get Bartok? I looked around wildly and saw that Jan was looking at me – he must have seen Anna being dragged past him. He mouthed something to me, but I couldn't make out what it was.

The music suddenly seemed louder, the dancers faster. I couldn't grasp onto a thought; I couldn't make my eyes concentrate properly on what Jan was trying to tell me.

I felt someone bump into me and looked to my left to see Magdalena, a teacher at the school. She was just a little older than me, but in this light and with the make-up she wore, she suddenly looked much older.

'Are you all right, Irena?' she asked me over the din.

'I – Anna—' I started to say, then stopped as a short, thin uniformed man appeared and cupped her elbow with his hand, drawing her away from me.

I don't know how long I stood there trying to decide what to do – but I knew the minutes were ticking by, and Anna was in that cupboard. Finally, my legs started to move, and propelled me across the dance floor towards her.

I reached the door. Should I knock? Simply open it?

Then I heard Anna yell out, followed by a muffled sound. My hand went to the doorknob, and I yanked it open.

It wasn't Anna I saw first. It was Richter. He had Anna in his arms, the shoulder of her dress pulled down low. He stared at me and I at him. Neither of us spoke.

Anna realised that I was there and turned to me, revealing a tear-stained face. With the shock, Richter had let go of her, and she seized upon the moment and hustled her way to me.

'Go to the kitchen,' I whispered in her ear and ushered her out.

'Well, well, look who it is, *Irena*. I haven't seen you for some time.' Richter licked his lips and smiled at me. 'Are you here to take your friend's place?'

I stood in the doorway and could feel the heat of the room on my back, the music seemingly becoming a feeling and not a sound, thumping down on my skin too.

'Come in, Irena. Come in and see me. We haven't seen each other in some time.' Richter held out his hand to me in almost a gentle manner as if we were friends.

'I have to go back to the kitchen,' I tried, my voice coming out barely above a whisper.

'You can't leave me here all alone. You keep avoiding me – I know you do. You scuttle off into that kitchen every day, too shy to talk to me.'

I shook my head. I wasn't shy. I was afraid.

'Such a nervous little sparrow, aren't you?' He grinned. 'Come. Come and see me.' His hand was still held out to me, all ready for me to take.

'I don't want to,' I managed to say.

His smile dropped then. So did his hand and, for a moment, I thought that I was free, that I could simply leave and it would all end.

But in less than a second, he was upon me. His hands on my shoulders, his face close to mine. 'But you're *mine*,' he said, his voice menacingly low. 'And I like it when you're scared. Nervous. So much more... *fun*.'

He pulled me into the cupboard and threw me down. He must have closed the door, but I didn't see him do it. All I knew was that he was on top of me, kissing my neck, the stubble on his face scratching my skin.

I didn't move. I couldn't. My arms were pinned under his weight, my legs I knew were between his.

'No. Don't,' I mumbled underneath him, but the more I protested, the harder he pressed himself into me, the more he kissed me.

Then, his hand slid between my legs. In that moment, I stopped protesting. It was as though my brain knew that there was no escape, so I stayed as still as I could and closed my eyes.

I felt pain. I smelled alcohol and sweat. I could hear the band. Laughing. Talking. It all seemed so far away as if I wasn't alive any more. I couldn't understand it. I just wanted it to be over.

I don't remember him getting off me. I don't know how I got back to the kitchen. I don't remember how I got home.

All I do remember is sitting on the toilet, seeing scarlet in my underwear and bruises appearing on my thighs. I remember that.

How could I forget?

TWENTY

IRENA

Pinamar, Buenos Aires, Argentina
5 January 1994

The street was dark. It was not like it had been during the day. There was no man with a harmonica on a balcony, no people shopping, no one talking.

'I don't like it,' Anna whispered.

I squeezed her hand tightly. 'It's all right.'

'We should have asked that nice boy Peter to bring us. Why didn't you ask him?'

'Because the less he knows the better. What was I to say anyway? That his friend, Santiago, is someone I want to talk to, someone I want to look at to see if he is the man that raped me?' I said, my irritation barely concealed.

'Sorry,' Anna said. 'And don't say that word.'

'What word?'

'You know. *Rape*.'

'Well, what was it, Anna? What am I supposed to call it?'

'I know what it is, Irena. I just don't like the word. When

you say it, it makes me think about what he did to you, what he almost did to me. I just don't like it.'

I could hear the quiver in her voice and squeezed her hand again. 'I know. I don't either.'

We walked a few more yards to Santiago's bar in silence, Anna now and again looking over her shoulder at the taxi that I had asked to wait for us.

'He won't leave, will he?' Anna asked. 'He'll wait for us?'

'If he wants to be paid, he will.'

Within the minute we were standing outside Santiago's bar, a garish blue light lighting up the words next to the green painted sign I had seen that day.

The tables outside were empty, the yellow umbrellas still erect even though they were not needed. A sandy dog sat next to one of the chairs and eyed us, then wagged his tail happily as we approached.

'Should we go inside?' Anna asked.

I could only hear the thrum of male voices coming from the bar and music that I did not know and felt was too loud.

'We'll sit outside,' I answered. I did not want to go inside and have men stare at us. I did not want to try to ask for Santiago in the little Spanish that I had learned from the guidebook I had bought.

We sat on the plastic chairs, and Anna immediately bent down to pat the dog, who rose up on his hind legs and placed his front paws on her lap.

'Look, Irena! Look, he likes me!'

'Be careful,' I told her. 'He might have rabies.'

'He doesn't have *rabies*.' Anna grinned. 'You don't have rabies, do you?' she asked the dog in a baby voice. The dog, not understanding Polish but understanding her pitch, wagged his tail even more furiously so that it batted against the table leg.

I knew I should go inside – they might not see us out here. But – I hated to admit it – I was scared to do so. I had never been in a bar on my own before. Never had to. I was always with Mateusz, and without him by my side, I had lost my nerve.

'Are you sure you still want to do this?' Anna asked. She had asked this so many times now that I was beginning to get a bit frustrated with her.

'I have to,' I said firmly.

'You don't, you know. You don't have to. It won't change anything.'

I didn't answer her. I knew she was right. No. It wouldn't change anything. It wouldn't change the fact that he had raped me. It wouldn't change the fact that he was the reason that my baby had died. It wouldn't change that. But I still had to try. I had to do something. I had been waiting until Mateusz had died, until I could let myself think of the pain of the past again, let myself wallow in it and find the resolve to do what needed to be done. Richter could not live any more. I could not allow it. I had to see this through.

'That Sara girl, she was no use then?' Anna asked.

'No. Her father has retired. I think it might be worth trying to find him. He knows who he is, I'm sure of it.'

'Well, he did help the Liebermans, didn't he?' Anna said hopefully. 'He gave them the address of that Obersturmführer, and they came here and...' She trailed off.

'Yes. They came here,' I said, not saying what we both knew. That the Liebermans had had the Obersturmführer found, and then dealt with. Whether by their own hand or someone else's, they saw it through and never told me the details.

'But they didn't seem any better, Irena. When they came back. They were still the same. I don't think it will give you what you need.'

'Maybe not. Maybe it won't.'

'I suppose, though, that Obersturmführer they got. He deserved it, didn't he? Their whole family bar two of them gone in Auschwitz. You can't blame them for wanting to seek him out.'

I knew she was trying to rationalise what we were doing, or rather what I wanted to do. She was trying to find a moral reason for it, as there was no legal one. I let her continue.

'I mean, we could get him arrested if we find him, though. Isn't that what Carlos said had happened to others – that they had been arrested?'

'It's too late for that,' I told her, as I had told her many a time. 'He's old. No one will care. It has to be done this way.'

Anna nodded and diverted her attention back to the dog. She knew she could not talk me out of it. I had vowed years ago to do it, but then, my life with Mateusz – well, it changed things for me. It changed things enough so that I was able to find a semblance of a life, joy, excitement.

But there was always something hidden, deep down, things I never voiced to my husband, and not for some time to Anna either. I couldn't say them out loud, I couldn't voice the feeling I had – for me it had no name. The best I could describe it was as being like a furball that one of our cats once threw up. It was a mixture of food, of fur, all matted and congealed. That was what was inside me too. Anger, hate, revenge, pain, sorrow – all of them mixed up like a disgusting hairball, but one that I could not vomit up. It had to sit there. Festering. Waiting.

And as soon as Mateusz got sick and I saw the end of my own life nearing me, I knew there was only one thing that would perhaps make it go away: death for Richter, but it had to be by *my* hand. I had to see him suffer. I had to see the pain. It was the only thing I thought might help.

'Buenas tardes, Damas. ¿Qué puedo conseguirte?'

I looked up. There stood the man from earlier that day, his face half hidden in the dark. I felt my heart quicken. Could it be him?

'Ola,' I tried. Then I forgot what I had practised saying all

afternoon and dug around in my handbag for the guidebook. I flipped to the back and tried to ask him his name, but it came out wrong.

'Santiago?' I asked again.

'*Si*. Yes,' he then said in English. 'You are English?'

I shook my head. I knew a little of the language, though. 'Germany,' I said, not wanting to say Poland, not wanting to give any part of who I might be away.

'Ah! Welcome. I speak no German. Only little bit English. You want to drink?' He mimed drinking from a glass.

'Yes please,' I said.

'Yes? Okay. I find you something nice. For nice German ladies.'

He waddled back inside, and I felt disappointment wash over me. I didn't need to see his face. I knew it wasn't him. It wasn't Richter.

I said as much to Anna, who agreed. 'He is Argentinian, isn't he? I don't think that Richter would ever be able to look that native. But then maybe? Maybe look closer?'

Santiago returned with two short glasses filled with a dark liquid, and a can of Coke.

'It is Fernet-Branca,' he told us. 'Very nice. Very good. You mix it see.' He poured the bubbling sweet drink into the liquor. 'Very good.'

He then leaned forward and placed a candle on the table and, with a flick of his lighter, sparked the wick. It was then that I could get a good look at his face – the eyes brown, the skin quite tight. It wasn't Richter. Even if his eyes had been that dark grey-blue, he simply was not old enough.

'I sit? Is okay I sit?' He nodded at the other chair, and Anna told him to sit and join us.

'Is nice seeing ladies here. From Germany!' He slapped his hand on the table and laughed. I wasn't sure what he was laughing at, but Anna seemed to understand – then I saw she had already drunk all of her liquor.

'You have many Germans?' I asked him. 'Living here?'

'No. No so many. Maybe some. I don't know. There is one man he is going to swimming at the Hotel Pinamar every day and Ric—' Then he stopped talking and shook his head. 'No. Not Ricardo. No German. He is no German,' he corrected himself. 'He goes there, yes, Ricardo, my friend. But he sees other men there too. Maybe they are German,' he rambled.

Anna then began to talk to him, using her hands to express what she could not in words, and they seemed to understand each other as she patted the dog and pointed at things.

Santiago went back inside to retrieve the bottle of the liquor that Anna liked so much.

'We should go,' I told her.

'What are you doing?' she asked.

I quickly wrote the name of the hotel that Santiago mentioned on a piece of tissue paper, and the name – *Ricardo* – hoping that I had heard him correctly. She leaned over. 'But he said that the man wasn't German, didn't he?'

'He might have said that. But there was something about the way he said it, Anna. Like he wanted to correct himself not because he was wrong, but because he *shouldn't* have said it.'

Back at the hotel, Anna went straight to bed. I knew she would be suffering the following day from the amount she had drunk with Santiago, but I didn't care much. I sat at the little desk in my room and spread out a map. It took me a while to find the hotel, my eyesight being not what it used to be.

Should I ask Peter to take me? I had paid him for two more days in case we needed him. No. I would do this on my own and keep Peter in case this was just another dead end. I'd visit Sara too. Maybe if she saw me again, maybe if I asked her a few more questions or told her a bit more about myself, she might ask her father for more information. Maybe, just maybe...

I did not go to bed straight away but instead sat on the balcony, enjoying the sea salted air that blew over my skin. I tried to look at the stars, the moon, and marvel in their beauty, but I could not find an ounce of peace. Not like earlier that day when I had been sitting in the park and had that moment of *just not thinking*. But then, it had been short-lived, hadn't it? The music, the dance. I shuddered.

I remember how I felt afterwards. I still felt the same now.

Shame.

Fear.

Hatred for me. And for him.

TWENTY-ONE

IRENA

Zakopane, Poland
December 1941

The fire roared into life the moment the match touched the dry wood, letting the scent of pine, of cedar enrich the air of the sitting room. I sat by the fire, letting it warm my feet, my toes, finally reach my legs and creep its way up my body.

I was alone. My father and mother were in the basement with Abel and Henryk, eating dinner together. I hadn't joined them – I couldn't, someone had to be here to open the door if anyone knocked. But I couldn't anyway. I could barely talk.

A depression had taken over me. Dulled me. Taken away any light, any joy. My body did not feel like my own, and whenever I bathed, I would look at my skin, noting each blemish, each crease, each mark, and wonder whose body this was.

Every time I tried to think back to the dance, it was as though a veil came down, blocking my view. It wasn't that I wanted to remember what had happened, it was just that I was scared that if I didn't try and remember, it wouldn't be real. But,

I knew it was real. I knew it. And yet my mind was trying to tell me it had been a nightmare that should quickly be forgotten.

I remembered that the morning after, when I had returned to work in a daze.

Outside everything looked different and the same. A cat sauntered atop a wall, then stopped, looked at me, then with a flick of its tail jumped down and disappeared. A car rumbled past. A man wearing a hat grumbled as he passed me, telling me that I was in the way.

Was I in the way? I wondered. I looked either side of me. Yes. I was walking in the middle of the pavement as if I owned it. How selfish of me. I moved to one side, then looked at my feet as I walked. I wore black shoes. Boring shoes. And yet I now hated them and wanted to stop and take them off my feet and throw them into the street.

As soon as I got to the kitchen, I acted normal. I laughed with Bartok, I chopped vegetables, but it was as though I was outside of myself – sort of hovering above my own body, watching myself act out a life that I had no interest in any more.

It was only when I went into the dining room to serve lunch that I came back into my body with a thud. Richter was there. Smiling, laughing.

He waved me over, asked me how my morning had been, asked if I could come and see him the following evening in his office. He did not touch me as he usually did, his hands roaming my body as I served him, and the other men seemed not to notice, or perhaps they simply did not care.

I said yes. I couldn't say no. I knew that now.

On my return to the kitchen, I lost myself. My ability to hold or listen to a conversation was lost. It was as though everything was muffled, sounds, touch, smell, like I was so close to it and yet I couldn't grasp it.

Everyone noticed – of course they did. Overnight I had gone from being me to being someone else.

'Go and talk to Abel and Henryk,' my mother said that evening. 'You don't seem yourself.'

I shook my head and stared at the wall.

'What's wrong, Irena? What happened?'

'Nothing.'

I scraped my chair back and went to bed.

I remembered then, the following evening when I went to Richter's rooms in the hotel. I took him his evening meal so that Bartok would not ask questions, knocked and waited outside his door. *Room 12* hung on it in polished brass. I hated that it was polished. I don't know why. I just wanted it to be dull, tarnished.

'Come in,' he called out. He did not come to the door. Perhaps he was too important for that.

I had to place the tray on the floor, open the door, then pick it up again and keep the door open with my foot. Twice I almost tripped. Twice I almost cried.

'Irena.' He welcomed me into his sitting room cum office. Behind him the double doors were open to reveal his bedroom. 'How was your day?' He kissed my cheek. Took the tray from my hands.

'Good. Yes. Thank you.' The words came out of my mouth with no meaning. It wasn't really my voice. I wasn't sure whose it was, but it wasn't mine.

I turned immediately to leave and then felt his hand on my shoulder. 'Stay a while. Talk to me.'

I did not turn, I was determined not to. I felt him grip my shoulder tighter, painfully.

'Sit down,' he ordered.

I did as I was told and chose a chair by the window, perching on the edge, smoothing my skirt over my legs.

He sat on a plush soft pink sofa and crossed his legs. He

smiled at me.

'I enjoyed our time together,' he said. 'Did you?'

'No,' I muttered. I knew I was supposed to say yes. But there was no way I was going to do that. I wasn't going to give him that too.

'No?' he asked. He unfurled his legs and leaned his elbows on his knees. He shook his head softly, almost sadly.

Then he stood and walked the few steps towards me. He placed his hand on the top of my head, then stroked my hair, then finally let his hand find my cheek. He let it sit there for a moment, then with a shock I felt pain heat up my skin. He had slapped me.

I raised my hand to my cheek and held it there. He had already returned to the couch and sat down again. He lit a cigarette, then blew smoke up towards the ceiling.

'No?' he asked again.

'I meant yes.' I fumbled the words. My cheek hurt. I wanted to cry. I didn't move. Didn't dare.

'See!' Suddenly, he was happy again, his face softer. 'I knew you did. My nervous little sparrow. You just don't like to admit it, do you?'

I didn't answer, just watched as he dug around in his trouser pocket, his cigarette balanced in his lips.

'Here.' He drew out a small red velvet box and handed it to me.

I stood, took it, then sat back down again.

'Go on, open it!' he urged.

I opened it to reveal a gold pendant of a tiny bird.

'I saw this and thought of you. My tiny sparrow. You shall wear it always.'

He came up behind me and took the necklace, clasping it round my neck. I felt his breath on my skin.

'You'd want to show me your appreciation, wouldn't you?' he whispered.

I nodded.

'Come with me. And it's all right if you are scared.' He took me by the hand to his four-poster bed. By the time we reached it, I was crying, but he didn't seem to care. If anything, my tears made him more excited.

This time, it took longer. This time all my clothes were removed, and only the necklace, so bright against my pale skin, remained.

This time, I remembered too much. This time I cried, I fought. And then, when it was over, exhausted, depleted of everything, I got changed and let him kiss me on the cheek as a farewell.

The same cheek he had slapped. The same cheek that still bore his fingerprints.

'My little sparrow,' he said.

'*Irena!*'

I looked up from the fire. How long had I been thinking about it all? What time was it?

'I've been saying your name over and over for a minute! What is wrong with you?' My mother stood in front of me, her hands on her hips.

'Nothing,' I told her.

'Abel and Henryk want to see you,' she said. 'You've barely been talking to them lately. They're doing well. Your father thinks Henryk might be leaving us soon.'

'I said he *might* be.' My father appeared from the hatch.

'That's what I said, *might*,' my mother huffed.

I stood and made my way down the steps to the basement, to find Abel and Henryk sat across from each other, my father's chess set in between them.

'Sorry, I didn't mean to interrupt your game,' I said.

'No! No, we haven't started yet, just setting it up for tomorrow. Your father was kind enough to lend it to us.' Abel waved me over.

I sat on the edge of his bed and watched the pair as they placed the pieces on their designated squares.

I reached out and picked up the queen, the white queen, a crown atop her head, a face carved into the marble revealing a smiling, almost motherly appearance.

'Ah the queen!' Abel said. 'She's the one that protects the king. You know how to play chess?'

I agreed that I did.

'Well then, you know that she is the strongest piece of the lot. She is the one to protect really, because once she is gone, the others would find it hard to protect their king.'

'Maybe someone should protect her at all costs?' I suggested.

'Maybe,' Abel said. 'A king should protect his queen. I always tried with my wife, but...' He trailed off.

'I'm so sorry, Abel.'

'You have nothing to be sorry for,' he said.

'Irena.' Henryk looked to me, his voice soft and even. He barely spoke, always allowing his grandfather to do most of the talking. But when he did speak, everyone listened. 'Irena,' he started again. 'I'm worried about Grandfather.'

'About leaving him, you mean?'

He nodded. 'Your father said it might happen soon. I want to go. I want to help people. I want to fight. But I am worried about leaving him here.'

'*Him* is in the room, you know!' Abel chimed in. 'And him – me – I will be fine. You don't need to worry. It is me that must worry for you.'

Henryk smiled at his grandfather and did not say more.

'I promise I will take care of him,' I said.

'Like the queen protects the king?' Henryk asked with a large grin.

'Definitely.' I laughed, and he held out his hand for me to shake. Our deal was struck.

I stayed around half an hour until Abel sat on his bed, his eyelids drooping, when I stood up and made my way to the stairs.

'Goodnight, Henryk,' I whispered.

'Irena, please can you stay a while longer?' he whispered back.

I took my foot off the first stair and went to Henryk's bed at the other side of the room. He patted the mattress for me to sit next to him.

'I hope this is all right?' he said, his eyes flitting to the staircase. 'I wouldn't want your father to think anything improper.'

'It's fine,' I said. 'What's wrong? Did you want to talk more about leaving? About your grandfather?'

'No. I just wanted to tell you what happened to my parents and to my grandmother. I know my grandfather told you some of it, but he didn't tell you everything.'

'There's no need, Henryk. I know it is hard for you to talk about—'

'No. No, you don't understand. I *have* to talk about it. I have to tell *someone*. Grandfather won't speak of it, and I understand that. But what if I die? What if he dies? Someone should know our story. Someone *needs* to know what they did to us.'

A part of me felt guilty because I did not want to hear what Henryk had experienced. But I understood his need to talk. I hoped that one day soon I would feel that need to express what was happening to me and perhaps feel the weight of it had lifted enough to give me some semblance of peace.

I let Henryk talk. I did not interrupt. It was his story to tell. I simply listened with patient ears and promised I would always remember his story.

. . .

'It had been coming for a while, you know. Bit by bit it was coming for us, so when it happened, when we were taken to the ghetto, it didn't come as a surprise to me. I knew that things were only going to get worse.

'First, they came for our possessions, our jobs, they made us wear the star. You know all this. We were lucky then. It sounds stupid to say that we were, but some of the things that happened to our neighbours, our friends, it made us feel lucky.

'I was seventeen when I first found out what was happening to others. A girl I knew, I won't say her name, I can't. Anyway, she was sixteen. Really beautiful, you know – she had that kind of smile that made you smile back. Everyone liked her. She could play the piano and sing and dance. She was just one of those girls who you only really ever meet once and you can't ever stop thinking about them.

'Anyway, she lived two streets away. Just two streets. One morning, my mother left the house in a hurry. She said she had to visit the girl and her family. The way that she ran from the house made me run after her. I knew something was wrong – the way she ran – the way her face was tighter – like scrunched up with worry, or fear.

'We got to their house and their front door was hanging off its hinges. Just hanging there like a loose tooth, and inside it was all dark, like the dark of a mouth. I'm sorry. I'm not good at describing it, but I want you to see what I saw – this mouth, all dark, a tooth hanging off, and I half expected to see blood dripping from the brickwork.

'There was no blood outside. There was inside, though.

'They had come. The Gestapo, at 3 a.m. They liked to wake you up in the middle of the night and say that you had done something or had something that they wanted. They did it to us and took things. But like I said, we had been lucky.

They hadn't broken anything yet. They hadn't broken us either.

'So, inside was my friend's mother, crying over this lump on the floor. But when I got closer, I saw it wasn't a lump. It was her husband. He had no shirt on and all over his back were black and blue bruises. Deep, you know. Like it wasn't just on the skin. I could feel those bruises.

'He wasn't dead, but he couldn't move. There was a red rug underneath his head. But when I looked closer, I saw that the rug was moving. I saw then that it was blood. My mother immediately helped. She helped get him sat up, mopped up the blood. I didn't look as she did it because I was already feeling sick. And I felt guilty that this man was in so much pain, and I was going to vomit.

'I went to find my friend instead. I looked in each room, and each room was turned upside down. Furniture, chairs, paintings ripped off the walls.

'I found her in the parlour. She was sitting on the piano stool staring at the keys that were all broken – like teeth. See again, I'm no good at describing it. But they were broken, all of them, like broken teeth.

'She had bruises on her face. Her nightgown was ripped. There was blood on it. She told me what they had done, Irena. How they had taken her into the parlour, made her play them some songs as they drank vodka and laughed at her. They made her parents sit in the living room. They didn't close the door. They wanted them to see, you see. Oh God, they wanted them to see *her*, and for her to see *them*!

'They made her dance for them. That's what she said. They made her dance as another soldier played the piano. Then – oh God – they – well – you know. They took turns on her. She could hear her father shouting, screaming, trying to help her, to get to her. But another man had this stick she said – maybe a baton – I don't know. So he started to hit her father, over and over, whilst these men took turns on her. She's screaming for her father, he's screaming for her. Her mother was frozen, she said. Couldn't move. Like a statue.

'So you see. We were lucky so far. That hadn't happened to us, yet. But it made us more aware of what could happen. It made me realise that nothing was going to get better. The girl, my friend, she died. That's why I can't say her name – I can't make it real just yet. They had raped her so badly and beaten her so much that she bled from the inside out – that's what my mother had said – from the inside out.

'We lost everything. Just like everyone else. We were sent to the ghetto. You know, the wall around the ghetto, they built it like gravestones – did you know that? Just another reminder that death was literally all around us.

'In the ghetto we worked – all of us did. We didn't have much choice. We lived, all of us, plus two others, in one room in a large house and there was never enough food, never enough water.

'We tried to barter to get what we needed, but everyone was doing the same. In the end, my grandfather bartered education. He read to children, taught as if he were still in a lecture hall. It got us a little more bread, a little more water.

'But my grandfather, he wouldn't eat much. He let my grandmother have his portions. She was frail anyway, and even though we tried, we couldn't give her what she needed. Couldn't get her the medication. Every day, he had to watch as she simply disappeared in front of his eyes. Imagine that. Imagine the pain he felt. He wanted to help her – do something – but there was nothing he could do.

'She died in July. We had been in the ghetto for only two months. Two days after she died, my mother died. But this was different. This was because she took a risk for us all.

'After watching her mother waste away, she decided to risk leaving the ghetto to take some of our belongings – a watch, a ring – to some friends on the outside. They could sell it for us, and, in return, we then had something better to barter with – money. Money could bribe guards too. She knew that, so she took the risk.

'The problem was when she was trying to get back in. Imagine that. Dying trying to get into a place that was obviously going to kill us all.

'Shot, once in the head. I was the one who saw her. Someone saw it happen and fetched me. Grandfather wanted to see her, but I wouldn't let him. I couldn't let him have this image on his mind forever.

'So, you see. That's our story. And we got out. We are still lucky. Mateusz, that baker, the others who are strangers who helped us – all of them risked their lives for us. And you too. You and your parents. I just thought you needed to know who you were risking your life for and why.'

Henryk looked exhausted. Each word had been painful for him, I was sure. I had not interrupted him, not once. I knew how hard it was sometimes to say the things you were scared to say – to put a voice to the fear.

I wasn't sure what to say to him. Instead, I leaned forward and took him in an embrace, knowing that he was braver than I ever could be.

He had spoken. And I could not.

TWENTY-TWO

SARA

Pinamar, Buenos Aires, Argentina
5 January 1994

The sky bruised its way into night and yet Sara still sat at her desk, the small electric fan whirring and making the pages on her desk flap.

Since the old woman had left, she had gone through her father's files trying desperately to find a mention of her. All she found were four or five manila folders, each of them marked with a simple 'X' in place of a name, with no papers inside.

She rubbed at her temples, where a headache was beginning to make itself known. Sensing defeat, she packed up her things, and decided that on her way home she would go and see her father.

Outside, the evening still held on to the day's heat, but a slight breeze lifted the temperature just enough to make the short walk to her parents' house enjoyable.

As she walked, she could not help but notice the families who sat outside restaurants, small children, their faces smeared with ketchup as they bundled fries into their mouths, the parents talking to each other, laughing with each other.

Her hand immediately went to her stomach and that morning's appointment came rushing back at her. *Pregnant*. That was what the doctor had told her. The tiredness she had been feeling, the headaches – all of it was because she was pregnant, not some mysterious illness as she had thought it might be.

What was she going to do? She obviously had to tell Peter, but she wasn't sure what his reaction would be. Sara was always prepared, always two steps ahead with everything she did in her life, so this had thrown her completely. She wanted to be happy about it, but instead she was scared. And the thought of saying it out loud, of putting a voice to it, made it too real. She wasn't brave enough, not yet.

Would he cry? she wondered as she walked. Would he get down on one knee and finally make their relationship official? Or would his eyes immediately seek out the horizon, his mind perhaps preparing a new life, far away from her?

Why did he make her feel this way? He loved her, she knew that. But there was something about him, especially lately, where she felt him pulling away slightly and he would not talk to her about it, would not tell her what was on his mind.

Before her thoughts could continue on this downward spiral, she realised that she had reached her father's house – a one-storey whitewashed building, wedged between two terracotta-brick homes. The jasmine that climbed over the doorway gave a welcome sweet freshness as she used her own key in the heavy wooden door to enter the cool, blue-tiled hallway.

She pushed open the front door and was greeted immediately with the scent of grilled meat, the voice of Mercedes Sosa coming from the old gramophone in the sitting room, and the stuffy heat, held inside all day.

She found her father in the kitchen, his back turned to her, a glass of red wine in one hand, the other stirring something on the stove. She leaned in to kiss his cheek and saw the surprise on his face as he turned round. 'Ah! My daughter! Where have you been?'

Before she could answer, he took the wooden spoon he was holding and placed it on her lips, making her open her mouth. 'Tell me, too much salt? Too little?'

She tasted the rich tomato sauce and saw that her father's eyes were bloodshot. This wasn't his first glass of wine. His shirt was crinkled, misbuttoned, and splattered with what she could only hope was the sauce, although it resembled blood.

'So? Salt? No, yes?' he asked.

'It's fine as it is,' she told him.

'Aha! I knew it was! I was testing you, you see. To see if you have a palate like mine. A chef's palate!'

He turned away from her and stirred once more at the sauce.

She sat at the kitchen table and felt a sudden wave of nausea rise up. She swallowed it back and stared at the wood grain until she felt normal again. As her father chatted about his latest hobby – he was going to be a painter, he had decided – she thought of how much in this moment she would dearly love her mother to be there. She didn't remember her – or perhaps she did a little; a sort of ghost at the edge of her vision when she thought back to being a child. But she could not remember her voice, nor her features.

And it was not as though her father was much help. He had seemed to think that it was better for her, and maybe for him, that her mother was never spoken about. It was as though she had never existed at all, and as much as Sara had probed him over the years to at least give up something about the woman he had married, he had always told her to leave it be.

'What is the point?' he had asked her angrily one evening when she was a teenager. 'What is the point of trying to bring the dead back to life?'

It was then that she saw tears in his eyes, his jaw clenching and unclenching as he fought them back. He wasn't speaking about her mother, not because he didn't want to, but because it hurt him too much to do so. Sara saw that and never asked about her again.

'Papa,' she said, making him turn away from the sauce. 'I need to talk to you about something. About... *someone*.'

'Ah yes.' He dragged a chair out away from the table and sat. 'What is it? Peter?'

'No, not Peter. Why do you think it would be Peter?'

He shrugged. 'Just wondered.'

'No. Not him. This client that I asked you about. She came to see me.'

'Ah.' He stood, went to the counter and found the bottle of red. He splashed a generous amount in his own glass and had just gone to reach for a glass for Sara when she told him no.

'No? You? No wine?'

'Not tonight. I have a headache,' she said. She wasn't about to tell him about the baby – not yet, not before telling Peter.

He sat back down, drank and then smacked his lips together in satisfaction. 'Go on then. What did she say? What do you know?'

Sara could see that her father was fishing. He knew everything and she needed to play along as if Irena had told her everything too – it was the only way that he would tell her the truth.

'Well. Everything,' she said, making sure she looked him dead in the eye and did not blink.

'Everything?' He raised his eyebrows.

'About Christoph Richter.' She said the name slowly, wanting to see his reaction.

Her father gave a low whistle, then smiled. 'Richter, she said? She wants to find him? That's what she told you?'

She nodded.

'Did she tell you why?'

She considered whether to simply say what Irena had said to her, but she knew it wasn't enough. 'Maybe.'

'Ha! Maybe.' Her father poured more wine into his glass, took a swig, then leaned across the table towards her. 'She wants to kill him,' he said. This time, he did not blink, his eyes did not leave hers. 'She wants to kill him for killing her only child.'

She felt like laughing. It was absurd. An old woman here, looking for someone to kill? But the way her father was looking at her made her realise that this was no joke.

'She didn't tell you that, did she?'

Sara shook her head.

'Ah, Sara, my good girl.' He leaned away from her and raked a hand through his hair. 'I suppose it's time you knew. I wasn't going to tell you, but ever since you reminded me about it, about her, I thought that maybe you should know. That it would help you in some way. Help you to see what I see – that there isn't just right and wrong, there's a grey area.'

'Not this again!' Sara raised her arms in exasperation. 'You've said this for *years*! We don't see things in the same way, that's true, but I don't think I can practise law the way you have done. I mean, you got your licence taken away!'

He didn't react angrily like she thought he would. Instead, he laughed. 'And with good reason! I went too far with that politician. Them taking me my licence is fine. But I did good things Sara – very good things – it's just that I was worried that you would never see it that way. But now. Now you should know.'

'Know what?'

'I've been working, for some years now, with some people. People who could pay a lot of money if I could help them locate others – others not from here. You remember Eichmann?'

'Yes.'

'Well, not that that was just me. But people wanted to find

him, and you need someone on the ground, someone who knows others, someone who likes the grey.'

'So, you found him? And what does this have to do with an old woman?'

'No, you're missing the point. That gave me a taste for it, you see. Do you know how many Nazis came here after the war? How many evaded capture and punishment? Not just infamous ones. The ordinary ones. Ones that governments weren't looking for, but perhaps some of their victims were.'

Sara's mind whirred. She sat for a moment, piecing it together. Irena was looking for Christoph Richter, a Nazi. She had said he was her ex-husband, but she saw now that that had been a ruse. Then she remembered the one cream baby mitten that had fallen out of her bag and how Irena had reacted with a mixture of fear and sadness. A keepsake, perhaps, from a baby who was no longer there.

'She wants to kill him...' she muttered to herself.

'She does, but she won't.' Her father stood and went to the stove. He turned off the heat and placed the pot on the sideboard. 'She won't. There's someone else that has had eyes on him for a while. A different client. They get first shot. I gave Irena a fake name, Santiago. Said that was the man. I honestly didn't think she would come here, not at her age. But here we are.'

'I-I-' Sara could not find the words. Her father was helping others mete out their own punishment; he was allowing them to be judge, jury and executioner.

As if reading her mind, he said, 'I only find them. What happens next is none of my business.'

'But it's *wrong*!' Sara finally found her voice. 'Why not hand them over to the police? Why not send them back? Why not—'

'Why not what?' her father interrupted her. 'Like I said, it is for them to decide, Sara. You cannot know what these people have gone through to bring them to this decision. You cannot judge here. It might not be legal, Sara, but morally it's just.'

Sara scraped back her chair. She could not listen to this any more. 'Do you know where he is? Who he is now?' she asked, trying to keep her voice level.

'I do.' He turned round, the wooden spoon half in and half out of his mouth as he tasted the crimson sauce. 'But I won't tell you. You won't save him.'

'So, why tell me all of this at all? You don't want me to tell the police, you don't want me to tell Irena who he is – so, why tell me?'

He took the spoon out of his mouth and smiled. This time a gentle smile. 'Because, Sara. Your mother would have wanted you to know. This whole thing was your mother's idea because she worked with them. She was a Jew.'

TWENTY-THREE

PETER

Pinamar, Buenos Aires, Argentina
5 January 1994

Peter had a decision to make. A big one. It had been a decision that he should have made quite a few years now, but he had dragged his feet, hoping that maybe something would happen and make it easier for him.

Carlos, Sara's father, had spoken about it to him a lot lately.

'There isn't much time,' he had warned him. 'There's someone else and I've put them off for as long as I can. But it's coming to a head, Peter. You have to make a choice. You know I support you either way.'

His resolve to do what was necessary wavered daily, and most of it was Sara's fault. She had changed him, whether he wanted to admit it or not, and things were not so easy to make out any more. Like that shadow, there, on the beach. Was it moving towards him? Was it still? Was it a person?

The shadow was moving. It was a person. Whomever it was walked slowly, carefully, now and again appearing for a second in the moonlight and then disappearing again. It was only when it was a few feet in front of him that he could see who it was. *Irena*. The old woman from earlier that day.

'*Gówno!*' she shrieked.

'I'm sorry!' He stood. 'It's me, Peter!'

He could see the fear on her face, her pupils dilated. 'Oh my! I am sorry. I was at the hotel, you see,' she blathered. 'And I couldn't sleep, so I thought I would take a walk. I am sorry.'

'No, *I* am. I didn't mean to scare you.'

'It's all right. Not much does scare me these days. It was more of a surprise.' She chuckled. 'What are you doing out here?'

He saw her look to the sand where his fishing tackle sat. 'A bit of night fishing.'

'You won't catch anything unless you put the rod into the water,' she joked.

'I haven't got round to it yet. I was just sat here thinking.'

'Well. I won't disturb you,' she said, turning away.

'No. Please. Sit for a while if you want to.'

'Are you sure you don't mind having an old woman for company?'

He grinned. 'Not at all. I'd be honoured.'

They sat side by side, neither of them speaking for a few minutes, which gave Peter time to bait the hook.

'Do you catch much at night-time? I would have thought not,' she said, breaking the quiet.

'I do. Sometimes.'

'I always wondered if fish sleep. In my mind I thought maybe they slept at night. Oh God, listen to me! Rambling on. I sound like Anna!'

He gave a chuckle. 'It's nice to sometimes just say what pops into your mind. I wish I could do it.'

'And what would you say, do you think?'

Her voice was gentle, not prying nor demanding. It made him feel calm – safe, even.

'I would say that I wish I could be more honest,' he said, surprising himself.

'Honest? With whom?'

'With myself mostly, but with my girlfriend too. She deserves better.'

'Honesty is important,' Irena said. 'I was married for years. Nearly fifty of them in fact. And I was honest, most of the time.'

'Only most?'

She laughed. 'I think we all keep a part of us hidden. Even from those we love the most. Usually, it is things that we are ashamed of. Or maybe things that scare us. And we don't want to pass that on to the other person. At least I didn't.'

He thought on what she had said during the next minute or so of quiet. It was as though she knew when to stop talking. It suited him.

He thought in those minutes of his past – of his adopted parents, how neither of them had really wanted him and how they had kept their own secrets from him too. Nature versus nurture. It seems that nurture had won out on that score.

They never told him who his real parents were, nor where he came from – not until his adoptive father, Maurice, was dying and eventually revealed a part of his past. A part of his past that had sent him here and one he sometimes wished he knew nothing about.

'You can be honest, though, with your girlfriend, I think,' Irena said. 'You don't have to be like me. When I think about it now, I think I probably could have been more open. But things were hard to say, to think about. The memories I had from the years made me a different person and made me think about things in a different way.'

'Like those people Anna spoke about today? Abel and that other one?' he asked.

'Yes. Them,' she said quietly. 'What they went through,' she added and shook her head gently. 'What we all went through. It was too much. It's too much to even put into words.'

'I understand,' he said softly.

'I think about it, though. Recently, I can't *stop* thinking about it all. It's as though now my husband is gone, something has been unlocked and set free. Not that I want it to be. I would rather not remember a thing. But here. In this stillness, my mind is not quiet. It is full of the past.'

'Think about it then,' Peter said. 'Just think about it all. Let it happen. Perhaps it's a good thing, to let it happen, you know?'

'And do you think of your past too? You sound as though you know what you are talking about!'

'Hardly. I know only parts of my past. Like glimpses of it. It isn't real yet – it isn't a full story yet.'

He could see, even in the dark, that she was confused by what he had just said. 'Just let them speak, I suppose is what I'm saying – the people from your life. Maybe just let them speak.'

'Are you going to be here a while?' she asked.

'I am. Can't sleep. Not yet.'

'Is it all right for me to sit here with you? Just to sit and to think? Do you mind keeping me company for a while longer?'

'Not at all,' he said and let out the line once more, feeling the tug of the waves and feeling the warmth of Irena's body next to his as she thought of the past, and as she let the ghosts speak.

TWENTY-FOUR

IRENA

Zakopane, Poland
December 1941

That night, I did not sleep. Instead, I wept.

I wept for Henryk, for his mother, for Abel and his grandmother. I wept for his friend, the girl who had been used like that, in front of her own parents, and then slowly bled to death from what they had done to her. I wept for myself too. I wept for what had been done to me and what I knew would continue to be done to me. I sobbed so hard into my pillow that it became damp with tears, and I had to turn it over, to the dry side, only to start all over again.

By the time the winter sun started to rise, I was already sitting next to my bedroom window, watching the world wake up, wondering if today would be any better for any of us.

The thought of what had happened to that poor girl haunted me. When I was fifteen, my mother told me about how babies were made. I remember sitting there, listening to her and cringing at the thought of her and my father doing what she said they did. I think she was probably more explicit than most parents were – she told me that it was a form of love, a way to show each other the most intimate parts of yourselves and feel safe. She also told me that it felt good.

What had happened to that girl was not love. It was brutal. It was more than animalistic. It was *evil*. And what I had with Richter was not what my mother had told me about either. It was not as evil, perhaps, but it was not done with care, with friendship even. I was just a thing to be played with and then one day possibly discarded in a bloody heap.

I left the house when the weak sun was high enough to shine on the snow, making it dance and sparkle. It snowed each year, heavily, and most of the time I enjoyed the change in the season. I liked to sit by the fire, to eat *bigos*, dumplings and thick slices of baked ham. I liked to read, to talk with my father, to ice-skate on the pond with Anna. But now, I felt nothing for the season. I was almost annoyed that the fresh snow had the audacity to look so clean, so inviting, so pretty. Would I ever feel any sort of joy again as a season changed?

The kitchen was a warm welcome as I arrived. Bartok was busy in his office with Emeryk, sorting out the menus, leaving me to wash pots, alone with my thoughts.

As I scrubbed, I wondered whether my mother had just been entirely wrong. Whether, in fact, it had nothing to do with love, but everything to do with hate. How could it be, that for her and my father it was an expression of love and yet for me, and for Henryk's friend, it could be so utterly different?

I watched my hands in the water turning red. The water was too hot and yet I did not care. There was a part of me that hoped Richter would see them and perhaps be revulsed by me – perhaps this would make him stop.

'Irena, *enough*!' Bartok came to my side and pulled my hands out of the too-hot water. 'What are you doing? What's wrong with you?'

I stared at him as if I didn't recognise him. I looked at his skin, plump from the fat underneath, small pores visible on his nose. Had he done to a woman what Richter was doing to me? I suddenly could not bear to be touched by him, and yanked my arms away from him.

I couldn't tell what the reaction on his face was – hurt? Worry?

'Take a break,' he said gently and stepped aside so that I could go and sit in the concreted courtyard.

The mouldy mattress was still there, propped against the wall. The crates were still stacked haphazardly. Nothing in this courtyard had changed, and I couldn't understand how this was possible. How had my life, my body changed so much and yet the world still moved, or stayed still – either way, it wasn't fair.

I sat with my back against a wall, feeling the cool brick on my skin. I wanted to stay here forever. I closed my eyes and hoped that when I opened them again, I would find out that this had simply been a bad dream.

'Sleeping on the job?'

I knew the voice. Mateusz. I opened my eyes and there he stood, one hand in his trouser pocket, the other holding a cigarette.

'How are things with Abel and Henryk?' he asked, then dragged a crate close to me and sat down.

'Much the same,' I said.

'What's the matter?' he asked, his brow suddenly furrowing with worry.

'Nothing.'

'There is,' he said, then reached out to take one of my still-pinkened hands in his. I immediately removed my hand from his orbit, and he stared at the empty space, then raised his eyebrow to me in question.

'I spoke to Henryk,' I said, deciding that this was something I could talk about. I just couldn't talk about me.

'Oh yes?'

'He told me what it was like in Kraków. What had happened to his friends and what happened when he was in the ghetto.'

'It's hard to hear, isn't it?'

'How did I not know? How could I have not understood how bad it is?'

He shrugged. 'Here, it's like it isn't as bad. I know, I know!' He raised his hands up in surrender at me as I raised my eyebrows at him. 'Look. It isn't as bad because the brutes have decided to make this their playground. You know that. Death's Head, yes, it's bad. But what's happening in the cities, what has been happening, it's worse.'

I wanted to tell him then about what was happening to me. How it might just be as bad, only we couldn't see it. But I didn't.

'Father would come back from the city and tell me and Mother about it,' I said. 'But he didn't go into the detail that Henryk did.'

'Maybe he didn't dare. Maybe it was too hard to put into words?'

'I suppose,' I said. I shivered. The cold was too much, I needed to go back inside, but I also wanted to keep talking to Mateusz.

I wrapped my arms round myself and tried to stop my teeth from chattering.

'I have a few things to drop off for Bartok and then I'm going to get Henryk,' he said.

I turned to look at him, but he was looking at the tips of the mountains. 'Best time to get him is in daylight – did you know that? Sometimes, it's better to hide in plain sight. Everyone expects you to do things in the dark, but sometimes the light is better.'

I wondered if that was what Richter was doing – hiding in plain sight. Doing it all in front of everyone, making it normal. I shivered again.

'You need to go inside,' he said, then stood and offered me his hand to take. I stared at it for a moment, then took it.

It was warm, in spite of the cold. For a moment, we stayed like that, my hand in his, and it was oddly comforting. Almost like we had had a whole conversation without either of us speaking a word.

'Tell Henryk I said goodbye,' I whispered to Mateusz as he let my hand drop. 'Tell him I promise to be a good queen!'

'A... queen?' Mateusz asked, puzzled.

'He'll know what it means,' I told him. 'Just tell him that I was lucky too. Lucky to have known him.'

Mateusz doffed his hat at me and with a wink and a smile left me in the courtyard, my arms wrapped round myself for warmth, my breath hanging in the air, the sun dazzling the iced snow, mocking us all.

TWENTY-FIVE

IRENA

Zakopane, Poland
January 1942

Christmas had been a sad affair. Our usual Christmas Eve feast had been depleted to just a limp piece of fish, potatoes and a few mouldy carrots that my mother had assured us would taste fine once cooked. They did not.

With Henryk gone, my father had spent as much time as he could with Abel, but there was a change in him – he could not seem to bear being away from his grandson, and refused to talk, to play chess or even eat very much.

I worried for him. Of course I did. But at the same time, my own worries took over my mind. Each day at work was a constant battle with Richter. I would hide from him, I would change my shifts until he complained to Emeryk, who told me to be there when Richter demanded it.

'Have you *any* idea who he is, Irena?' Emeryk asked me, pushing his slipping spectacles up the bridge of his nose. 'If he is not happy, then I can assure you he can make your life much, much worse. And mine,' he added.

However, it seemed as though the more I resisted Richter, the more he wanted me. If I was scared, if I told him no and fought him, he became more animated. It was only when I was in the courtyard one day, pouring dirty water down the drain, that I realised what was happening. In the corner of the courtyard was a tabby alley cat – one we fed copious amounts of food. We had nicknamed him Misiu as he reminded us all of a fat little teddy bear.

He was a good mouser, and that we were also glad of. That day, I saw him playing with a small brown mouse. The more the mouse tried to escape Misiu's clutches, the more excited he became, his tail swishing, a low growl emanating from his throat. As soon as the mouse stayed still, playing dead, Misiu left it alone and sauntered up to me purring, rubbing himself against my legs.

That was what it was with Richter. I was the mouse. He was the cat. And for some reason I had been playing along without realising the rules of the game.

The following evening when I took Richter his dinner to his rooms, I decided to change what I had been doing. Instead of saying no, I would say yes. It was a risk, I knew, but I was willing to take it. I wasn't sure how much longer I could do this.

Richter seemed, as always, happy to see me. He enquired about my family, about Christmas, and seemed upset that I had not asked him for extra food or gifts.

'Always come to me,' he said. 'You know I will take care of you.'

'Thank you,' I said, this time changing my usual silence for some form of conversation. 'Next time I will.' I forced myself to smile at him and was optimistic when I saw the look of confusion wash over his face.

'Ah well.' He came to me and placed his hand on my neck, his fingers finding the gold chain he had given me. He wound it round a finger until the chain bit into my skin.

I tried not to flinch, not to show any fear. He wound it tighter.

'So brave today!' he said. 'So *brave*.'

I thought I was winning. I really did. But with a quick movement, he got his finger free, threw me on the sofa, then turned me over, all of his weight on my back.

'This is what you get if you are a brave girl.' His breath was ragged on my ear. I could feel him pulling my underwear aside, only this time he was jabbing himself somewhere new.

I knew what he was going to do. I started to scream, to try to wriggle free from under his grasp, but I could barely breathe, barely shift an inch. He placed his hand over my mouth, and it was then that I bit him. I bit down so hard I didn't even stop when he yelled, not even when I tasted blood.

He let me go. I turned over and saw him standing over me, staring at his bloodied finger and then at me. I wiped my mouth with the back of my hand, glad to see it streaked red.

I stood and smoothed my skirt down and headed for the door.

All I heard him say to me as I left was, 'Stupid Polish bitch.'

It had been a week since I had bitten Richter. A week and I had not gone into the dining room, and he had not asked for me. I finally felt like I was free of him. That somehow it had changed and he would no longer be interested in me.

I wanted to tell someone about it. I wanted to be brave like Henryk and tell someone my story. I itched to get it out of me. There was Anna, I could talk to her. But I had barely seen her since the dance – she had been locked away in her house, not wanting to venture out into the world. I knew how she felt, but I didn't have the option of staying at home.

There was Mateusz – I liked talking to him, I liked seeing him, but how could I tell him what Richter had done? And what about Mother? Father? What would they do if I told them? It was then I realised I didn't really have anyone to talk to and it would have to be my burden to silently bear.

As I reached home one evening, I found my mother standing on the doorstep, a shawl around her shoulders.

'Mother, get in. It's freezing. What are you doing?' I asked as I reached her.

'Abel's gone,' Mother said. 'He said he wanted to leave, he didn't want to be a burden. Your father has gone out to look for him.'

'But it's past curfew,' I said, but my eyes roamed the street as if I might suddenly spot my father with Abel by his side.

'We should go too, shouldn't we? We should look for him?' Her voice had taken on the pitch that I knew well. At any moment she would cry and become hysterical. Not much had to happen for her to have one of her 'turns', so I knew that this would make it come much quicker.

'Mother, please. Come inside. I'm sure Father will find him. He can't have got far. There's nowhere for him to go.'

Inside, my mother sat beside the fire wringing her hands, pushing herself up to stand, then sitting back down again.

'It's my fault,' she cried. 'It is. I should have done more. He wouldn't talk, though. Your father, he tried to get him to talk. To eat. But he misses Henryk. He kept telling me that he had nothing left. He said he had lost any hope.'

Her rambling continued. She went over each conversation she had had with Abel, trying perhaps to pinpoint the one thing that was said, or even unsaid, that would have stopped him.

'If he's caught – I mean, think of what will happen to us? But that's selfish of me, isn't it?' She stood and screamed this at me now. 'I mean, he could freeze to death! That's worse than what could happen to us, isn't it? What do you think? Am I selfish? Tell me, Irena, what should I have done?'

I took her by the shoulders and made her sit down. There

was a little *wiśniówka*, vodka with fermented cherries, left in the cupboard. I got it for her and poured her a healthy measure.

'I can't drink this!'

'You can. Drink it,' I demanded of her.

She looked at me with tears in her eyes and then drank it back, handing the glass back for me to fill it up again.

The door opened and closed and both of us looked to it hopefully. It was just my father, his black coat dotted with snowflakes, his cheeks red.

'They got him,' he said.

We didn't say anything. We let the words hang in the air for a moment so that the weight of them could be fully understood.

'I saw him. Stood at the end of the street next to Dubanowski's bakery. He was just stood there, looking in the darkened window. I was going to shout out, say something, when headlights appeared. Then they stopped.'

My father lowered his head and shook it. I knew that he was crying, or fighting back tears.

'I watched. I saw them talk to him. I don't know whether he spoke back. They just hit him over and over, then bundled him into the car, and it disappeared.'

My mother stood and went to him, not caring about the snow still on his coat. She took him and rocked him in her arms and shushed him like a baby. All at once her own hysteria, her worry, her emotions had been put on hold so she could comfort her husband.

'What will happen to us?' her mother asked in a small voice.

'I don't know.' My father took a step out of her embrace. 'He might not say anything.'

As they spoke, as they discussed where he might be, what might be happening, my mind was whirring. I knew exactly where he would be taken – Death's Head Resort. And I knew that once he was there, he would have no choice but to talk.

Before they could stop me, I raced out of the house, their voices disappearing as I ran.

The snow was falling more quickly now, blurring the streets. The only lights still burning in the night came from the Stamary and the Palace – Death's Head itself.

My feet sank into the snow, once, twice, three times, the third time forcing me to fold in on myself, so my knees collapsed under me, letting me fall flat on my face in the icy mounds.

Dragging myself up, I carried on, and soon reached the gates of the Palace, where a lonely and cold guard was standing in the driveway, stepping from foot to foot to keep warm.

As soon as he saw me, he aimed his gun at me. '*Halt!*' he yelled.

I raised my hands up in surrender. 'I need to speak to Hauptsturmführer Richter,' I told him. I knew he would be there – he always was in the late evenings.

'And you are?'

'Irena. Please. Tell him Irena is here to see him.'

'Irena who?'

I shook my head. 'He just knows Irena. Tell him his little sparrow is here. He will understand. Please.'

The guard laughed at me. I knew how stupid it must sound. Perhaps he thought I was a love-struck young woman, obsessed with the Hauptsturmführer. Perhaps he thought I was crazy. Either way, he told me to wait a moment and went to the front door, opened it, spoke to someone and then walked back to watch me.

'A few minutes,' he said. 'Little sparrow, eh? You need to be careful, little sparrow. You know, hawks, eagles, they'll eat you right up!' He laughed at his own comment, then eyed me as I shivered in the cold.

Finally, a figure appeared in the doorway. Richter.

He was dressed in a thick black coat, the silver of the eagle and skull on his cap shining under the moonlight. His hat was pulled down low, so I could barely see his eyes.

'Little sparrow,' he said when he reached me. There was no warmth in the greeting, no excitement about seeing me. I was suddenly very aware that he had once promised me he could make me disappear. And I was standing outside a place where people went into and did not come out of.

'I think there is someone here that I know,' I said.

'I think there is too.' He stepped closer to me. 'Abel, is that right? Your family have been very busy.'

I nodded. I was admitting it. What else could I do? 'I know it is wrong. I know that we shouldn't have done it. But *please*. He's just an old man.'

'Perhaps a Jewish man too, no?' he asked.

It was then that I realised that he did not know who Abel was. He had no *Kennkarte*, he was simply an old man with no identification. And they would keep going with whatever torture they had already started inside Death's Head in order to find out who he might be.

'No. No, not Jewish,' I rambled. 'Just a family friend. He had nowhere to stay, so we said he could stay with us.'

'Oh really? Not quite what he has said. Something about you helping him, hiding him even.'

'Not hiding.' I tried to force myself to laugh. 'He's old. He gets confused...'

Richter looked over his shoulder at the lighted windows. Then he looked back at me and let out a sigh. 'And what do you want? You want him back?'

'Yes, please.'

'And what do I get in return?'

I stepped towards him and placed my hands on his chest. 'You get me.'

'And why would I want you? I believe the last time I saw

you, you made it very clear what you thought about me. In fact, I'm still coming up with a suitable punishment for you.'

My stomach dropped. He wasn't done with me yet. He had just moved on to the next step in his game.

'Please, I am sorry. I will never do it again. I was just scared,' I said, noting how he leaned into my touch a little as soon as I said 'scared'. 'I was nervous. You know I am.'

'My nervous little sparrow.' He took his gloved hand and stroked my cheek.

I made myself lean into his touch too.

He sighed again. 'This is the last favour I will do for you,' he said and stepped away from me. 'And from now on, you'll do as you're told, is that clear?'

'Yes. Absolutely clear.'

'And your, *Uncle* Abel – let's call him your uncle, eh – he won't be here much longer, will he? He won't become a problem for me?'

'No, he will go and stay with another family,' I agreed.

'Well then. Goodnight, my little sparrow. Wait here a few minutes and he will be returned to you.'

He tipped his hat at me as he walked away and left me standing, the snow up to my ankles, worrying not only about Abel, but what I had just agreed to.

TWENTY-SIX

IRENA

Zakopane, Poland
January 1942

I waited an hour. By the time Abel came out of those doors, the snow had soaked through my shoes and my stockings and had left me with toes that I was sure had turned to ice.

Abel walked slowly and seemed to weave from side to side. I went to him and saw that his face was a bloodied mess.

'Irena?' he asked, trying to open his half-closed, swollen eyes to see me.

'Yes, it's me, it's Irena,' I told him.

'I'm sorry.'

'You don't have to be sorry.'

'I was just trying to go home.'

When I finally managed to get Abel back to the house, my parents were sitting waiting for us in the sitting room.

'Oh my!' My mother lunged at Abel. 'What happened?'

As she sat him down and ran about trying to find cloths

and warm water, I told them I had found him at the Palace. That he had been let go. I did not tell them how, nor why. They did not need to know the deal I had made on Abel's behalf.

'He has to leave, soon,' I told my parents as they tended to him. 'They said he had to leave.'

'But where?' my father asked, exasperated. 'Where would he go? They don't know he's Jewish?' he confirmed.

'They don't. We need to ask Mateusz to get him somewhere safe.'

'I won't say I'm not who I am. I won't pretend,' Abel mumbled through bloodied lips.

'Hush now. You will if you need to. You will if you want to live,' my mother soothed. 'It will be fine. It will all be fine.'

I had heard those words repeated before. Only, they had come out of my own mouth. *We're fine. I'm fine. It will be fine.* But nothing was fine. Nothing was right and nothing would be.

'I don't know how I will get in touch with Mateusz.' My father was pacing now. 'He wasn't expected to come back after he got Henryk.'

'He wasn't?' I asked. He had left me in the courtyard, and not said a proper goodbye?

'Well, I mean, I don't know exactly. He might, I don't know.' My father continued to pace.

'I'll ask Bartok,' I suggested. 'He might be able to get word to him through the couriers who bring produce.'

'Brilliant, Irena!' My father clapped his hands. 'I knew you had my brain. I knew it.'

Exhausted, I slumped in the armchair as my parents continued to talk over each other, as they argued how best to treat Abel's cuts and bruises.

I stared at the fire as it grew low, trying not to think about what I had agreed to – what might happen to me now.

Perhaps an hour went by, perhaps more, until Abel had

fallen asleep in a tightly curled ball on the sofa and my parents had finally made their way to bed.

I wanted to stay with him, and perhaps needed the company too. If I could see what had happened to Abel, then maybe it would give me the courage I needed to follow through with Richter. I couldn't let this happen to my parents. I couldn't let anyone get hurt – or worse.

I must have fallen asleep when I heard a distant voice.

'Thank you.'

I swam against my dreams and opened my eyes to see Abel sitting upright. 'Thank you,' he repeated. His lips and face were still so swollen that it came out mumbled, and I almost felt the pain of him mouthing each word.

'I didn't do anything,' I told him. I stood and wrung out the cloth that my mother had left in a porcelain basin, then went to him and placed the damp cloth on the cut that ran from his right eye down to his chin.

'You did. That man – that one – he said your name.'

I knew that Abel was looking at me under the deep hooded lids. I tried to keep my face as straight as possible, but it was as though he could see through me, all the way through to what had happened.

'He said you made him a promise. What did you promise him, Irena?'

I ignored the question and went back to the bowl, soaking the cloth again, noting the way the water was slowly taking on a pink hue from the blood.

'You don't have to say,' he mumbled behind me. 'But you should tell someone. It is hard when there is something bad happening to you and you have no one to talk to about it. Henryk, he always wanted to talk about what had happened, but I couldn't. It was too hard. But I could see that he needed it. I should have done that for him. I should have done that for myself – told my story. Now I have no one to tell it to.'

'You have me,' I said, looking at him. 'You can always tell me anything.'

He tried to smile, but instead, the pull on his skin made him wince. 'It is not right to tell a young lady of what has happened to me. It would give you nightmares.'

'I already have plenty of those.'

'Come, sit.' He patted the sofa, and I did as I was told.

Neither of us spoke for a few minutes. I stared at my feet. My shoes had been discarded upstairs as blood had stained them. A few flecks held on to my stockings, and I itched to wipe them away. Abel's blood was everywhere, it seemed.

'How are you still alive?' I said quietly, almost to myself.

'I am not sure,' he answered. 'Honestly, I am not sure.'

'Do you want to tell me what they did?'

He did not answer for a minute, and I was sure he was not going to.

'They wanted to know who I was. Why I was out after curfew. They wanted to know if I was a Jew. They asked me. And I am ashamed to say it, I told them that I wasn't.'

'You shouldn't be ashamed,' I told him. 'You did what you had to do to survive.'

'No, I shouldn't have dismissed myself like that. I *am* a Jew. I should be able to say it. I won't ever deny it again. It was just the screams...'

'The screams?'

'There was someone else. In a room next to me. I don't know what they were doing. I don't know who it was. But the screams were not human. Not even an animal. It was something I had never heard before and it scared me to my very soul.'

The weight of my decision pressed down on me. I was right to have made the deal. But I had now firmly placed myself in a position whereby the person screaming in a locked room could one day be me or my parents, if Richter ever became displeased with me.

'What did you promise that man?' he asked again.

I looked at him, his kindly eyes that were barely visible underneath the swollen skin. 'I made a promise to keep you and my parents safe.'

'That doesn't make sense,' he said.

'I can't make it make any more sense than that.'

He nodded and looked away for a brief moment. Then he looked back at me, smiling. 'Like the queen. Like the queen in chess. You are protecting your king.'

TWENTY-SEVEN

IRENA

Tatra Mountains, Poland
February 1942

The sky was clear, hanging over the iced landscape, speckling it with starlight. The moon was not quite full but still seemed like it glowed from the inside. As we climbed, our breath hung in the air, and I wondered when we descended if there would be tiny puffs still hanging there.

'Are you all right?' Mateusz asked, a few steps ahead of me.

'Fine,' I gasped, trying not to show how out of breath I was. He laughed. He knew. He slowed his pace, and I concentrated on placing my feet in the grooves of his footsteps, delighting in the silence of the night, peppered only with my laboured breathing and the satisfying crunch of snow as we walked.

I enjoyed the silence that a heavy snowfall brings. There is nothing but the slight flutter or whomp as bare branches shake free some of their icy burden. Everyone tucks themselves away, leaving the world to turn on its own – we are no longer needed.

But this night, this night, I needed.

I looked to the trees, naked of their spring and summer

clothing. They stood proud, cold, knowing perhaps that they would be dressed again as soon as the season changed. There was no shame for them in their nakedness, they did not question it. Their limbs were weighted by snow and yet they would shake it effortlessly away as if they perhaps wanted to be bare for all to see. They knew who they were. Not like me.

I stopped and looked down into the valley below, hoping foolishly to be able to see my home amongst all the white. Nothing was distinguishable and no one's lights shone from windows. I knew that my parents and Abel were tucked away inside, curtains closed, a fire roaring in the hearth, and Abel, poor Abel, lying on the couch next to it, a fever burning his skin as it had done for a few days now.

'He will be all right.' Mateusz was by my side, his eyes scouring the valley too.

'I'm just glad that Bartok was able to find you,' I said. 'Henryk needs to know about his grandfather.'

'We're nearly there,' he said, making me turn away from the chocolate box scene in front of me.

I turned and followed, my muscles screaming with pain, as we hiked further and further upwards, soon disappearing from the icy slopes into a thicket of pine trees. Here, the ground was a little easier to traverse. The twigs and rocks beneath the snow gave my feet some anchorage and we seemed to move faster.

I made myself listen to the sounds of our laboured breathing, the snapping of twigs underfoot, the screech of an owl, and told myself to think only of this – not to think of Richter, not to think about the deal I had made with him.

But it was hard not to think of it.

The memory of returning to the hotel, to his rooms, the day after Abel had returned home would not leave me alone.

He had been there, sitting on his couch, waiting for me. He didn't look at me as I walked in but kept staring at the wall in front of him as if the gold swirls on the wallpaper were saying something to him. He had known that I would have to walk round the couch and stand in front of him to be appraised.

The room had been warm. Too warm, and the thick cardigan I wore scratched at my sweating skin, making me want to tear it off my body. Then I realised that it would soon be taken off, and all of a sudden, I wanted it to act as my second skin, my armour.

So many thoughts had swirled through my head in the few seconds it took to get to him. Would he still be mad? Would he punish me? What part of the game was this now?

By the time I was standing in front of him, he had lit a cigarette and was blowing smoke rings above his head.

'So, my little sparrow returns,' he had said.

'I'm sorry,' I'd said because that's what I'd thought I was meant to say.

'You know. I could have any woman here. In this town. Any woman. But I chose *you*. And yet you are so much trouble, so much, it makes me wonder whether I have made a mistake. Have I, little sparrow? Have I made a mistake?'

'I-I think – I'm sorry...'

He laughed, then placed his arms on his knees and leaned forward, staring now at the carpet. 'Little sparrow can't talk. That's good. Maybe this time you will listen.'

I didn't say anything. I just waited for him to stop staring at the carpet and do something so that I knew what I was meant to do.

He raised his head slightly at me and looked me in the eye. 'Do you know how old I am?' he asked.

I didn't dare answer in case I was wrong and annoyed him, so I just shrugged.

'Twenty-seven. Can you believe it? At my age, the position I'm in?'

I was a little surprised. He was only a few years older than me, and yet his face wore a mask that was hard to define. Yes, his skin was still smooth, his hair not tinged grey yet, but there was a roughness about it, a sort of worn look that made him seem much older.

'Do you want to know how I got to be where I am at this young age?' he had asked, turning to look at me. 'It's simple. I show no mercy.'

He stood then and walked towards me and tapped the tip of my nose three times as he repeated the three words. '*Show. No. Mercy.*'

The hour or so after those words had been spoken was not an hour I wanted to think about. My body still ached. The bruises were still a deep shade of purple on my arms and thighs. I would not think about that hour. Not now. Not ever.

'Nearly there.' Mateusz's voice cut through the unpleasant thoughts. He had a small torch that he now beamed at me. 'I can use this now. We're safe here.'

I felt his hand grab mine and, at first, I recoiled from it. But then he grabbed it again, more firmly. 'So I don't lose you,' he said.

This time, I took it. It wasn't the same as when Richter touched me. It was for safety. To stay close. So I wouldn't get lost.

Within a minute or two, I saw the leap of an orange flame, small and alone in the darkness. As we got closer to it, it slowly illuminated faces – two of them; and one of them I knew; Henryk.

'Irena!' He grinned at me and stood up from where he had been crouched close to the fire.

We embraced. He smelled of woodsmoke and the ice-cold, and his frame seemed fuller under my hands.

'You look well!' I told him, and although I could not see his face that well, I could make out that his skin was dirty.

'I'm filthy!' He laughed. 'There's not much chance to clean up where we go.'

I noticed that his voice had changed. It was confident, adult. Working with the resistance had obviously brought out some happiness, or at least a feeling that he was doing the right thing – doing something.

My stomach turned with the thought. *I wasn't, was I?* I wasn't brave like him.

'Come, come sit by the fire,' Henryk said.

I sat next to him, noting that the other man had barely looked at me and also that it was the man from months ago – the wiry fellow with a moustache who had delivered goods to the kitchen before Mateusz had arrived.

'Tell me, how is Grandfather?' Henryk asked. 'That's why you're here, isn't it?'

'I warned him,' Mateusz said by way of explanation.

'He's not well,' I said, wondering if Mateusz had also told Henryk about Death's Head. 'He's had a fever for days, and it isn't getting better.'

'He'll be fine.' Henryk stared at the small flames that licked at the wood. 'He'll survive. I know he will. We have got this far.'

I knew he was talking more to himself than to me, and I let him reassure himself and said no more. I had thought I would tell him about Death's Head, about how it had taken so much out of his grandfather that there was little hope that he could recover. But I saw that Henryk in that moment did not need to hear the truth. He had to hope that they would be together again, and I did not blame him for thinking that way. He had lost so much family already, he couldn't bear thinking about losing Abel as well.

'I've learned to ski,' Henryk said, still staring at the fire. 'Tell him that, won't you? Tell him that I am doing well. That last week we got a whole family over the mountains and to safety.

Please, Irena, tell him that I am saving people. It will help him get better. It will give him some hope.'

I promised Henryk that I would tell Abel all that he had told me and then soon, Mateusz said that we had to leave.

'Already?' I asked.

'It isn't that safe for them to be here. They need to go back.'

'To where?'

'Higher up to a few places that we camp.'

I tried to look up, above the trees, and couldn't see past them. I knew we were not that far up the mountain, even though it felt like we were high up. It was then that I realised the risk they were taking – being so low down, near the town – just so that Henryk could hear some news about his only family.

I hugged Henryk goodbye and said farewell to the other man, who still did not look at me.

'I'll see you soon. When this is over,' Henryk said. 'Tell Grandfather that we will all be together again soon.'

As we walked away, I apologised to Mateusz for demanding that Bartok find him and Henryk. 'I didn't realise that it would be such a risk,' I said, annoyed that I was so stupid.

'It was worth the risk, I think. Henryk talks of no one else but his grandfather.'

'Maybe it would have been better for him not to know how sick he is?' I suggested.

'No, he needs to know. He needed to hear it from you. Let it sink in what you have told him so that when and if Abel leaves him, he's prepared for it.'

We walked a few minutes in silence. The rustle of snow falling from trees and the occasional crack and pop of wood breaking underfoot were the only sounds.

I tripped on a hidden stone. Not enough to fall, but enough that Mateusz took my hand. 'To keep you safe,' he said as if he needed to explain his actions.

'Can I ask you something, Nina?' he asked as we reached

the edge of the thicket of trees, the village visible again below us.

'You can.'

'Are you all right? You seem different. I mean, I know I don't know you that well. But when I first met you, you had this kind of light...'

I looked to see that he was shaking his head.

'Sorry. I'm not good at saying what I mean. I just mean that you were lighter. I know the war, it's affecting us all. But I'm worried about you.'

'You're worried about me,' I repeated back at him, and despite Richter, Abel and everything, I still felt a bubble of excitement at knowing that he had been thinking of me.

'I am. Is that okay, for me to be worried about you?'

'Yes,' I managed to reply, not daring to look at him again in case he could see that I was smiling, and I suspected blushing even in the cold.

'I like thinking about you. Worrying about you. Well, not worrying exactly. I'd rather not worry. I mean I don't when I see you, because I'm there with you, so I think to myself that I can help – you know. Protect you.' He was rambling now, his words coming so fast I was sure I would forget what he had said. And I didn't want to forget. I wanted to keep every word safe and remember them later.

'I just wondered.' He stopped walking, let go of my hand and stood in front of me. 'When all this is over. When it's all done and they have gone and life is normal again. I just wondered whether I might still see you. Whether you might want to see me?'

I could see in the moonlight that his hands had dropped to his sides and he was holding on to the hem of his coat, squeezing at it, like a small nervous child.

'I'd like that,' I said. 'I'd really like that.'

He laughed, letting out a stream of smoke into the air. 'I'm so relieved you said that.'

He came back to my side and took my hand again. 'I was thinking about it – about saying something to you for a while, but I wasn't sure. I mean, you seem so down, so distant sometimes when I've seen you that I thought maybe it was me. Maybe you didn't like me being around.'

'No, it's not you,' I said. This was my chance to tell him about who I didn't like. Who was making me different. But I couldn't tell him. I had to deal with this on my own.

It was my turn to stop walking now and stand in front of him. I did not let go of his hand. 'Please never think it is you. Promise me. No matter what, you need to know that.'

'I promise,' he said.

I don't know who stepped forward first, or maybe we did it at the same time, but we were suddenly nose to nose. I could smell the smoke from the fire on his clothes, the sweetness of his skin. And before I knew it, we kissed.

TWENTY-EIGHT

SARA

Pinamar, Buenos Aires, Argentina
6 January 1994

Sara sat at her desk. Another wave of nausea had sent her running to the rubbish bin, but nothing had come up, so she sat, her head in her hands, wondering what to do.

She had not left her father's house until the early hours of that morning. Their talk of the past, of her mother, had exhausted them both, sending her father to sleep in his armchair and her to walk home to her apartment just as the birds trilled their wake-up call.

'Your mother was a Jew.' His words were in her head again. 'Your mother's aunt and uncle, her cousins, her second cousins even, all from Germany, died in Auschwitz. All of them, Sara. Her mother and father came here before the war, in the 1920s, and for her I think she never really thought so much about her Jewishness. Her parents, your grandparents didn't really practise it, but during the war and then afterwards, she felt it keenly. She was Jewish and she wasn't going to be ashamed of it or hide from it.'

'Why haven't you told me this before?' she had asked him. No, *demanded* of him. 'Why did you hide it then?'

'When she died' – her father's faced had slackened, losing all of his natural confidence – 'I don't know, Sara. It was hard to think of her. I just couldn't cope. I had you. This four-year-old who asked me every day when her mother was coming home, and it broke my heart. The only way forward for us was not to talk about her, just to keep moving, keep living.'

Sara understood what her father had meant, but at the same time still felt frustrated and, yes, angry at him. Her whole identity was linked to her past as much as her present, and he had hidden it from her.

'I mean, her parents were dead, so it was just you and me. It was easier to create a life with just the two of us in it. There was no need to make it more difficult than it already was.'

'So I am Jewish?' she said.

'You are,' her father had said, offering her again a glass of wine, which she at first took, then remembered she couldn't drink it and placed it on the table untouched.

'In the 1950s, I was contacted by a man, a Jewish man, who said he worked for an organisation. He didn't tell me which, but it was obvious when he told me what he wanted. He had heard that I was the man to see in the city if one needed to know where, perhaps, the less desirable people were. I mean, I worked with them, for them, and used them from time to time. He told me that they were looking for some infamous Nazis who had disappeared – thought to be here – and wondered if I would help. I have to tell you, at first, I said no. It was exciting, yes. I had this thought in my head that I would be like a spy or something,' he mumbled, then drank deeply from his glass of red. 'But then I had a lot of clients already and was already working long hours, which was bothering your mother. But then, I told her about it. I mean, I told her everything. She was my best friend—' He stopped, and Sara saw his head droop a little.

He then raised his eyes to her, and she could see how watery they were, how talking of her mother was causing him so much pain. But she didn't let him stop. Not this time. This time, she needed to know because she too had been in pain, *was* in pain, and he had to give her this.

'She loved the idea,' he said with a sigh. 'She wanted to be a part of it too. Like I said. She was beginning to feel this part of herself, her history, keenly. It affected her – these people buying bread, living their lives after what they had done to so many in the camps. She became angry about it – so angry that I was a little scared of her myself!' He laughed, but Sara didn't join in with his attempt at a joke to lighten the situation.

'So, what happened?' she prompted him.

'Well.' He shrugged. 'We said yes. We worked together, seeking out people, following them, taking photographs if we could. Your mother was better at that part than I was. She could blend in, be sociable, talk to people and get them to open up. Even when she found out about the cancer, she didn't stop. Always reviewing files, pictures. She never stopped. Well. Until she did.'

Sara recalled something. A hazy memory. It was summer, she knew that. She was in her parents' bedroom and her mother sat, propped up by a mass of pillows. Her face was shrunken, and it had scared Sara. Her mother had patted the bed for her to sit. She didn't remember sitting, or if they spoke. But she remembered now all the manila folders scattered on the bed, her mother's skeletal hands flicking through pages and pages.

'She was a force,' Sara had admitted to her father. 'I remember her working.'

'You do?' His face had lit up a little. 'She told me that you were like her, you know. When we would talk about who you took after. She would say that you were your mother's daughter. That you would be like her when you grew up.'

'But I'm not,' Sara said. 'I mean, I'm not doing what she did.

What she was doing was right. It was just. But you said that you have helped others to find Nazis. Not just shadowy organisations, but actual people. People you know are going to kill them.'

'No. No' – Her father waved his hands – 'you have it all wrong, Sara. I don't always know what they will do. And your mother, she helped people too. People came to her, you know. Other Jews in the city. They asked for her help. She always said that it was right to help them. That morally it was right. And that whatever decision these people made, she understood why they might do it. All I did was carry it on. It was my way of remembering her. Of *honouring* her.'

'But you didn't tell me. Why?'

'Because, Sara, as you grew up, I saw that you were like neither of us. You were so clever, so so intelligent. You read, you understood the law. You understood everything. But you always had a keen sense of right and wrong. That's why I would always try and talk to you about the "grey" area. That part of understanding that is both right and wrong at the same time. But I saw that you couldn't or wouldn't think of things the way I and your mother did. I saw that you were your own person, and I wasn't going to drag you into something that you wouldn't be able to handle.'

'And yet you have told me now.'

He had nodded. 'It was time. I knew there would be a time. I just didn't really know it was now. But that client, Irena, I did let her come, let her speak to you. I wanted to see what you would do, how much you would question it. How you would deal with it. And when you walked in tonight, I don't know. The way you spoke to me reminded me so much of your mother, I don't know... It just felt right to tell you the truth.'

And now, she knew the truth. She knew that Irena was looking for Richter to seek some form of revenge. She knew that she was Jewish, just like her mother. She knew she was pregnant. She knew that she loved Peter. She knew she was still angry with her father. But what she didn't know was what to do. What she didn't know was who she was now.

She got up from her desk and saw that the rest of the office had already emptied. She had done no work and felt so tired and confused that she wished someone would come and fetch her, take her home, lie her on a couch and take care of her. In essence, she wanted to feel safe and loved, but she wasn't sure who could do that for her right now.

Of course there was Peter. She needed to talk to him about the baby, and about what she had found out. She wanted to be open and honest with him, and usually she was. It was him who always held something back from her, never really letting her in. But she couldn't divulge anything about Irena, even though she wanted to. She was still a client. Her father may have discussed clients with her mother, but she wouldn't do that. Right, wrong. No grey area for Sara.

She grabbed her bag and headed out. She would tell Peter this evening about the baby. That was something she could do. Then she would deal with her father, Irena, herself, another day. *One thing at a time, Sara,* she told herself as she locked the door to her offices. *One thing at a time.*

'I'm pregnant,' she told him again. His face remained the same. Slack.

She had blurted it out as soon as she had reached his house. It wasn't the way she had wanted to say it, but she was tired, angry, scared, worried – so many things – that the words had just fallen out of her mouth. Twice. She had had to repeat it.

'Pregnant,' Peter parroted back at her.

'You're not happy?'

'I-I-' he stuttered at her.

She felt her stomach turn. She had expected him to be

surprised, but his reaction was so blank, almost fearful, that now she wished she hadn't said anything. She stepped towards him and placed her hand on his shoulder.

'Look at me, please. Tell me what you think.'

He gave her a smile, then kissed her forehead. 'I'm thinking a lot. I'm happy, Sara. I am. And I know this isn't right. I know we need to talk. But I need you to trust me. I just need to deal with something. I'll be back soon. Do you trust me, Sara?'

Her head said no, but her heart said yes. And somewhere between the two she managed to say the word 'yes'.

She watched him leave, leaving the door open, letting the night-time song of the ocean creep inside. Wave after wave. A crash as one hit the rocks. The quiet as it pulled away from the shore. She stood and listened. She waited for each break on the shore.

She waited for him to return.

She waited a while, trying to decide what to do. She should have told him not to go. Not to leave her when she had just told him this news. She should have been stronger, more confident, bold. But she was tired of being strong. Of being right. She was tired of all the feelings that were threatening to send her running outside and screaming at the ocean.

A part of her knew she should just go home – give him some space to process what she had told him. Yet she couldn't quite bring herself to leave.

She did what she always did when her thoughts and feelings became too much – she cleaned. She started in the kitchen, wiping the table, the sink, then moved on to the bedroom.

Peter was never one to put his clothes away, and she had lamented about this many a time – although never doing it for him, always hoping that one day he would simply do it himself. But now she needed to be busy. She picked up a shirt that had been discarded on the floor, sat on the edge of the bed and folded it. Then she held the material to her face, smelling him, and felt tears prick at her eyes. What if he said he didn't want the baby? What if he was actually gone? Gone forever, leaving her to deal with it all on her own?

No, he wouldn't do that. She wouldn't let herself think that way. He would come back, fold her in his arms and kiss the top of her head and promise her that everything would be okay.

Shirt folded, she moved on to a pair of jeans, a T-shirt, boxer shorts, discarding some in a pile for laundry.

She then opened his wardrobe. She remembered once, when she had first started staying over, looking for space inside, hoping to hang up a few of her clothes. But what she had found was a bulging rail full of his clothes, then bags, suitcases and boxes stuffed at the bottom. He had promised her that he would clean it out – but it was another thing he had promised, like stopping the gambling, and had never followed through.

The wardrobe was in much the same state as it had been the last time she looked inside. She tried to shove some of the clothes to one side so she could hang up a few things, perhaps place the folded items on one of the boxes below.

As she crouched down to put his clothes on top of a battered suitcase, she noticed some writing on the side of a box. She recognised it; she knew the handwriting, and it wasn't Peter's. It was her father's. It was a box like the ones they had in the office. Their yellow logo was stamped on the side.

Christoph Richter written on the side in her father's hand. Christoph Richter, the man who Irena had said she was looking for. Why would Peter have her father's documents? What was going on?

Dragging the box out, she unfolded the cardboard flaps and dug out file after file. Some of the files were in German, others in Spanish. She flicked through one and saw a black and white grainy photograph of a man, presumably Richter, wearing a Nazi cap. He smiled at the camera as if he were proud to be wearing that uniform and having it memorialised forever.

She shuddered.

Her already tired mind tried to process what was in front of her. *What are the facts, Sara?*, she asked herself. *Look at the facts.*

Irena was looking for Richter, but her father had said that Irena would not find him. He had given her a false name, Santiago, as he had another client, another person who was looking for Richter.

So, why did Peter have the box?

Suddenly, she could see pieces of the jigsaw coming together in her mind.

Irena was looking for Richter. And Peter was looking for Richter. But *why*?

Then she thought of the small pieces of information Peter had revealed to her over the years. He had been an orphan from Germany. He didn't know who his parents were. Could it be that Richter was Peter's father? No surely not.

Then she remembered something else her father had said. Why Irena had wanted to find Richter in the first place: 'He killed her only child and she wants to now kill him.'

If Richter had done that to Irena's child, was it possible that he had also killed Peter's parents?

As night fell around her, she went through the files, reading testimonies from people who had known Richter, detailing what he had done to them.

'Shot in the back of the head… my son… twelve years old.'

'Took my mother in the dead of night to Death's Head Resort… she never came out.'

'Interrogated me for four days. Broke both my arms and legs…'

'Beat my father in front of me… I was ten years old. My father died the next day.'

On and on the testimonies went, each one brutal. Each one stated as fact, with no hint of emotion. She placed them aside for a moment as she went over and over the questions and the possible answers.

Peter knew Richter. But the question was why – and had Peter already found him?

TWENTY-NINE

PETER

Pinamar, Buenos Aires, Argentina
6 January 1994

Peter did not think. He drove.

He had told Sara he was going for a walk, but as soon as he saw his beaten-up van, he knew what he was going to do, and where he was going to go.

As he drove, he thought of the past. Of the choices he had made that had brought him here and finally made him realise that he had come here to do something – to find out who he was, and then to take whatever he could away from the man who had made him this way.

He thought back to the conversation that had started this – what was it now – ten years ago? His father, Maurice, had had cancer. That much he knew. The man he had always been slightly afraid of, his bulk, the booming voice, had shrunk in on itself, leaving a man with yellowed skin and hollowed-out eyes that sat each day in a chair, his legs covered with a blanket.

Peter had been an only child, but, just as he had once joked to his friends, he may as well not have been there at all. His parents were not overly interested in him. His father, an ex-politician and as right-wing as they come, and his mother, an obedient housewife, had never tried to conceal the fact that Peter was adopted and had told him so as soon as he could understand what they meant.

They made it clear, from the outset, that he was not theirs, that he did not belong. The only thing they ever did seem to like about him was the fact that he had come from Germany and was not a Jew.

He grew up in a semi-detached house in rural Kent. His life was as plain as his parents could make it until, at eight, he was shipped off to boarding school and, after that day, never really returned home.

At eighteen, he took odd jobs in London, then travelled around Europe, never speaking to his parents, and never asking who he really was nor who his real parents had been.

It was only when he heard the news that his father was dying that he felt the need to return home, just the once, just to say a final goodbye.

'Ah-ha, so now you come and see your old man!' his wrinkled, tiny father gasped at him as he walked into the heavily carpeted living room, every sideboard weighted down by tatty porcelain, the gas fire burning, stuffing up the room even more.

'Maurice,' he said, nodded, then sat opposite him on the couch.

'Dad? Father? You could say either of those.'

Peter shrugged. 'You never wanted me to call you that before.'

'Well, things change,' the old man said, then began to cough, hacking up something and spitting it into a tissue. He then reached to the side table and picked up a packet of cigarettes. He shook one from the packet and lit it, filling the already stuffy room with smoke.

'You should stop,' Peter said.

'What's the point now?' he half laughed.

'So,' Peter said. Then he stopped. He wasn't sure what else to say.

'Cat got your tongue?' Maurice asked, scrunching up his brow. 'Always were a quiet one. Not sure where you got it from – I mean your father—' Maurice suddenly stopped and shook his head.

Peter had never asked Maurice about his real parents, never really wanted to know. But the way that Maurice compared him to his 'father' made him curious now. 'Tell me. I am not like him, so am I like my mother?' he asked, his tone laced with a hint of sarcasm.

Maurice waved the question away with the hand that held the cigarette, the fingers stained yellow from tobacco. 'It's in the past.'

'Who was he?' Peter felt suddenly emboldened. Here was this man who had 'raised' him – a man who he had always been a little afraid of, but who now was shrivelled almost into nothing. Why not ask now? There wouldn't be another chance.

'You want to know?' Maurice leaned forward with a strange smile. 'Really. You wish to know?'

Despite an odd churn that had started up with Maurice's unsettling smile, Peter decided, yes, he did want to know.

'All right. I'll tell you. Your father was a Nazi. Ha! How do you feel about me now?' Maurice laughed, his chest crackling. 'A Nazi! And you treat me with so much disdain.'

Peter swallowed. Maurice was playing with him again, he knew. He was a bitter man, a mean bastard, and this was just another thing that he had concocted to try to upset Peter.

'He was all right, mostly,' Maurice continued, not looking at Peter, his eyes fixed on the gas fire as if his memories lay within the heat. 'I didn't know him that well. I wasn't like him, per se, but I sympathised – you know? There were a lot of us that did.'

This wasn't right. This wasn't Maurice's usual way of taunting him into an argument. This – this felt *real.*

'You're serious?' Peter finally asked.

'Absolutely.' Maurice looked at him. The smile was now gone. 'He had to leave – get away after the war – and he couldn't very well take a small child with him. He'd left you in an orphanage, told the nuns he'd come back for you when the war was over, but obviously he couldn't in the end. So he asked me and your mother to take you in.' Maurice shrugged as if taking in a child were no different than taking in a stray cat. 'It wasn't much really. We just went and picked you up from that orphanage. He sent money for you now and again.'

'My mother?' Peter asked, almost not wanting to hear the answer.

'No idea,' Maurice answered. 'Maybe dead. Yes, maybe that was it – he said she was dead.'

'And where is he now? Is he alive?' Peter asked.

'Sure. He's in Argentina. Why, are you going to see him? Make a new family now I'm on my way out?' Maurice laughed again, this time dropping the cigarette onto the carpet.

Peter bent down to pick it up and stubbed it out in the ashtray, then turned and left Maurice sitting by the fire, hacking up a lifetime full of bile.

Peter had returned to see Maurice a few days later. He wanted a favour from the old man. It was true he had got into a slight bit of bother with the police over selling stolen goods on a market stall. But Peter had not known that they were stolen. He needed a change, needed to get away. The realisation that his father, no matter who he was, was alive had stirred something in Peter. He wanted to know the man – know where he came from at least, and maybe find something out about his mother too.

Maurice agreed to the favour. He would contact Peter's

father and see if he would send money for him to go to Argentina.

'Do not tell him that I know who he is,' Peter had told Maurice.

'Why?' Maurice had asked.

'Because I want to tell him myself. Just say that you need him to do you this favour.'

'And what do *I* get out of it?'

Peter had shrugged. 'Maybe it will grease the wheels for you with God. Maybe he won't send you to hell.'

'Ha! Maybe, maybe...' Maurice had said.

Now here he was. Ten years later. He knew who his father was: Christoph Richter. He knew his new name too: Ricardo Hernández. He knew everything about him. When he went swimming at the new Hotel Pinamar, where he drank, who his friends were.

Indeed, Peter had made it a point to spend time with the man. He wanted to see something in him; maybe himself – a link perhaps. He wasn't sure. Maybe he had wanted to hear from the old man that he wasn't a Nazi, that he would trust him enough to tell him about his past. But Ricardo, or rather Richter, spent his time drinking, never really speaking of the past, no matter how persistently, but subtly, Peter tried.

He thought back to a few days ago, when he had been drinking with him at Santiago's, how Ricardo had offered to tell him his secrets. Why had Peter not taken him up on it? All he thought now was that perhaps he didn't really want the old man to say it – to tell him the truth.

He pulled to a stop and sat for a moment in the van, letting the engine tick over and looking at the front door. It was late and he knew he probably shouldn't go in, but he had to talk to him – he just had to.

He turned the key in the ignition and stepped out onto the pavement. From somewhere in the darkness, an alley cat meowed and then hissed.

He knocked on the door and waited. No one came. He tried again, harder this time, and heard the scuffle of footsteps.

THIRTY

SARA

Pinamar, Buenos Aires, Argentina
7 January 1994

Sara sat at the kitchen table, the papers from the cardboard box strewn across the wood. She again picked up the document that she could not take her eyes away from, even though she wished she could. It was a testimony, a photograph of Christoph Richter, a file written in German talking about a sixty-two-year-old man who had been interrogated by Richter. A man who was allowed to leave with a broken nose, burn marks from where electricity had been run through him, three broken fingers and his left foot devoid of all toenails.

Even though her head hurt with all the information, with all the horror, she could not help herself. She just had to find the link between Richter and Peter.

She checked her watch: 2 a.m. Then she heard it. The familiar rumble of Peter's old van, the rattle of the exhaust as it came to a stop.

'You're still here.' Peter opened the front door, and for a

moment, he smiled. Then his eyes roamed the tabletop, and he scrunched up his brow. 'What's going on?'

Sara stood. She kept calm. She had to keep calm. 'Peter,' she said. 'We need to talk.'

'Look. I'm sorry about before...' His words suddenly rushed out – so unlike him. He came towards her and began grabbing up the papers and then placing them back down as if it were all too much and he was unsure of himself.

'Peter,' she tried again, stepping towards him now.

'I'm sorry, Sara, I really am. It was a surprise. That's all.'

'I know. I know it was. But we need to talk about all this first. You need to talk to me, Peter. You've been hiding something from me – something big. Why wouldn't you tell me?'

His eyes widened, his mouth opened and closed, but he said nothing.

She could yell at him, she knew that. She had every right to. He had left when she had told him she was pregnant. He had a box of documents from her father's office. There was so much he hadn't told her, and she had every right to know who he was, this man, the father of her child.

'Where were you? What's going on? Who is Richter to you?'

Peter dragged a chair back from the table and slumped in it. 'I went to see your father.'

'Why?'

'Because I needed to know what to do. I needed him to tell me that it was the right thing.'

'I don't understand!' Sara screamed at him now. Her voice was edgy with tears. 'Just tell me, as plain as you can. What is going on? How do you know Richter?'

'Ricardo,' Peter said quietly. 'That's his name now. Not Richter. Ricardo.'

It took Sara a minute to realise what he was saying. Then

she remembered his friend. The old man with leathery skin who drank heavily and gambled.

'You found him? Richter is Ricardo?'

'Yes,' he said. 'And... he's my father.'

Sara sat across from him and saw that he could not look her in the face. All of a sudden, he looked like a small child. Frightened, worried. Not at all like a fifty-one-year-old man.

'I wanted to tell you. I did. I just didn't know how to. I already knew he was my father when I came here. I don't know – at first, I wanted to get to know him. Maurice, my adopted father, had told me that he was a Nazi. That he had given me up. I just wanted to know if it was true.'

'And you found out that it was... That Ricardo, or Richter, really is the man you thought he was?'

'I didn't know much at first. Then, I heard through a few people about your father. How he was helping people find Nazis in hiding. How he had even helped Mossad. I went to him and asked him to see what he could find out about my father. I wanted to know everything – the truth about who he was. And he found it all.'

She looked at the documents that were spread on the tabletop between them.

'I read some of them,' she said. 'What he did...'

'I know. I've read them all many times,' he said.

'So, what now? What are you and my father planning to do?' Sara asked, even though she was not sure she wanted to hear the answer.

'I don't know,' he said. 'At first, before I met you, I thought that I would do something to him, confront him at least. But then I met you and things changed.'

She remembered how they had met. Just outside her offices on a hot day. How he had bumped into her and apologised with a lopsided smile. How he had invited her for a drink, and she had accepted.

'How do I change anything?'

'Before, the only thing I had to think about was myself. Nothing much mattered to me. But then I met you – you are so strong, beautiful, so, so...' He waved his hand about as if trying to grasp the right word. 'Good,' he finally said.

'Good?'

'You work so hard and always help the right people. You know right from wrong. If I had told you about who my father was, I was worried that you would judge me— no, wait, don't get mad,' he said.

She had already opened her mouth to yell at him. To tell him she would never judge him based on who his father was. But he silenced her.

'Please. Just let me say what I need to. I've been trying so long to tell you and I feel like if I don't get the words out now, I never will.'

She wanted to argue, to yell, to demand a better answer. But she knew she had to listen. He had to talk.

'I was worried that you would look at me in a different way. And, I was conflicted, every day, about what to do about him. I mean, your father had told me about others who had come here before and what had happened.'

'They were killed.' She said it for him.

He nodded. 'There were days, after I read all the testimonies, that I wanted to kill him too, you know. There were days when I was so full of rage, I was sure I was going to do it. But then, I don't know, it would flow away. I think because of you. Because I knew if I did it, it would change me, and even if I didn't tell you, if you never knew, you would be able to see it on me – does that make sense?'

'So you're not going to do anything?' Sara asked cautiously. 'You and my father are not going to do anything stupid?'

'I'm not,' he said. 'I promise I'm not. I don't know what the right thing to do is. I don't know if any authorities in Germany, or Poland or anywhere, want to deal with him. I don't know whether we just wait it out for him to die. But I promise I won't do anything stupid.'

'So why run off and see my father when I tell you I'm pregnant? What has all this got to do with what I told you?'

Peter stood and took a step towards her. He crouched down on one knee and placed his hand on hers. 'When you told me that I was going to be a father, I knew I had to speak to yours. I had to get his permission to do something, something I should have done a while ago.'

Sara watched as he took a small, blue velvet box from his pocket. She knew the box. She knew what was inside. Her mother's engagement ring.

'I can do this now because you know everything. You know who I am. All my secrets. I'm telling you the truth. All of it, because I want to let it all go. I want a life with you. I don't want to live in the past like this any more.'

The weight of the past two days and the tiredness that it had brought made Sara burst into tears. She couldn't tell him her answer because, every time she tried, another bout overcame her.

After a few minutes of crying into Peter's shoulder, she managed to squeak out her answer. 'Yes,' she said. 'Yes, I'll marry you, Peter.'

As Peter laughed with relief and pulled her up to hold her close, she felt a worry that although this was what she had wanted – honesty, openness and for Peter to want her and this child forever – there was something still not quite right.

There were still questions that were unanswered.

THIRTY-ONE

IRENA

Hotel Pinamar, Pinamar, Buenos Aires, Argentina 7 January 1994

Ricardo – that was the name of the man that Santiago had said was a German. I was sure of it. Even though he had tried to backtrack. I knew a lie when I saw one.

Anna and I had come here the day before. To this hotel where this Ricardo apparently came to swim every day. We had arrived at 2 p.m. because Anna had faffed about all morning complaining of her bunions, so that we needed to stop off in the city and buy her some new shoes.

Yesterday, I had not seen a man who resembled Richter. Not even in the slightest. We had sat under the shade of an umbrella and looked hard at each man who got in and out of the pool. But nada. Nothing.

As the sun began its lazy descent, I had asked at reception about a man called Ricardo, telling them that he was an old friend of mine.

'*Si*, yes,' the young man behind the counter told me. 'Ricardo. Every day he swim, but he come at eleven. Every day at eleven he come here. I tell him you want to see him?' he had asked, proffering a notepad and a pen for me to write down my name.

'No, it's okay,' I told him. 'I want it to be a surprise.'

This morning, Anna would not get out of bed. 'I'm sunburned!' she wailed at me, indicating her feet, which were red and puffy, latticed with white stripes from her new sandals. 'I can't go. Please, Irena. Let's just stay here and we'll go tomorrow.'

She was my friend. My very best friend. She had been with me through everything, and I felt that I couldn't leave her, so I said that I would stay. But as the morning wore on, as that clock ticked its way to 9 a.m. and then onwards to 10 a.m., I knew I couldn't sit there and do nothing.

'I'll go, but just for an hour,' I told her, grabbing up my things and heading for the door before she could argue with me. 'I'll be back by 2 p.m., I promise.'

'I called Peter!' she yelled at me as I was leaving. 'When you were in the shower, I called him and told him about my feet and how I think I need a doctor. He's going to take us at 1 p.m.'

'Yes!' I yelled back at her as I opened the door. 'I'll be back by then. Just give me one or two hours. I'll be back by one, I promise.'

I was almost glad that Anna did not come with me. As much as I loved her company, sitting here by the pool, watching people and just waiting, gave me time to think – to really think about why I was here.

I took the cream baby mitten from my handbag and held it in my own hands. It was so small, so delicate. I imagined my baby's hand going into that mitten. How that night had been so cold that I had put the mittens on him, even for bed.

I wished I had the pair. But where the other one was now was anybody's guess. I could imagine it lying lonely on a pavement somewhere, people walking past it, not realising where it had come from or who it had belonged to.

I supposed, though, that it didn't really belong to anyone now. My baby, my son, was gone. First taken from me, then, when I had searched for him after the war, I had found out that he had died in an orphanage in Berlin.

So there was just me. Just me and my memories of months that seemed to blend into one, of time that rushed on, taking me to the year that meant everything to me. To a memory that was so beautiful, but became so ugly, that it has taken me years to actually think about it again. But now, sitting here by the pool, this memory was the only one I needed to think about. All that had led up to it was fragmented to me now. It was a blur. The only thing that mattered to me was January 1943.

When I had my son.

THIRTY-TWO

IRENA

Nowe Bystre, Poland
January 1943

Time had marched on. It had not thought of what it was taking from us each time the seconds, minutes and hours ticked by. It had not thought of Abel, and how Henryk had needed him to live. Instead, it had cruelly taken him away almost a year ago now, just two days after I had seen Mateusz and Henryk on that snowy mountain.

Time had carried on and carried people away with it. Death seemed to be everywhere. Constant reports of battles fought and lost, news from my father's colleagues about the deportations from ghettos, people loaded onto trains to be sent to places that my father tried to tell me about, but which I could not bear to hear.

When I had seen Mateusz a year ago, I had at first come away from him, from that small kiss in the cold, with a slight feeling of hope and joy. I had held it to me; even after Abel had died, even during the meetings with Richter in his hotel room, I had nurtured it, cherished it and hoped that it would bloom one day in the future into something more.

But the year, time, as it had dragged me onwards, had taken it bit by bit. First, I was told I was not to work at the hotel any more. Richter wanted me to be his girlfriend. He showered me with gifts all the while, constantly reminding me physically that this 'relationship', as he saw it, was controlled by him. I was just something to put on his arm at dinners and dances. I was just another 'thing' that he could own.

I remembered how one day I had seen, Magdalena, crossing the street. She had a purple bruise under her eye and had tried to style her hair in such a way that it covered it. It didn't.

I remembered that she had been at the party at the hotel with a Gestapo officer. The short one. His hair too slick.

'Magdalena!' I had called to her. She had turned, seen me, then carried on walking, more quickly now. I didn't know why, but I couldn't let her go. I had had this urge to talk to her.

'Please, Magdalena!' I'd called out again, quickening my own steps to get closer to her.

Whether she had given in and reduced her speed, or whether I had been quicker, I was suddenly near her, and I reached out and placed my hand on her shoulder.

She'd flinched at my touch, then turned to face me. 'You look well, Irena,' she'd said, her eyes looking me up and down.

'I – well—'

'I know.' She cut me off. 'You got the big fish, a Hauptsturmführer, no less.'

'I didn't want to,' I'd admitted to her, keeping my voice low. 'I had no choice...'

'That's what I told people too. But no one listened to me. Spat at me. Called me a traitor. As soon as he left and didn't take me with him, I lost my job at the school. My ration tickets go missing. When I go to buy bread, it's sometimes filled with sawdust.'

Each word she spoke was filled with a mixture of spite and resignation. This was her lot now.

'Tell me, did he tell you he would take care of you? That's what Ansel told me. You know my mother is sick – can't walk. I had no choice. I needed extra medication, money. I tried to tell people, but no one would listen.' Her words rushed out, the tone replaced with one of worry, of sadness. 'Now you see this' – She moved her hair to the side, revealing the bruise on her eye in all its glory. 'Got a new one. I had no choice again. No job. No money. But this one, this one is mean. Is your Hauptsturmführer mean too?'

She'd leaned in close, too close, and it made me step back. She'd taken that to mean that I was offended by her. Then she'd given me a weak smile and turned on her heel, leaving me standing on the pavement thinking about her last question – *was my Hauptsturmführer mean too*?

Yes. Yes, he was. If anything, his obsession with making me afraid of him had got worse. It was a constant game for him – he would be nice one minute, allowing me to relax, but only for a second. Then he would snatch any peace away from me. Beatings. Humiliating me. Making me stand naked as he ate dinner, as he ignored me.

Once he made me dance, and it made me think of Henryk's young friend who had died in such a devastating way. I had never felt so ashamed, so frightened in my life. And he loved every second of it.

Now though, a year had passed, and I was away from him. I was happy in a way that you can be happy only when all around you the world is falling apart. I tried daily not to think of the past, of what had now brought me here, but now and again snippets of those months would break through. I just had to remind myself of one thing: that I had something now, something I cherished more than anything else in the world.

I had a *son*. He was mine. And no part of the past could ever take away the love I felt for him.

THIRTY-THREE

IRENA

Nowe Bystre, Poland
4 January 1943

'Are you going to give him a name or not?' Anna asked me, sitting on the side of the bed. My saviour. My friend.

'Soon... I don't know yet what will suit him.' It had been almost a month since his birth and yet I could not think of the right name to give him.

'You'd better get to it,' she said, rising from the bed and going to the door. 'I'll tell Zofia that you're awake and to bring you some dinner.'

She left me sitting in a bedroom that had been mine now for six months. A room in a house that was not mine, in a town I did not know and with people who were not my family.

It was the house of Anna's cousin and her husband. Her cousin had heard of my plight – I was pregnant with Richter's child. And Anna, darling Anna, had come up with a plan to get me away from him.

It had been simple in its way, and effective. The day I had found out that I was pregnant, I had rushed to see Anna, desperate to tell someone, needing comfort. But she had been more than just comfort. She had told me I had to hide away from him – I simply had to disappear.

'I'll help you. I will. My cousin, you can go there. Nowe Bystre, it's not too far and she will help you – her and her husband, I know they will,' she had said.

'He'll find me,' I sobbed into her shoulder. 'He will. There's only one way he would stop looking for me and that is if I were... dead.'

'Dead? Oh no, Irena! Don't do anything stupid. We can do something, I know we can.'

She had held me as I cried into her. It was the only way, wasn't it? Either have his child and be tied to him forever, or just end it all. It wasn't as though I hadn't considered it recently. After every beating, after each time I saw him, there was a temptation to simply walk into the mountains, lie down in the snow, and just wait for it to be over. Once, I had even picked up my father's razor, eyeing the shining blade and testing it gently against my skin.

It had left a thin line of blood, and I had stared at it for some time, knowing that if I pushed down hard enough on my wrist, it might just work.

'You know' – she let go of me – 'you might just be right. We tell him you're dead.'

I started to laugh. 'Dead! How, Anna? How can we do it?'

She smiled at me. 'Well, because my cousin's husband is a doctor. And he can make him believe it. You go there, saying you're just visiting a friend. Then he will come forward and say that you died – I don't know, a motor car accident, or you fell, and your body wasn't found – *something* – we can make it work.'

'And my parents? We tell them to go along with it?' The idea seemed so absurd, so utterly stupid, but Anna seemed so sure, so adamant that she could help me that I wanted to let her take control and make it happen.

She was quiet for a minute and chewed on her bottom lip as she thought. Then she clicked her fingers. 'We tell no one. I know it would be hard for your parents, but if they knew the truth, there's a chance they might let something slip. Let me talk to my cousin tomorrow.'

'How can you be so sure that she will want to help? How do you know that her husband would risk helping someone he doesn't know?'

'I don't. But I know she is kind, and I know that her husband is a good man. We have to try, Irena. This is the only option you have.'

I let that sink in for a moment. It was the only option. Again, I had no choice. It was like I was constantly being moved about against my will – just like a chess piece, I thought. Then it occurred to me. I was the queen. I was the one who had to protect my king.

And now my king was my baby.

That one day, that one conversation with Anna had spurred time on again. Changing my life, moving me forward whether I liked it or not. It worked. The whole thing worked. I simply went to Anna's cousin's house and stayed there. Her husband was a good man and told Richter, and my poor parents, that I had died in an accident.

Did I hate doing that to them? Of course I did. The shame and guilt kept me awake at night; but I had to protect them as best I could. If they knew the truth, there was always a risk that they would tell someone, or that it could be beaten out of them.

This was the only way.

That evening, as the snow fell outside, I sat in bed, my newborn child nuzzled against me, cream knitted mittens on his tiny hands, and felt, for once, calm. It was all going to be all right. There was talk that the Germans were not doing well, that the Americans would soon end the war, and when that happened, I would be free to go home, to beg forgiveness from my parents, to live a life without fear, without lies. And without Mateusz.

As soon as I had found out I was pregnant, I had stopped myself from daydreaming about him, from thinking about him in the slightest. I had to. No man would want a woman with another man's child – not even a man as good as Mateusz. I had to face the fact that it would be me and my child now; and that was okay. I could live with that.

My son made a noise, a sort of squeak in his sleep, and I smiled. I loved that each day he would make a new sound and I would have to learn what each one meant.

I leaned down to kiss his head, feeling his soft hair on my lips. He was perfect.

As I placed him in the crib next to me, I noted, and not for the first time, how I had been so afraid to have Richter's child, afraid that he would be like his father, or even look like him, which would always bring up memories that were best kept locked away.

But as soon as I gave birth, those fears vanished. I looked into my son's face, so new, so fragile that I could not feel anything but love for him. He would not be like his father. He wouldn't even be like me. He would be himself.

I got back into bed carefully, still sore from the birth, and rested my head on the pillow. At first, I could not sleep. Every noise he made had me turning to check on him – was he breathing? Was he cold? Too warm?

But soon my eyes began to close, and that heady feeling of falling into a slumber took over my brain, sending me, for once, into a deep sleep.

The baby woke me. His cry was different, almost as if he were afraid of the freezing wind and sleet that now battered against the windows, sneakily trying to let itself inside and disturb our dreams.

I leaned over to look at him, my hands already outstretched ready to take his warm plump body towards my own, to let him nuzzle at my breast and settle down into sucking with a rhythm that matched my heartbeat.

Before I could reach him, the hairs on the back of my neck alerted me to something – something in the room that certainly should not be there. Had the storm snuck in? Had it brought nightmares and danger inside with it? Then a voice. It wasn't a *something*, it was a *someone*.

'Irena,' the voice said. I knew whose voice it was. 'Irena.' Richter said my name again, lower, making the baby cry louder now. 'You lied to me, Irena. You let me think you were dead.'

I couldn't speak. I couldn't even lift the baby out of his crib. My hands shook in the same violent way as they had the first day I had met Richter in that stuffy dining room, as the smell of the officers' sweat mingled with the harshness of the red wine that they drank.

I tried to breathe. To tell myself that I was not back there. That this was not happening, that the storm had come inside and replaced my dreams with nightmares brought from beyond.

I heard him step forward, out of the shadows. He looked at the child, then back at me, and I was sure that he was going to kill us both.

As if sensing that something was not right, that he should in fact be quiet, be still, my son stopped crying and stared at the man above him.

'So, this is why you hid from me? You hid my baby away from me? What was it, Irena, did you not think I would make a good father?'

I knew his questions needed no answer from me. He didn't care about what I thought or felt. I knew that. I stayed quiet.

'So, what are we to do?' He took a step closer to me, then another. He sat on the edge of my bed.

I could feel the warmth from his body on my legs, and I wanted to kick out at him, to push him away, but I was frozen. Even my thoughts were frozen. I tried to think, but nothing came to me – no plan, no answer, no way out.

'Boy?' he asked, not looking at me but at our son.

'Yes.'

'Name?'

'I-I haven't named him yet,' I said. I could hear how small my voice sounded, how childlike.

'So, what are we to do?' He looked at me and smiled. 'Here is a woman, a woman who I bestowed gifts on, who I took care of, who I gave favours to, and this is what she does to me. Tell me, Irena, what would you do if you were in my position?'

He dug around in his pocket and produced a silver cigarette case. He opened it and offered me one.

'No?' he asked. 'I would have thought that the occasion was right for a cigarette and a chat. Suit yourself.'

He lit a cigarette and smoked silently.

I did not know what to do. Not that I had ever really known my role in the games that he played with me, but this was different – this wasn't him wanting me and me trying to hide. This was him angry. Silently angry, and it felt worse, so much worse than it ever had done when he simply lashed out and hit me.

'You know,' he said, 'I believed it. I really did. I thought you were dead. Your parents, they had a funeral for you. I didn't go. Of course not. But I saw the mourners. I believed it. I even left Poland. Did you know that?'

I gave a slight nod. Anna had told me that he had left for Germany with some other officers.

'A promotion. A house. All the things I was willing to share with you. But then, you were dead, so that was that.'

I was sure I should apologise, or say something that would calm him. Yet words failed me. What could I possibly say or do?

'I found you, though,' he said. 'You know how?'

'How?' I squeaked again.

'I came back. Just for a week, for a holiday, of all things. I had leave and I thought to myself, where shall I go? Then I remembered this place, the skiing, how so many came here for leave, and I thought, why not? A trip down memory lane might be nice.'

He placed a hand on my leg before he spoke again. Heavily. As if he thought that at any moment I was going to leap from the bed and run.

'So here I am. On holiday, and I see a friend of yours – Anna. In her arms she's got all these bags, and she's talking to some woman – a woman I know now is her cousin, Zofia. They didn't see me, but I could hear them. How they talked about you. But not in the past tense, not at all. No, they talked about how you were doing well, how the baby was so beautiful, how you had slept, how Zofia was going to make you dinner and get your strength up. Can you believe it, Irena? How I must have felt standing there, wondering if I had heard correctly?

'I doubted myself at first. I was sure I had misheard. So I sent a few of my men to follow her, to see where she went. And then, now, here I am.'

There was a buzzing sound in my ears. It was making it hard to make sense of my thoughts, as jumbled as they already were. He had left, I was safe, but now here he was, by chance, by luck.

As if reading my mind, he grinned. 'I always told you I was a lucky man. Promotions at a young age, living in a grand hotel! I mean, I always thought I was lucky, but then when this happened, I realised that I am invincible – that's what I am, Irena, invincible. You, and no one else can get rid of me. I will always find you. I will always be here. Just waiting. Just round the corner.'

I felt as though he were going mad. His talk of invincibility went on for some more minutes. Much of it I did not understand, but the more he spoke of himself, of his luck, of his power, the more animated he became. He waved his arms about to demonstrate how brilliant he was, he leaned close to me, and then close to the baby, all the while ranting about how I would never be free from him.

In a way, I was glad. It meant that I was to go with him. Me and my son. It meant that he wasn't going to harm either of us, not yet anyway. And it actually made me hope for a second that perhaps we would be safe in some way.

Then he reached down into the crib and immediately I tried to stop him. Whether it was instinct, I do not know, but I hadn't even had the thought to try to stop him from touching the baby; I just did it. He backhanded me across the face, knocking me back into bed and against the pillows.

By the time I had righted myself, he was standing with my son in his arms, half holding him in such a way that I thought he was going to drop him. There was no care, no love for what was in his arms, I saw that, and I launched myself towards him, trying to get to my son.

'Now, now, Irena.' He pushed me back with one hand. The baby was crying now. He was being held in an uncomfortable way, his head was not supported, and it sort of lolled over one of Richter's arms. 'You do that again, and I might just drop him.'

'No!' I shrieked. 'Don't hurt him! Do what you want to me, but please don't hurt him!'

Richter laughed, then turned away from me, opened the door and left.

I followed as quickly as I could. I was still in some form of pain from the birth, and I could feel my delicate skin tearing as I tried to run after them. Finally, I made it to the front door, which was wide open. I could hear the hum of a car's engine ticking over outside.

I stood barefoot in the snow that was now melting with the rain and sleet that was falling. I did not move. In front of me, Richter held our child. Two men held guns. Both pointed at me.

I cried out for my baby, for my son. But my cries dissolved into the icy air, and it was as though I were shouting, screaming at a dream.

'*Please!* Please give him back to me!'

I heard Richter say something to the soldiers and both of them looked at me, surprise on their faces. I knew what he had told them to do – to shoot me. They raised their guns.

At that moment, a scream came from behind me. It was Zofia. Her husband was with her. They raced outside and each one held onto an arm each, holding me back from heading straight towards Richter and those guns, all the while trying to bargain with Richter, with the men with guns.

I could hear the voices, pleading, but my mind was racing – frantic – and I didn't know what they were saying. My focus was on my child. I tried to think what I could do, could say. Then Richter said something to the men, and they lowered their weapons.

He took a few steps towards me.

'I'm not going to kill you, my little sparrow. Not even your friends. You seem to forget what I am good at. I can make anyone do what I want them to do. I can make them say what I want them to say. I see the fear in someone, and I exploit it for myself. I could kill you, yes. But what would that do? You'd be dead, you'd feel no pain. This way, and only this way, will you feel pain for the rest of your life. You will always wonder where your son is, but you will never find him. You may, even, one day, feel safe in a new life, but then you'll remember who I am and that I can always find you. And you two' – he turned to Zofia and her husband – 'you'll get your punishment. On a day when you least expect it.'

I felt Zofia's grip on my arm tighten. It had worked. Not knowing when or how the punishment would come for her was scaring her more than standing in the snow facing officers with guns.

Richter handed the baby to one of the men, then stepped away from us and turned to the car. I saw one of the officers open the door for him.

I took one last lunge towards him, falling headfirst into the snow. As I lifted my head, the car was already moving away. I screamed, yelled, cried, long after the car was gone. Long after Zofia had tried to drag me inside. I would stay there and freeze. I would die, here in the snow.

I felt Zofia's husband pull me up. I fought with him, but he was strong and would not give in. Bit by bit, he dragged me inside, and then gave me a sedative to drown out the screams. The screams from a madwoman whose heart had just been shattered into a million pieces.

THIRTY-FOUR

PETER

Pinamar, Buenos Aires, Argentina
7 January 1994

Peter woke tightly curled up next to Sara. He did not want to move away from her; he wanted to stay like this for a moment more, because it was the first time, he thought, in his life, that he was truly happy.

He had told Sara everything, and she had not looked differently at him. She had accepted him, wanted to be his wife, trusted him to be a good father. He felt free now from the constant questioning of what to do about Richter. None of that mattered any more. The only things that mattered were Sara and his child.

But he could not stay in bed any longer, as the telephone in the living room would not stop ringing. He tried to wait it out, to let whomever it was give up, but as soon as it stopped, it started again.

Groaning, he got up, careful not to wake Sara. She had seemed so exhausted last night; even the way she had talked had been slower, her eyes red, dark bags under them too – he had to take better care of her. He could not let her worry like this again.

He went to the phone, not really knowing who would be bothering to call him at this hour – 8 a.m. – and found that the voice on the other end belonged to Anna.

'I am so sorry to wake you,' she began. 'Did I wake you? It is Peter, isn't it?'

Despite the annoyance of the call, he couldn't help but smile. He liked the way she rambled on. 'It is, yes. What can I do for you?'

'I have this sunburn. Irena thinks it isn't anything to worry about, but then I remembered this story someone told me once that they had had sunburn and the skin had peeled off and they almost lost their arm! So, I was wondering if you could perhaps take me to see a doctor later today? Say 1 p.m.? We'll pay of course. We could get a taxi, I know, but I thought that you would probably know the best place to go to, and I don't want to go to see a bad doctor because that could end up being worse than the sunburn if you see what I mean? And—'

'Yes,' Peter interrupted her before she could carry on. '1 p.m., the hotel. I'll be there.'

'Wonderful! Oh, you are so good. So good. 1 p.m. I'll tell Irena.'

She did not say goodbye, and he thought that was funny. She could talk and talk but then suddenly just put the phone down.

'What are you laughing at?' Sara walked towards him. She was wearing an old T-shirt of his with a surfboard in garish colours right in the centre of it. She looked beautiful – her long dark hair all mussed up from sleep, her cheeks flushed from the warmth of the bed.

'Some woman. Anna,' he told her and took her into his arms.

'Your other girlfriend?' she joked and pulled away from him. 'I need coffee.'

He followed her into the kitchen and was going to ask her if she should be drinking coffee when she was pregnant, he was sure he had heard about that somewhere before. Then he thought better of it. She would know what to do, and he wasn't about to start the day off bickering.

'Anna's this old woman,' he told her as he foraged about in the cupboard for the coffee. 'Go sit, I'll make it.'

Sara moved away from the counter and sat at the kitchen table. He watched her for a second and saw her smile.

'Who is this old woman exactly?'

'Ah, she's here with her friend. From Germany— no, *Poland*,' he corrected himself. 'Something about finding a friend from years ago.'

He heard a rustle behind him and saw that Sara was staring at something on the table, something he could not quite make out.

'What was the other woman's name?' she asked, not looking up at him as she spoke.

'Irena. Why?'

He placed the cups on the counter and went to the table to see what she was staring at. It was then that he saw she was looking at a cream knitted mitten.

'Where did you get this?' she asked.

'It came with me when I was adopted. It was the only thing I had with me, apparently. The nuns who arranged the whole adoption told my new mother that it was a keepsake. They said I played with it all the time.'

'And you kept it all these years?' She looked at him now, tears in her eyes.

'I did. Why? I mean, it was the only thing I had from my life before. Why's it upsetting you?'

'Did you ever find out who your mother was? You know who your real father is. But your mother?'

'She died. That's what I was told. I wasn't given a name or anything.'

Sara stood and embraced him. He could feel her cheek, damp with tears, on his own.

She pulled away and cupped his face. 'Last night there was something bothering me. It felt like, and I don't know why, there was still something left unanswered. But I think I've just answered it for you.'

THIRTY-FIVE

IRENA

Hotel Pinamar, Pinamar, Buenos Aires, Argentina
7 January 1994

I placed the mitten on the table for a moment so I could pick up a glass of iced water that was dribbling condensation on the tabletop. I remembered how the day after my son had been taken, Zofia had come to me, holding the cold wet woollen thing.

'I found it outside,' she had said.

I did not answer her. I took it from her and held it to me and wept. That was all I did for months on end. Not caring if Richter found me again. Not caring if he killed me. I just wanted my son. He had been right; this was a worse punishment than death.

Poor Zofia and her husband moved – disappeared, so scared they were that their punishment was just round the corner. Perhaps Death's Head, perhaps one of the camps. Within two days of my child being taken, they were gone, leaving me in their house crying into Anna's shoulder. Anna eventually took me home to my parents.

I could not let my thoughts linger on that time in my life any more. I could not think about the person Richter had made me into, because in that moment a man caught my eye. An old man.

He was leathery, as though he had been sat in the sun his entire life, wearing blue, tight swimming trunks that seemed wrong on a man so old. I didn't need to get up and go to him to know it was Richter. I could tell by the way he walked, by the way he flung a blue and white striped towel on a sunbed. How he sat down, stretched out and placed his arms under his head. I knew him. Every movement.

In that moment, I had no feeling. No thoughts of joy at finding him. No fear at finding him either. It all just sort of felt right. That this was the moment my whole life had been leading up to and there was no need for emotion now.

I could see him there, behind the palm trees. I knew he could see me too, but I was sure that he didn't know who I was. I was just an old woman. Sitting on the other side of the pool. Drinking iced water.

I watched him carefully and I looked for the one definitive mark that would put any small doubt aside. I looked for a scar on his right leg, a scar he had once proudly pointed at and told me how he had got it; a Jew had tried to fight back. He had told me that the scar made him remember to always fight first. Never wait. Never talk. Action was the only thing needed. But really he didn't mean action; he meant violence.

As I waited for him to move again so I could look at his leg, I noticed green coconuts hanging in thick bunches, not yet ripe, from the tree next to me. I never knew coconuts could be green.

It was surprising to me to find my mind so calm. I had always thought that my mind in this moment would be a flurry of thought, or of fear. But instead, my mind was wandering, thinking about coconuts.

I made myself look away from the palm tree and at him; he

was still lying there, not giving me a glimpse of that right leg. I could wait. He didn't know how long I could wait, but I could – I already had.

Finally, he moved. He stood and went to the pool's edge and then I saw it. The half-moon scar, white against the tan of his right calf. I saw it as clear as day. It was him. It was definitely Richter.

A waiter approached me and asked if I wanted another drink, and I said yes and ordered myself a cocktail that I could barely pronounce the name of. I didn't particularly care what it would taste like, I just wanted the Dutch courage that alcohol is supposed to give you.

I watched him get into the pool, where he dipped under the water for a moment before surfacing and then floating on his back.

I had to think what I was going to do. I hadn't ever really thought about the actual event; perhaps I had never thought I would find him. But here I was, and I suddenly did feel something. Unprepared. Worried.

What if he got out of the pool and left? Should I follow him? Did I do it here, where everyone could see me? How was I going to do it? Did I just confront him and see what happened? It was then I wished Anna were with me. I needed her now. I needed someone to tell me what to do.

He did not swim for long before getting out of the pool. My heart quickened. He was leaving. What was I going to do?

Although he was old, he was quick. He'd already grabbed his towel and was making his way inside the hotel. I tried to gather my things as quickly as I could, and knocked over the water in my haste.

It soaked the mitten. My son's mitten. I picked it up and squeezed the water out of the damp wool. It would be fine.

I was about to step out from under the umbrella when I

suddenly felt a hand on my shoulder. Turning round, I saw Peter with Sara and Anna.

'What are you all doing here?' I asked, trying to move away from them.

'There's no need to rush after him,' Sara said.

She knew? I looked at Anna.

'Richter. There's no need to rush after him,' she explained. 'We know who he is. We know where he lives.'

Perhaps it was the shock of seeing him, or the heat, or seeing Peter with Sara – how did they know each other? – or thinking about my son, how he was gone, how the man who had taken him from me and left him to die in an orphanage was within reach. Either way, I took a turn. My legs felt like jelly and a sudden wave of nausea overcame me.

'Sit down,' Peter said. 'You're sweating and pale.'

I sat because I had no other option. There was a buzzing sound in my ears and head, and everything felt a little out of focus.

'Just breathe.' Anna was by my side. And then there was a fresh glass of water on the table. How did that get there?

I drank it, then remembered how I had already spilled my water before. How it had soaked the mitten. How careless I had been!

In my befuddled state, I kept trying to rummage around in my handbag to find it. All the while the three of them were trying to take the bag off me, telling me to breathe, be calm.

As soon as I found it, felt the wool, although wet, beneath my fingertips, I was calm. I placed it on the table, wanting it to dry out a little.

Then, as if by magic, another mitten appeared. Its twin. I was sure I was seeing double and rubbed at my eyes. Two mittens? No.

'Irena.' Anna's voice broke through my strange delirium. 'We have something to tell you.'

THIRTY-SIX

IRENA

Hotel Pinamar, Pinamar, Buenos Aires, Argentina
7 January 1994

I had to wait for a few more minutes until I was compos mentis enough to listen to what they were all saying. Although, when I say all, it was just Anna and Sara who were talking. Peter sat next to me, looking at me, but not saying a word.

'It was the mitten,' Sara said again. 'I saw it this morning and I remembered then, the mitten you had. And it was the same. I mean it *is* the same—'

'Peter and Sara came to the hotel,' Anna butted in. 'I said 1 p.m., but they came earlier. They wanted to talk to you, and I told them where you had gone – looking for Ricardo – and then Peter, he says that he knows the man and that the man is his father and then I said to Sara, could it be? And then they showed me the mitten and then—'

I raised my hand to cut her off. I needed a minute to think.

'It's a lot, isn't it?' Peter finally spoke. 'Take your time.'

I nodded and didn't look at him. I was scared to. I was

scared to look at him and not see my son. I had spent time with this man, and I hadn't got a feeling or anything. Surely, a mother would instinctively know her son?

But he was dead. That was what the nuns had said. I'd tracked him down – it took years and money away from me. A private detective had found the trail, found that he had been placed in an orphanage and that their records said that he was dead.

'But why lie? Why do that to me as well?' I asked myself out loud.

'Do what?' Anna asked.

'Richter. He wanted me to never find you. It was his way. He wanted me to feel pain forever. He knew how to do it. That's why he did it, wasn't it? To make me feel pain?'

I looked now at Peter, staring into his face, at his blue eyes, the crinkle in his brow. Trying to see some resemblance of me – some mark to say that he and I had once been one and the same. Could it be true? Could he really be my son?

'It all adds up,' he said gently. 'The timing. The mitten. Richter, you, the whole thing...'

'So you are...'

'I am. At least if you want me to be?' he asked, then he smiled. And I saw it. I saw in that smile that it was like my father's. Wide, generous. A smile of a good man. It suddenly struck me that it was my smile too.

I wasn't sure how to react. My heart was beating too fast, my mind going over and over the years at full speed, trying to make sense of this new past. I saw Peter place his hand on the baby mittens, just an inch or so away from me.

I raised my hand and slowly placed it over his. In that moment, it was as though all the pain I had carried around with me all these years began to seep away. I could feel his skin under my own – warm, soft. He didn't pull away from my touch but neither did he rise to embrace me as silent tears started to fall. It was as though he knew me – knew that I would be awkward, unsure of myself, just as he was.

I stared at our hands, mine old, his ageing. So many years had gone by, so many moments that I had never had with him. He had a white circle of a scar near his thumb. *How had that happened?*

There were so many stories, etched into our skin, displayed in each wrinkle, stories that we might not ever learn about each other. Could we fit our pasts together now and be in each other's lives?

'Irena,' he said gently. 'Are you all right?'

I nodded that I was, too scared to look at him – to look at my boy – because I knew that the silent tears would not stop, that I would not be able to contain everything I felt.

So, we sat. My hand on his, the tiny mittens under his hand, and let the past erase itself whilst I quietly sobbed.

The afternoon was spent back at Peter's small home on the seafront, not far from our hotel. I remembered how I had sat with him on the sand that night as he had fished and I had thought about my past. How close we had been to never knowing who the other person really was. But now we did know.

Sara, it turned out, was Peter's fiancée. She showed us the ring, told us of how they had met outside her law offices, how her father had secretly helped Peter and had fobbed me off with Santiago's name in case I ever came looking.

'I think Papa wanted to let Peter talk to Richter – to sort it out in his way. I think maybe he thought that you wouldn't really ever come here too,' she said, clearly trying to atone for her father.

'It's all right now,' I said. 'It's all clear.'

In fact, though, it wasn't completely clear. Yes, I knew what had happened. My son was taken to Germany, given to an orphanage, adopted and sent to England. My son had found out about his father and wanted to meet him, to find out who he was. And all the while, Richter had played games with us all. Making sure I thought Peter was dead, hiding in plain sight, probably proud of himself for being able to pull it all off and get away with it.

'Coffee?' Peter asked me, handing me a chipped orange mug.

I took it from him and had to remind myself again who he was. My son. Alive. My son.

We all talked that afternoon, about everything we could, without settling on the one subject that still needed to be spoken about. That thing that still wasn't cleared up, which sat messily in some grey area.

Anna told stories from our childhood. I tried to fill in as much as I could about what had happened between Richter and me, and Sara showed me some documents proving that, in the years after he left Zakopane, he had continued his reign of terror.

As I told them about the night Peter was taken from me, Peter stood up and came to sit by me on the couch. He did not try to hug me – perhaps it was too soon – but I felt his strength and his presence keenly. When I had finished telling them about the day Peter was taken, 4 January 1943, Peter went to the kitchen table, where all the documents about Richter sat in messy piles.

He brought a piece of paper back with him. A document signed by a nun at the orphanage that stated he was brought into their care on 7 January 1943.

'He hadn't even kept you with him until the end of the war?' I asked.

'Nope. Dropped me off and left. I didn't know until much

later when I went there on my travels and found this one really old nun, who told me I had been left there. She never told me who did it, nor that it was my own father. It was only afterwards that I realised. But she did tell me one thing. That my date of birth was wrong. That on my birth certificate it said 4 January 1943. She said that I was at least two weeks old when I came to them. She asked the man who dropped me off why this date had been put on the certificate. And the man had told her, apparently, that that was the day I was saved from the enemy.'

'I'm so sorry that you had to go through all that,' I said. My voice was dense, my throat all bunged up. I knew I was going to cry, but I didn't want to. I didn't want him to see me cry.

'It's all right, it's not your fault.' He crouched down in front of me, and I bowed my head so that he would not see the tears.

'I could have done more. I should have. I should have fought him. I shouldn't have let him take you – all this time...' I sobbed.

That was when my son, my Peter, hugged me to him. He held me like the silly old woman I was and let me cry until I felt myself regain some composure.

'I'm sorry,' I said again, sniffing and then blowing my nose on my hanky. I looked about and could see that Anna and Sara had been crying too; both of them were wiping at their noses and their faces.

'Look at the state of us!' I exclaimed, making them laugh. 'This is meant to be a happy occasion and here we are, all blubbering!'

'It's bittersweet,' Peter said, and sat by my side.

He was not crying, not a hint of it. Instead, he had his fists balled up, resting on his knees.

'You're angry,' I said simply.

'Yes.'

'Peter.' Sara said his name in a way that was meant as a warning. 'You promised.'

'And I won't,' he said. 'I won't do anything stupid.'

'Is this about Richter – what were you going to do?' Anna asked. 'Irena here has had it in her head for years that she would find him and kill him. I'm not sure how. I mean, we never really had that conversation, did we, Irena? I mean this morning, when you went to the pool, I thought to myself, gosh, I hope she doesn't find him – she won't know what to do!'

'You were going to kill him?' Sara asked.

'Yes. But Anna's right. I had never got to the actual event. I hadn't planned it that far. In a way, I think I thought I would never find him. And I also thought that if I did, I would just instinctively know what to do.'

'And do you still want to?' Peter asked. I noted that his fists had unclenched.

'I do,' I said. 'Honestly, that's still the same answer. But I won't. I think I realised that today when I saw him. There was still a voice of reason or something in there that told me I wouldn't be able to. That's obviously why I hadn't planned on how to do it. I knew I couldn't. Not really.'

'So, what do you want to do?' Sara asked. 'We can call the police, show them what we have? We can speak to my father?'

I thought for a moment. Here I was, at the age I was, with a son sitting next to me who I had to get to know. And, he had told me he was going to be a father, which meant I was going to be a grandmother. Did I want to call the police? Did I want to have to go to court? Did I want to waste what precious time I had left dealing with Richter?

'He's taken enough time away from me,' I said.

'So we do nothing?' Anna was incredulous. 'Really? After all this time. *Nothing*?'

'No, not nothing. I want to see him. I want to confront him. I want him to know that I am not living my life in fear any more and that he can't take anything else away from me. I want him to know that. And, Peter' – I turned to look at him – 'I want you there too. If you feel you are able. I want him to see that we found each other, in spite of him. I want him to know that I found my son.'

THIRTY-SEVEN

PETER

Pinamar, Buenos Aires, Argentina
8 January 1994

Peter sat across from the man who for the past almost fifty years had called himself Ricardo, and watched as he slept.

Each rise of his chest made Peter want to reach over and grab a pillow and place it firmly on his face – yet he did not. He waited. He could hear Irena, Anna and Sara, in the sitting room, whispering just a little too loudly. He wanted them to be quiet – he wanted complete silence so that maybe, just for a moment, his mind would fall silent too and the thoughts that were running riot would be banished.

He had promised Sara that he would not do anything stupid to the old man. He had known for years what a piece of shit he was, but after hearing Irena, his mother, tell him about what he had done to her, how he had played games, cruel games, and tried to ruin everyone's lives, Peter had wanted to renege on his promise. But he wouldn't, because he was going to be a father and he did not want to start out like his own. A murderer. A vile excuse for a human being. If, in fact, he was human at all.

Richter stirred. He turned onto his side so that he now faced Peter, but he did not open his eyes. First, he yawned loudly, then rubbed at his face with his hand and smacked his dry lips together. It was then and only then that he slowly opened his eyes.

The shock on his face at seeing someone sitting beside his bed, watching him sleep, made Peter feel emboldened. He wanted him to feel uncomfortable – he wanted him to feel unsure of himself, he wanted to see the old man, his father, squirm.

'Peter! What the hell?' The old man sat up in shock. 'What's wrong? Has something happened?'

'It has,' Peter replied. 'Something has happened.'

'What? Is it Santiago? I knew he wouldn't last much longer, not with that weight and the amount he drinks. Wait, how did you get in here?'

'Your door was open.'

'Was it? I don't know – it might have been. I had a few drinks. I left it open? Are you sure?'

'I am. I am certain of it... Christoph.'

As soon as Peter said the man's real name, he saw a blanket of shock on his face. Then it slackened. His mouth opened and closed. And then just as quickly, the old face returned. 'So you know?' he asked. 'That's why you're here.'

'I've known for a long time,' Peter said quietly. He didn't yet want to alert the others to the fact that Richter was awake – he needed this moment with him, with this man, his father. He still needed to understand him, he still needed to feel that this man held some trace of humanity.

'How?'

'My father, your friend Maurice in England, told me.'

'He never would have,' Richter said.

'He was dying. Maybe he thought that it was a gift for me. Or maybe he just wanted to be cruel. Either way. He told me.

Just when I'd got into that spot of bother, and you came to the rescue.'

'Why didn't you say anything when you arrived? I mean. It could have been different. Why not tell me that you knew? I wouldn't have been mad about it.'

Peter shrugged. 'I needed to know who you were – who you really were. And if you knew that I knew, you'd try and squirm your way out of the truth. What you did to me, to others. Why would I tell you that I knew I was your son? You didn't care that I was. You left me in an orphanage.'

'I did that for your own good!' Richter smiled at him. 'I mean, how could I bring you here? I had to hide who I was. All these people after Nazis, Germans and things and, well, I mean I worked for them, but I wasn't a bad man. I just did my job! I did as I was told. But then I had to hide myself away for my own protection, and yours!'

'You can argue it whichever way you want. But I know who you are.'

'If that's true, then you'll know I am not a bad man,' Richter said. 'I did my job. I got you a nice family eventually, didn't I? I sent money sometimes when Maurice asked for it. I did what I could. Why are you so angry at me?'

Peter suddenly laughed. Was that what he thought? That he had presented himself to Peter all these years as a good man? That everything he had done was for Peter's own good, that he had nothing to be sorry for.

'Why are you laughing?' Richter sat up, suddenly angry. It was then that Irena appeared in the doorway, and Richter gasped.

'Christoph,' Irena said softly. 'Nice to see you again.'

The confusion on Richter's face was laughable. He looked to Peter, then back at Irena, and Peter could imagine that he was trying to figure out exactly what was happening and why.

'It can't be,' Richter said. 'Irena, is that really you?'

Peter could see that Irena was holding on to the doorframe for support. He knew how hard this must be for her, how she must be feeling so much all at once. It did not go amiss that she had almost fainted the day before at the pool after seeing Richter, and Peter knew that this was affecting her much more than she would ever say.

'It is her. She found me,' Peter said, then stood. 'We found each other.' He went to Irena's side and placed his hand on her shoulder so that she would know he was there, that he would not let anything bad happen to her.

'Won't you join us in the sitting room?' Irena asked politely.

'*Us?*' Ricardo asked.

'Anna. You remember her, don't you? And Sara. You should come and sit. We have a lot to talk about.'

THIRTY-EIGHT

IRENA

Pinamar, Buenos Aires, Argentina
8 January 1994

It was strange to see Richter close up.

I had seen him at the pool, of course, but at a distance. Now I could see how much he had aged – more, worse than me – and I was glad of it. I was glad to see that his wrinkles were much deeper, his hair whiter, his teeth yellowed by tobacco. He was no longer a handsome man; he wasn't even frightening any more. Now, he was simply an old man.

Peter stayed close to him, perhaps thinking that Richter might try to turn and run at any moment, but there was no chance of that. Richter, despite being confused, was interested in what this was about – I could see that look in his eyes, the way he looked at each one of us in turn, how he was turning it over and over in his mind, ready to charm, to argue, and if necessary be brutal, evil even, in what he would say and perhaps do.

But still, I was not scared of him. Not any more.

We all sat. Anna was the only one who could not look at him. Her fear was still palpable – she had never got over that night at the dance, she had never got past what he had done to me.

Richter seized upon her as the weakest in the group. 'Ah, Anna! How lovely to see you again!' he said, and I noted that Anna flinched.

'Still so beautiful. You have aged like a fine wine!' He chuckled. 'So nice to have old friends all back together – and new ones. You have met Peter and Sara, I see.'

Anna did not respond, so I decided that it was up to me to take charge; I knew that otherwise Richter would try to wrangle the conversation to his own purposes.

'Anna knows Peter is my son,' I told him.

'*Our* son.' He laboured the 'our' so much that it made my fingers itch with anger.

'He's *mine*!' I yelled. 'You *took* him from me! You took him from me and then you let me think that he had died!'

'How did I do that?' he asked calmly. 'How could I take something that was mine in the first place? If anything, I gave him a life that you could never have given him.'

'You gave him away!' I was on the verge of tears. 'You didn't even want him. You just wanted to hurt me.'

Richter shrugged. 'Maybe, maybe not. It wasn't as though I could turn up here with a child in tow, so I gave him to a friend of mine. You had a good life, didn't you, Peter? And you got to know me, your father.'

Peter did not speak. I could see a small muscle jumping in his jaw as he kept it clenched.

'Who told you?' Richter asked me.

'My father and I did,' Sara answered for me. Her voice was level, strong, and I felt like going up to her and wrapping her in my arms. Not that she needed it. It would be more for me. 'He tracked you down for Irena at first, but Peter stopped him from telling her who exactly you were. Peter wanted to deal with you himself.'

'*Deal* with me?' Richter laughed. 'And how were you going to do that?'

Again, Peter did not speak.

'Cat got your tongue, boy? You've always been too quiet. Letting women do the talking, and making decisions for you.' He spat this last part at Sara, who smiled at him.

'You have no idea how close you have come to death—' Sara started.

'Death! Ha! Irena sends me letters every year, don't you?' he asked me.

'Letters?' I asked.

'You know, the ones where you tell me you are going to kill me? Such a joke. I should've figured out it'd been you the past five years.'

'Five years?'

'Yes. A letter each year for five years,' Richter said, but it was his turn to look confused.

'I only contacted Sara's father three years ago,' I told him. 'I have no idea what you're talking about.'

It was then that Peter decided to break his silence. 'It was me.'

'You?' Richter said. 'But why? I thought you wanted to get to know me, spend time with me – that's what you said.'

Peter shook his head. 'I wanted to see who you were. I wanted to see if you were the man Sara's father told me you had been. There were other people looking for you – Jews you tortured at that hotel in Poland. But I made sure that no one else found you. I wanted to be the one to do it.'

'So. All of you are here to see me die – is that it? You're going to what? Shoot me, strangle me?' Richter laughed again, but I could see now the uncertainty in his eyes. He was scared.

'We're not going to do anything,' Sara spoke up, and Peter opened his mouth, perhaps ready to argue with her, but she ignored him. 'Killing you won't change anything. And I won't allow my fiancé or his mother to lose their humanity. I won't allow them to become *you*.'

Richter did not respond to Sara but looked at me. 'Why would you want to kill me, Irena? You were the one who broke my heart. You were the one who lied. You were the one who loved that Mateusz and not me.'

He must have seen the surprise register on my face. Love? How dare he. What he thought love was was not what I had felt for him.

'Ha! Yes. You think I didn't know about Mateusz? Of course I did. I assume you married him, yes? Had a brood of ugly Polish children?'

'How *dare* you say his name to me!' I stood now. I could feel every muscle in my body twitching. I wanted to strangle him, stab him. I wanted to watch as the life went from his eyes. 'How was anything my fault? Your heart? Yours?' I spat. 'You raped me day in and day out. You took my son away from me. You—'

'I what?' he demanded, cutting me off. 'If I remember correctly, you liked it. If I remember correctly, I did nothing wrong. Didn't you come to me and beg me to take you back if I let that Jew go? Didn't you say you were sorry? You had a choice, you always did, but now you're rewriting history to suit yourself. If anything, I spoiled you. I ruined you.'

'Spoiled me?' I gasped. Was he joking? Had he actually thought that we had been in a relationship? Those nights he took me to his rooms and grunted and sweated over me, then told me to leave and come back the next day – he thought that was some form of love?

'I had no choice,' I said, but my voice was wavering. Had I been complicit? Had I had a choice and not taken it?

'You had a choice, Irena. What else could I do but take my son away from a lying whore? I couldn't leave him with you!'

'Enough!' It was Anna. Her voice had taken on an edge I

had never heard before. She looked at him now, her eyes narrow, a flush on her cheeks. Oddly scared, I sat back down.

'Enough of this! You fucking bastard! You fucking, fucking pig!' she screamed. 'You tried to rape me. You raped Irena. She did what she had to do to save me. To save Abel, her parents, Mateusz, Bartok. She did it for us, not for you. Tell me. What would you have done if she had refused you, eh?' She laughed. 'Let her choose. Let her get away from you? I doubt it.'

Richter had the common sense to stay in his seat and say nothing as Anna spoke. Indeed, I don't think any of us moved an inch. The anger that came forth from her commanded the attention of the whole room, and I was not sure now exactly what she was capable of.

'You killed others. I know. We all know. We've seen the evidence,' Anna said, emphasising the word 'evidence'.

She let it linger for a moment, and I could see Richter shifting in his seat and his eyes darting about the room. *Evidence.*

'Yes. We know. Do you know what we could do with you? I saw one thing in the papers. Something that caught my eye, and I read it and reread it. It was about you in Berlin, and there was a woman and a child. Do you remember?'

Richter blinked a few times. He opened and closed his mouth, and I could tell he wasn't sure what Anna was going to say. It made me sick. The thought that he had done so much to so many that he could not narrow it down to what Anna was describing.

'There was a woman and a child. This time, you didn't let them go. You shot them – both of them – and walked away. People saw you do it. People heard the woman cry for help, and you didn't care. You shot her anyway.'

'That never happened,' Richter said, but his voice was small.

'It happened. You almost killed Irena. You took her child,

then a year later, you stood on a street in Berlin and murdered a woman and her child. You did that.'

'I was just doing my job,' he tried. 'It was a job. What was I meant to do? I didn't have a choice.'

His argument made me boil over with rage. I stood and took the two steps towards him and bent down so that our faces were close together.

'Do you remember what you once told me? You told me that you showed no mercy. That was what you said. Maybe now it's time for us to do the same.'

I saw his pupils dilate; I knew then that it had clicked in his mind. There was no talking his way out of this; he wasn't invincible any more. He was now scared.

I stepped away from him. My hands were shaking with rage. I can't describe the feeling of anger in that moment. It took over me, made my thoughts jumbled. My muscles twitched under my skin as if preparing themselves for what might happen next.

'Sit, Irena.' Peter was by my side. I felt his hand on my arm. 'Sit. It's all right.'

I sat, feeling that same feeling I had had at the pool. Dizzy, sweating, nauseous.

'If I could do it all again, I wouldn't change a thing. I would try harder to get rid of the vermin Jews, Poles, gypsies – anyone who defiled our race,' Richter blustered. His voice was loud, but not threatening. He was trying to be the old Richter, to scare us, to make us listen to him and do what he wanted us to do. But that Richter was gone, and he had only just come to realise it.

'But you can't do it again.' Peter's voice had changed. It was still soft, like he normally spoke, but it was quieter, slower.

He took a step towards Richter. I could see his fists clenching and unclenching. I looked to Sara, who looked back at me with fear in her eyes. This wasn't part of the plan. We were going to confront him, mock him, make him understand that he had no power over any of us. But Peter now – the way he spoke, the way he moved towards Richter – told us all that he was taking matters into his own hands.

'Peter.' I heard Sara's voice, but it sounded like it was coming from far away.

My head still wasn't right. My breathing was fast, my palms sweaty. I knew I should say something, stop what was about to happen, but it was happening too fast and too slow at the same time. It was like being in a dream and you know what is going to happen, but there's nothing you can do to stop it.

'*Peter!*' I heard Sara yell.

Peter was on him. He had picked the older man up out of the chair, his large hands holding him by his arms so he was an inch or so off the ground. He slammed Richter into a wall, knocking a picture of a farmhouse onto the floor.

Richter's eyes were wide with fear. His mouth was flapping open and closed again like a fish. Sara had stood and was grabbing Peter's arm, but he either didn't notice or didn't care.

I don't know how, but Peter had moved his hands to Richter's neck. Still holding him off the ground, against the wall, squeezing at his neck.

His face was red, his teeth gritted.

'No! Stop, Peter! *Stop!*' Sara screamed at him.

I looked to Anna. She sat still. Staring. I had expected her to want to stop this – she had never thought it was a good idea – but in this moment, she simply watched the scene unfold without any emotion.

'Peter.' My brain finally worked and let me say his name, quietly at first, then louder. 'Peter!'

My voice had an effect. He let go of Richter, who fell to the floor in a heap, breathing loudly, holding onto his own neck, where red marks had already appeared.

'Don't do it.' I went to him. He stood staring at Richter.

'Peter.' I tried again. 'Look at me.'

He obliged and I could see the confusion in his face – he was questioning what he had been about to do, he was wondering what he was capable of. I didn't want that for my son.

'It won't change anything,' I said gently. 'We agreed. Let's leave him here. Leave it now.'

'Peter, please. Please stop. He means nothing. He is nothing. Leave it now. Please,' Sara begged him.

I saw his eyes flick to Sara as she spoke, then to me, then to the heap on the floor that was his father.

Sara took his hand, and he looked at their two hands, fingers intertwined. I knew what was going through his mind. I knew he was thinking about his life now, his future.

'I could have you arrested!' Richter had managed to sit up, still holding his neck. His voice was raspy.

'Try it,' Peter said. He stepped away from Richter, still holding Sara's hand. It was time for us to leave.

'So that's it?' Richter was still blustering. 'You can't go through with it? Weak. All of you are weak. And you, Peter, are a disappointment! You're not my son. You have no backbone! No balls!'

Peter, thankfully, did not react. I hoped he could see now how pathetic Richter was. He could shout and scream and mock us, but it meant nothing.

Peter and Sara went to the front door.

'Anna, Irena.' Peter looked at us.

'You all go,' I told them. 'I want just a minute on my own with him.'

'I don't think that's a good idea, Irena,' Sara said.

'Please. One minute. Just one.'

Anna stood and gave me a slight nod. I wasn't going to do what she thought I was. To be honest, I wasn't sure what I was going to do. I just knew that the end of this had to be me and Richter.

The two of us for the last time.

Once the others had left, I sat back down on the tattered green armchair that I had occupied just a few minutes before.

'Why don't you get up off the floor and take a seat?'

Richter watched the door, I suspect expecting that Peter might burst back in.

He had to get on all fours in order to push himself up to standing and, as he took the few steps to the chair opposite me, I saw that his legs were shaking.

He sat and stared at me.

'Do you remember what you said to me the day that you took Peter away?'

'What is this with you all and trying to remember everything?' he croaked. 'I can't remember.'

I stood, went to his kitchen, found a glass and turned on the tap. I took the glass of water to him and saw that he hesitated, confused at my kindness, before taking it from me. He eventually took it, and eyed me as he drank.

I sat again. 'Do you? Do you remember?' I asked him again.

'I don't know what you're talking about.'

'Then let me remind you. You told me that you weren't going to kill me that day, not even physically hurt me. You told me that you knew what would cause me pain and fear. And you said that you wanted me to know that you could find me at any time you liked. I want you, now, to know the same.'

Richter had the audacity to smile, and that red-hot rage began to burn again inside me.

'My little sparrow has finally learned something. I knew I could change you. I knew you wanted to be like me. So weak you were. *Yes, sir, no sir!* Always doing as you were told!'

I stood and walked towards him. As before, I bent down so that my face was inches from his. 'You taught me one thing. I'll give you that. You taught me how to be strong. How to be patient. Because, *Sir*, I will get what I want. It will happen. But when you least expect it. You can live with that now. You can know that I can find you and I will.' I spat at him.

As I backed away from him, I saw the fear in his eyes. Richter was afraid of death. Everyone was, and for him to think that he was invincible, or somehow immune to pain or fear – well, it had finally dawned on him that that was no longer the case. He didn't want to die. Just like the rest of us.

'You don't mean it,' he stuttered. 'I mean. Irena, we had some good times, didn't we?'

He had changed tack, and I liked it. His fear was palpable.

'Look, I have money,' he tried next. 'How about I give you some and we just go our own ways. You've said your piece. It's all in the past now. Like you said to Peter, I'm not worth it, it won't change anything.'

I picked up my handbag and walked to the door. All the while Richter repeated back to me various arguments for why he deserved to live.

'It won't change anything, Irena, it will make you like me!'

Another step to the door.

'You wouldn't do it. You couldn't!'

Another step. My hand was on the doorknob.

'I'll just disappear again! Ha! You won't find me!'

I turned the knob, letting the warm air of the evening seep into the room.

'I was just doing my job! How can you condemn me for that?'

I stepped out, closing the door behind me as I heard his last plea.

'Irena! Don't be like me...'

THIRTY-NINE

IRENA

Pinamar, Buenos Aires, Argentina
8 January 1994

Peter's house, whilst a ramshackle affair, felt safe and warm after we returned from Richter's.

I sank gratefully into his cream couch, noting the odd stain here and there. Normally, it would bug me seeing a stain, dust and dirt, but his house told a story of his life. I found myself asking him random questions about each thing that my eyes rested on.

'This stain?' I pointed to an orange mark on the armrest.

'Spaghetti mishap,' he told me. I noticed that he raised his eyebrows at Sara and Anna as I asked questions. I was acting odd. I knew I was, but I couldn't help it.

'It's the adrenaline.' Sara handed me a glass of red wine. 'It will calm your nerves.'

'I'm not nervous,' I said. Then I saw my hands shake as I took the glass from her.

Anna sat next to me, Sara and Peter opposite. Sara was in the armchair, a pretty pink colour that I was sure was her doing, and he sat on a woven bamboo chair that I quite wanted for myself.

Anna wedged herself close to me, and all of them let me babble on for a while.

'I'm talking rubbish, aren't I?' I asked.

'You're in shock, I think,' Anna said.

I nodded. That made sense.

'Shall we talk about what happened?' Sara tentatively asked.

'Maybe tomorrow,' Peter answered.

'No. No, we should,' I said. 'Sara's right. We should talk about it.'

But no one spoke for a while. What could we say?

It was Anna to the rescue as usual. 'What did you say to him when we went outside? When you got in the car to leave, you just stared out of the window. I asked you, but you wouldn't say.'

'I wouldn't?' I couldn't really remember getting in the car. I couldn't remember looking out of the window. Shock. Yes, shock and adrenaline. I drank the wine back in one go and handed the glass to Sara for a refill.

'No. So, what did you tell him?' Anna asked.

'I just told him he couldn't hurt me any more. I just told him that I wasn't scared of him.'

'That's it?' Sara handed me back a full glass.

I drank two mouthfuls and let the warmth of the alcohol numb my brain.

'I don't believe you,' Anna said.

'It doesn't matter what I said,' I told them all. 'They were just words. They don't mean anything, really. I just wanted to scare him a little bit.'

'How? What did you say?' Anna was persistent.

I glanced at Anna, my friend, my dear friend. 'Anna, it was between me and him. It honestly doesn't matter any more. Besides, why were you so quiet when Peter had hold of him?'

Anna gave a wry smile. 'I never thought I wanted it to happen, you know. But then the things he said, the way he was. It was like being back in the past again. Sorry, Peter' – she looked at him. 'I'm glad now that you didn't go through with it. Really I am. But in that moment – I don't know. I just froze and sort of wanted it to happen. Does that make me a bad person?'

'Not at all,' Sara replied. 'I have to admit, even though I stopped you, Peter, there was a feeling that it was inevitable – that he had to die. I don't know – it was all a bit confusing.'

'Peter? Are you all right?' I looked at my son, who was staring into his empty glass.

'You're not a bad person, Anna,' he said quietly. 'None of you. Me, on the other hand – I'm not so sure.'

'Oh Peter!' Sara reached her hand out and he took it. An anchor for him.

'In that moment, I really thought I could do it. I thought about what he had done to you, Irena, to you, Anna, to the others. I thought about what he had done to me. And I thought about you, Sara. About our baby, and the thought of him, living, walking about, having a life, I don't know – it just...'

'Broke you,' I said.

'Yes, I think so. It broke me.'

'But you didn't really break, Peter. You listened to reason. Your reaction was normal. You're not a bad person. You just wanted to protect us all, and yourself,' I told him.

He nodded slowly, and although he was listening, I knew it would take some time for him to believe the words. I knew his thoughts, because I was having the same ones. I was questioning my decisions, what I'd said, what I had wanted to do. It would take me time, too, to process everything that had happened and come to a place of peace about it all.

'You know what I wish?' Anna sighed. She had flopped

back into the couch and placed her still sunburnt, swollen feet on the coffee table. 'I wish that Mateusz were here now. He would know how to cheer us up. He'd know the right thing to say, wouldn't he, Irena?'

I knew what she was doing. She knew I couldn't resist thinking about Mateusz. She knew how much joy he had given me in my life.

'He would,' I agreed. 'He was very good at making people happy. He could see if you were sad before he'd even spoken to you and then he would make it his priority to make you happy again. I honestly don't think that I ever saw him sad one day in his life.'

I could feel a smile tug at my lips as I spoke of him.

'I wish I could have met him,' Peter said softly.

'You would have liked him. He would have liked you too. Especially the fishing. He liked to fish. I was rubbish at it – couldn't get the fish off the hook, and I'd always throw it back. I couldn't kill it. That's what's funny, isn't it? I couldn't kill a fish and yet all these years I'd had it in my mind that I could kill Richter. Silly, isn't it?'

'I don't think it's silly at all,' Sara said. 'It makes sense. The fish hadn't done anything to you. It was innocent. You were the hunter, it the prey. With Richter, he was the hunter and you were his prey.'

'I suppose,' I said.

'But Mateusz,' Anna steered the conversation. 'He helped me a lot after my husband, Alec, died. Remember Irena, how he would come round with you each day and when I said I wouldn't get out of bed, he got all those cakes and chocolates and he made that trail from the bedroom to the sitting room? Like Hansel and Gretel? It was so silly, so funny, that it made me get out of bed!'

I saw Peter and Sara relax as Anna spoke, their hands still holding each other's, tired smiles on their faces. Mateusz, even though he was gone, was still working his magic, still making people happy again.

'When did you marry, Irena?' Sara asked.

'Oh goodness, when was it? 1946 or 1947 I think. I honestly can't remember.'

'But you remember that day he came back, don't you?' Anna said. 'I do. I mean I know *you* do. It was like that weight you'd been carrying lifted off you in an instant.'

'I remember,' I said.

'Tell us. Tell them,' Anna said. 'Cheer us up. Give us something else to talk about.'

I nodded my agreement and thought for a moment. I remembered the day Mateusz came back as clearly as if it were yesterday. There was nothing fragmented about this memory.

It was one I cherished.

FORTY

IRENA

Zakopane, Poland
February 1946

The skies had opened and sent down freezing rain, turning the once-pristine snow into a grey slush.

I sat by the window, watching the sheets of water fall. My mind was quiet for once. I let it concentrate on the rain, thinking about how cold it would feel as it touched skin, how those who were caught out in it now would soon hurry home and warm themselves by the fire. Outside, a whole world was still turning – time was moving, and yet I had stopped.

I reached out and placed my hand against the glass, feeling the cold against my palm. I didn't know why I did it. To be honest, I didn't know why I did a lot of things these days.

Three years. It had been three years now. *No. Don't think about it. Don't try and imagine what he's like now, a three-year-old, tottering about on chubby legs, his hands reaching up for a cuddle. Don't think about it. You can't think about it,* I told myself.

'Irena.' My father stood behind me. I felt his hand on my shoulder. It was warm. 'Irena,' he said again.

I knew he wanted me to come away from the window. He wanted me to sit with him and my mother by the fire, to talk, to eat, to be normal. I knew he wanted that not just for me, but for him too, but I couldn't give it to him. How could I be normal? What even was normal? I wondered.

'Irena,' he persisted.

I sighed and turned away from the deluge outside and faced him. He smiled at me, a smile that used to bring me comfort, but now I saw it was tinged with sadness and regret.

He went to his chair and sat by the fire. My mother joined him and sat on the sofa. She patted the cushions as if I were a small child and needed to be told where to sit.

Oddly, I did need to be told. I had relied on her and my father to try to show me how to live again, and to their credit, they had not once wavered in their support of me. They had never shouted or berated me after what I had done to them. They had every right to, because I, their only child, had allowed them to think that I had died. I had let them grieve, cry and miss me and I had never said I was sorry, and they had never asked for an apology.

I think that the day that Anna brought me home, she had already explained everything to them, and perhaps they had had it in their minds to give me a piece of theirs; but when they saw me, this living-dead thing, they put it aside and took care of me.

I had been dead. Really, I had. I was sure of it. That first year, I certainly was. I didn't leave my bed unless my mother made me bathe. And even then, most of the time my father had to carry me to the bathroom whilst I sobbed. Sob at being touched, at being moved, at the effort to simply bathe. It was too much. I wanted them to leave me in the bed, sobbing, not eating, not drinking. I wanted them to leave me so my body could die, because I knew my mind was dead. That was what it felt like.

They never gave up. My mother slept by my side. Between her and Anna, they sat me up in bed and force-fed me broth. They even spoke to Bartok, and he cooked me elaborate meals and would sit next to my bed and tell me jokes. I never laughed. I never really noted that he was there. But he never gave up either. Joke after joke, hoping that one would seep through.

My father read to me. Sometimes from the Bible, perhaps hoping it would provide some form of comfort. But I was sure that those words were not meant for me. I mean, why would they be? I was dead already.

I don't know when or how things changed. Perhaps it was the medication that they made me take, perhaps it was simply time moving on. But during the second year, I was able to go to the bathroom myself. I slept less. I began to dress myself.

My moods were still odd, though. I would talk of strange things, things that didn't matter. I wouldn't talk about what happened. I couldn't put it into words, and I didn't want to. It was like it had been with Richter – saying it out loud was too painful, so I simply didn't.

I wouldn't leave the house. Not ever. I wouldn't even go into the cellar when planes flew low and when air raid sirens screeched in the air. I didn't care about what was happening out in the world. I knew it was full of pain and loss, and I knew that I couldn't cope with hearing about it, seeing it, living it.

Even when the war ended, I still did not leave the house. There were parades, parties; people were finally free. But I could not take part in their joy. I could not feel that again, I was sure of it.

At Christmas, Anna bought me a puppy. I didn't want it, I told her I didn't, but she left it in my bedroom and closed the door.

I ignored this tiny white and brown puppy for as long as I

could. I let my parents feed it, fuss it, and whenever it whined, I would put my hands over my ears like a child.

One day, however, my parents had both left the house, which was unusual. Either one or both of them were with me every day, and they hadn't told me that they were going out.

I sat in the sitting room, unsure of what to do without them. They had to tell me when to eat still, or if I needed to bathe or change my clothes. I still needed that.

The puppy, who my father had named Igor, chewed at the edge of a rug. His bum was in the air as he pulled at the tassels. Each time a tassel escaped him, he would yap at it as if telling it off, and then start the process of attacking it all over again.

I watched him for a while, and felt the anxiety of being alone, adrift, begin to ebb. I sat on the floor next to him and saw him look at me with curiosity. I hadn't bothered with him so far, so he was unsure of me.

I flicked one of the tassels on the rug. He saw it and pounced on it. I did it again and again. He was so wound up that he jumped on me and licked my face. I pushed him away, but he wasn't going to give up. The third time he licked me, I felt myself smile. I couldn't help it.

Igor soon tired and wanted to sleep. He curled up in my arms, and I held him close. I wept as I held him. I knew why, but I didn't want to put thoughts or words to the feeling. I just held him, and something, something small shifted.

Now, sitting on the sofa next to my mother, Igor on my lap, kicking his tiny legs in his dog dreams, I felt a little more at ease. My father had been right to make me move away from the window. He knew that sitting there, I would get fixated on staring and being quiet, and would withdraw a little each time I sat there. I needed to be part of the family, of life, again, and he knew how to do it.

'You know, that puppy will soon be a dog. He's growing up and will soon need walking,' my mother said. 'You can take him out on a lead for a walk soon – wouldn't that be nice?'

I hadn't been outside in three years, and the sudden thought of being out, amongst the world, the noise, the people, sent my heart racing.

'But only when you're ready,' my father added. 'You'll know when you are.'

I stroked Igor's pink belly until my heartbeat quietened. In his sleep, he licked my hand as if he knew I was always there – he was always thinking of me, even in sleep.

I smiled, then felt eyes on me. I looked to my parents and saw them smiling at me. They had seen my smile. They thought I was almost better.

There was a knock at the door that woke Igor. He launched himself from my lap and waddled off, yapping at the noise.

My father groaned as he stood up, already annoyed by the puppy's yapping, and picked him up before going to open the door.

I heard a male voice, not my father's, and assumed it was Bartok. He was now bringing food for Igor and not me, and I was sure that he was overfeeding him, but it brought me a sliver of happiness to see how happy Igor made others too.

'Nina.' I heard the voice. It was close. I knew that, if I turned my head, Mateusz would be there.

'I can't believe it!' he said, then he stood in front of me.

I stared at him and tried to smile. Tried to be polite; but I knew it was forced. I saw his own smile falter, and he glanced at my parents and then back at me.

As he did, I tried to remind myself that I had once liked Mateusz. That we had shared a kiss on a wintry mountain. That I had daydreamed about him. But there was no feeling now. Nothing. But then, I didn't feel much for anyone or anything.

Perhaps Igor came closest to getting any form of emotion from me.

'You look well,' I said. He didn't look well. Not at all. He had lost weight and already had grey streaks through his hair. There were wrinkles under his blue eyes too. He looked older and tired.

He sat across from me and rested his arms on his legs, his hands placed together as if in prayer. Maybe he was praying for me? I wondered. Another random thought. More evidence that my mind was still not right.

'You do too. I mean, I thought, I heard...'

'You thought I was dead,' I finished for him.

He nodded. 'I went to your funeral!' Then he forced out a laugh. My parents joined in. It was as though no one knew how to address the whole mess. Make a joke of it? Get angry about it? Or somewhere in between, where it felt a bit awkward.

'You have a dog,' he noted.

My father handed me Igor, and I held him up so he wriggled. Mateusz's face broke into a wide smile that crinkled up the corner of his eyes. I couldn't help but mirror it.

'He's still a puppy,' I said, drawing him to me. 'He's still learning things.'

'Yes, he's learning to chew my slippers,' my father harumphed and plonked down in his armchair.

'And my heels,' my mother added. 'Are you back here now?' she asked Mateusz in her usual direct way. 'Or are you going back to Kraków? Where have you been – I mean, we thought we wouldn't see you again. And Henryk, how is he?'

Mateusz looked to my father, who duly saved him from what would no doubt be a barrage of questions.

'Mateusz is staying here for a while, aren't you?' he said.

'Here? As in our house?' my mother asked. 'No one said anything to me. Why didn't you say something?' She directed this at my father.

'I didn't say anything because it was only decided yesterday. I saw Mateusz in town, and we spoke and he was looking for somewhere to stay and I said we had a spare room.'

My mother opened her mouth to say more, but I saw my father widen his eyes at her – she should stay quiet for now.

Mateusz was going to stay *here*. I repeated that in my mind. How odd. How odd life is, I mused, how it was obvious that Mateusz knew more about what had happened to me than he was letting on. How my father obviously thought that this could be my next step into becoming myself again.

'I hope that's all right with you?' he asked me.

'I don't mind. I mean. I'm in the house a lot. I don't go out much.'

'You don't?'

'Not for a while.'

He nodded. 'It will be spring soon, though. Flowers poking their heads up, no more snow, no more cold and grey. It might be nice to see it?'

'It might,' I said.

'Look now, it's stopped raining.' He pointed at the window, where the sun was peeking out from behind a cloud.

'It's still cold out, though,' I said.

'Maybe. I don't mind the cold much. How about you and I go for a walk, just a little one? Show Igor where he lives?'

'One day,' I said. 'Maybe.'

He nodded again and rubbed at his face, then he clicked his fingers. 'I tell you what. Take a walk with me now. Let's just walk a little. We don't have to talk, unless you want to. And if you do that with me, if you would keep me company for a little while, then we'll stop at the chocolate shop. I know it's expensive still, but we'll stop. Have one chocolate each. How's that for a deal?'

I wanted to tell him that chocolate would not tempt me out of the house. I wanted to tell him about why I felt this way, but I didn't. I didn't know why, but when he held out his hand to me to take, I took it.

I let him help me into my coat, I let him lead me outside. I let him hold my hand as we walked.

He was like magic, how he made me feel as we walked, how he made everything seem somehow better. He joked with me, he let me be silent when I needed it. After just a short walk, I felt safer. I felt like I had when I had given in to Igor and his puppy ways; like something had opened up.

It was as if I wasn't dead any more. As if slowly, oh so very slowly, Mateusz was bringing me back to life.

FORTY-ONE

SARA

Pinamar, Buenos Aires, Argentina
15 January 1994

Sara sat on the love seat, wrapped in a thick woollen blanket, watching the waves crash noisily onto each other. She could hear Anna bashing about inside, telling Peter that he needed to fix up the place for the baby, clearing away stacks of books, tidying, polishing surfaces.

The last week they had been here, they had spent a lot of time together, Irena telling her stories from the past, her more pleasant memories of her life with Mateusz, and Anna cleaning, always cleaning!

She didn't want Irena to leave. She had grown close to her, even in such a short time, perhaps looking to her to be the mother that she did not have.

'I am sorry.' Irena suddenly appeared. 'She is loud. She won't stop until she has made sure Peter knows what he needs to do!'

'Come sit with me a while.' Sara patted the seat and Irena sat.

'It's a lovely view, I'll give him that,' Irena said. 'But it might not be suitable for a baby. Although. Who am I to say what's suitable?' She gave a self-deprecating laugh.

Sara placed her hand over the old woman's. 'You have every right to say. You did what you needed to do to keep your baby safe. I'm not sure I could ever be as brave as that.'

'You can. You will. As soon as you see the baby, you'll just know you will be able to be brave for them.'

'I hope so,' Sara said.

Irena sat quietly as if knowing that Sara had more to say. But she did not say what was on her mind; instead, she said, 'I liked hearing about you and Mateusz. How he came back and brought you back to life again.'

'He did. He was a good man.'

'You miss him.'

'Every day. The way he was with me after everything I had been through, that's just one small example of who he was. How he was magical in his own way. No one else could have got me out of that house. But he did. I don't know why, or how. I mean, I had no proper control of my mind back then. It was all a muddle. But he made it better.'

'Did he know? I mean, did he know about Richter and the baby?'

'He did. Yes. He had no idea what I felt about it all, though. Mainly because I didn't let myself think about it too much. It was too hard. But, I think, when I found out, or at least when I was told that Peter had died as a child, it changed me a little. I started to think about revenge. I started to plan a little. I think he knew there was something wrong – I never told him, kept it all a secret. In a way, I think I was like Peter. He told me that he never wanted to tell you things because he was scared how you would look at him, if it would change what you felt for him. I felt that way too.'

'You're more alike than you know,' she said. 'I'm glad there are no secrets any more, though.'

She waited for Irena to agree but saw that the woman was still looking out at the ocean.

'Secrets aren't good,' she continued. 'I mean, you have to be honest, don't you, about the way you feel and what you think, especially with your partner?'

'Something else is the matter, isn't it?' Irena asked.

'Not really. Just a lot on my mind.'

'About what happened with Richter? Don't give him another thought. You were right to stop Peter. You were right what you said. That there is wrong or right, no matter what others argue.'

'You stopped him,' Sara said. 'I tried to, but he wouldn't listen. He listened to you.'

The old woman nodded slightly. 'Yes, he did. But I didn't stop him right away. I think I wanted him to do it. I don't know. But you. You tried to stop him from the start. You saw what was about to happen, and you saw that it wasn't right.'

'But doesn't it bother you, knowing that he will get away with it all? That he will just keep on living?'

'It does. But not like it did before. Now I have something else to look forward to in my future. Richter – all of that is the past. I can't change it. Doing something to him wouldn't have changed it.'

'I suppose you're right,' Sara said.

'But I sense that you are not so sure?' Irena asked quietly.

'I just am not sure about a lot of things now. I don't know whether I told you, or Peter did – I mean we've talked so much about everything, but I can't remember whether I told you about my mother. About who she was, what she did.'

'You did. You told me.'

Sara turned her whole body to face Irena. 'I've been wondering if all these years I was wrong. I always thought that it was black and white. But my father, he would talk about a grey area. A moral grey area. And I never agreed with him. But after what happened, what I know – I can't help but think that maybe he and my mother were right. And maybe I take after them, after all.'

Irena shook her head. 'You are not your parents. You are *you*. Sometimes, you might be a little like them, sometimes not at all. Look at Peter. He is nothing like the man his father is. You decide who you are and what you want. You just have to ask yourself what that thing is.'

'I just don't know any more,' Sara admitted. She had not even been able to admit this to herself. But she could to Irena. She could be honest with her, open with her. 'I'm Jewish, just like my mother. I didn't know all these years, and really, finding that out shouldn't change things, but it does. It's changed what I think.'

Irena let out a heavy sigh. 'There were so many friends, families that simply disappeared back then. I am not Jewish, but I feel that pain that you must feel too. To know that your family was taken, killed in such unthinkable ways must be a burden for you to bear.'

'And bear it I must,' Sara said.

'You must, I'm afraid. There are things you can do, I am sure. Legal things. All sorts of clever things to make sure that this never happens again. But in the meantime, you have to look to the future, to your life with Peter and your child. Don't be like me, harbouring ideas of revenge for your whole life. It didn't do me any good.'

'Well, it brought you here. To us. To Peter.'

Irena looked into the house, where the argument between Anna and Peter was reaching fever pitch.

'I should go in and break that up,' she said. 'She'll win. She always does, and I don't want her and Peter to fall out over how you clean a toilet!'

Sara nodded and let Irena go back inside.

As she sat, watching the waves, she thought of what Irena had said. And of course she was right. There was right. There was wrong. There was no grey area. She had to come to terms with that.

'You don't think Peter will do something?'

Sara turned to see that Irena had not gone back inside, but was staring at the same waves, watching them break.

'I don't think so,' Sara said.

'It would change him. Doing that. I don't want that for him.'

'I don't think he will,' Sara repeated.

'But if he says something, if you think that he might be thinking of it, you'll telephone me right away, won't you?' Irena came to her side and took her hand. 'Promise me you'll tell me?'

'I will. But Irena, there's nothing to worry about. I'm sure he won't. And even if he did say something to me, or even to you, there's not much either of us could do about it. You saw how angry he was. You saw how it affected him. I really don't think he would do anything, but I also know that I wouldn't be able to stop him if he really wanted to.'

'Maybe not you. But between the pair of us, we could.' Irena gripped her hand tightly. 'I won't let him down again. I won't let Richter win. You must understand that.'

'I do – but what is it you're trying to say exactly?' Sara asked.

'I think you know.'

A moment of silence fell over them. They stared at each other, and Sara knew what she meant. Irena wanted to protect her son, and there was one way in which she could do it.

'I will let you know,' Sara promised. 'I don't want that for him either.'

FORTY-TWO

CHRISTOPH RICHTER

Pinamar, Buenos Aires, Argentina
July 1994

Each year Christoph Richter had received a letter. And each time it said exactly the same thing – *you are going to die.*

He knew he had received the last of the letters now. One last one, from his own son. And yet, Peter had not had it in him to do what he said he would do. And Irena had not done it either. How lucky was he? He even found himself whistling a tune – he was fine. He would always be fine.

He dressed and gave his face a cursory swipe with his almost blunt razor so that it left red tracks on his skin, and left his home to go to Hotel Pinamar, to sit under the shade of an umbrella and talk to one of his oldest friends for an hour.

As he walked under the shade of the jacaranda trees, he thought of all that had happened – Irena, Anna, Peter, Sara all sitting around, all waiting for him to apologise. But what did he have to apologise for exactly? Nothing. He had done his job. He had done what was needed.

As he walked, he did not really notice the woman across the

street. He saw her, but she meant nothing to him. Even when she crossed the street towards him, she still meant nothing.

He stood at the kerb, ready to cross the road himself, but as he stepped off, a car approached, going a tad too fast. It would slow down. He knew it would. But still, he didn't risk it. He'd wait for the car to go past or slow down. He wasn't stupid.

But, in the next second, he felt a push from behind. He tried to turn to see who had pushed him, but it was too late. There was no time.

The car was still coming and now he was flailing in the air towards it.

The woman. It was the woman. That was what went through his mind. But it couldn't be – could it?

The car did not slow; perhaps the driver never saw him. But he saw her. A woman wearing sunglasses. Two women.

That was the last thing he saw before the car hit him, sending him over the bonnet, the roof, rolling back onto the road in a heap.

The car sped off.

The woman from the street had disappeared.

He lay there waiting for someone, for a siren of an ambulance, but in the back of his mind, he knew it was too late. He could taste metal in his mouth; he felt no pain. And he knew that if there was no pain, then it was almost over.

Suddenly, he heard the cry of a child. They had seen him and were scared. The cry unlocked something in his mind – that memory. That damned memory. Was this really the last thing he was going to think of? he thought.

'Please let them go!' The woman's voice was back. *Irena.* Her voice in the past, not in the now. But it felt as though he was hearing her. She screamed and cried, then fell to her knees in the snow in front of him.

His feet were cold, and he could feel the sting of the air on his cheeks. *But that couldn't be,* he tried to tell himself. He was not in the snow. He was not in the past. But the woman, Irena, was still screaming. There was Peter in his arms, crying. He could smell the freshness that snowfall brings, he could hear the car's engine in the background, ticking over, waiting for him and his son.

Another memory came, jumbled up with Irena. Berlin. A woman on the street. He'd told her she was going to die. He'd killed the child, then killed her. He'd wanted her to see the child die, he remembered that now.

The two memories merged and separated, and he could feel himself falling.

The woman crying.

His child in his arms.

You are going to die.

This time he heard the words. Someone was above him. Someone had leaned down. Someone whispered it into his ear, just as his eyes began to close on the quiet street.

You are going to die.

And he did.

FORTY-THREE

IRENA

Zakopane, Poland
4 January 1995

The snow had come quickly overnight. I woke to see a clear blue sky, trees bowed by the weight of their now-white iced tips, and tiny snowflake-patterned ice on the insides of the windows.

I hoped that the snow would not stop them from coming. I had thought of nothing else for the past few months – my son, his fiancée and my baby granddaughter. It had filled me up once more with a kind of joy and love that I had never thought possible. The days of revenge, of hatred, of fear were now far behind me. I was free from it all.

I pottered about all morning, cooking *bigos*, which I was sure that they would love. I was relying on Anna to bake the bread and bring it over later. I brought in more dry logs and ensured that all the fires were roaring away. I couldn't have the baby being cold.

Every half an hour or so I would go to the window to check to see if their taxi had pulled up and, upon not seeing it, would find something else to dust, to clean.

As I did, I recalled that homely, lived-in feeling of Peter's small house. How the stains on the couch had in a way shown me his life. I looked about me, to my own pristine house, where everything was in order, everything had a place, and realised I was looking forward to them settling in, making a mess, leaving a stain or two for me to look at when they were gone back to Argentina, so I could feel as though they were still here with me.

By 3 p.m., I was in a bit of a tizzy. They should have been here by now, and I had worked myself up to the point that I was sure that they would not arrive. Their flight had been cancelled or diverted. Something wasn't right.

When I finally heard the splutter of a car engine outside the house, I almost wept with relief. They were here, my family were here!

I opened the door and went outside to greet them.

'Matka!' Peter said, holding me close and kissing my cheek. *Matka*, Mother, that was my name now. 'Go inside. I'll get the bags and bring them in. Go and see your granddaughter.' He grinned.

I didn't need to be told twice. I hurried Sara in, and the bundle that was in her arms, which was mewing for a feed.

'Was she good, on the plane?' I asked, helping Sara off with her coat. 'Did it scare her?'

'She was fine, Irena.' She kissed my cheek and sat in the armchair next to the fire, unravelling the baby from her blankets and showing me the two cream knitted mittens on her tiny hands.

I picked up my granddaughter, her blue eyes under those thick lashes watching me closely – this stranger. I kissed her, then held her close. At five months old, she was already alert, and placed a mittened hand on my face, her fingers wanting to explore all these wrinkles.

'I'm your grandmother,' I told her. 'And you're named after

me, little Nina!' I made my voice high-pitched when I said her name and it drew out a gummy smile. I said it again and again and soon had her laughing.

That sound, a baby's laugh! It was the most beautiful thing I think I had ever heard. Nothing came close to it – no composer in the world could evoke the feeling you get when you hear a baby laugh.

Before long, Nina decided that she would like to nap. I loved how she was the boss of the adults in the room, all of us bowing and scraping to make sure she was happy. It reminded me of Abel and our chess game, when he had said that I was the queen protecting my king. I still thought, in a way, I was the queen, and my granddaughter was now clearly the king, the ruler of us all. And that was exactly the way it should be.

Sara, Peter and I sat in the sitting room, drinking hot, sweet tea, and I promised them that dinner would not be long. Both of them yawned every few minutes, and I knew that the long journey meant that they all needed an early night. But perhaps they, like me, did not want to give in to it and would rather stay awake and be together.

'Anna is bringing the bread,' I told them. 'She makes the best bread. Don't ask her for the recipe, though, she won't tell you.'

'I think I'll have to stay away from the bread,' Sara said. 'Still have some baby weight to lose.' She patted her belly.

'You look so lovely,' I said. 'You were so worried about the baby weight last time I saw you, but it's just fallen off you. Not a thing to you any more!'

Sara shot me a look, and I realised what I had almost said. *Almost.*

But Peter didn't hear. He had gone to the hallway to root through his suitcase for some gifts he had brought.

It gave me a chance to ask Sara about him. 'How is he now?'

'Better,' she whispered back. 'Much better. After it all. I

mean, you know. He was going crazy I think. He knew what he wanted to do but wouldn't. You know it all. But now. It's better.'

'Calm? At peace?' I whispered.

'Yes.'

'And you?'

'I'm fine.' Sara gave me a tight smile. 'It was the right thing to do.'

'What was the right thing to do?' Peter was back.

'Come here and stay for a month,' I said. 'To visit your old *Matka*!'

He raised his eyebrows but did not question further. 'Do you have a pen?' he asked, waving about a piece of paper in his hand.

'For what?' I asked.

'This.'

He handed me the paper. It was a form to amend his birth certificate – to say who his father and mother were. Under *Father*, it said *Unknown.*

'I want you to sign it,' he said, looking at me hopefully. 'I want you to know that you're my mother, and I am your son.'

I felt a lump in my throat, but I did not cry – I would save those tears for later, when I was alone. I would cherish the tears, for they were ones of happiness.

'Unknown?' I said and pointed at the blank space under *Father*.

'Well, we know. But I don't want his name on there,' Peter said.

'Pens are in the top drawer of the bureau.' I waved my hand absent-mindedly towards it. Then I went to Sara and looked at my granddaughter again. Her chubby little hand reached out to grab my finger, and held it tight.

Before I knew it, I could feel tears on my skin. Silently making their way down my face.

'Do you want to hold her again?' Sara did not even wait for my answer, just handed her to me.

I took her to the window and explained in Polish that it had snowed, and that one day when she was older, we would go outside and play in it. We would build snowmen until our hands were ice-blue, then come inside and sit by the fire. Then I would read her stories – good ones, all of them with a happy ending.

As I looked outside, I saw Anna making her way down the path to the front door, her feet unsteady in the snow.

I opened the door, forgetting that I had such a tiny charge in my arms, and went outside to make sure she did not fall.

'So they are here!' Anna exclaimed; her hands were already outstretched to take the baby.

'Oh! I shouldn't have come out,' I said, turning to go back inside. 'The baby.'

That was when Sara and Peter came out, both of them looking up at the tips of the Tatras, at the snow that hid the chalet roofs.

'It's magical,' Sara whispered, her cheeks already flushed pink.

I could see what she meant. The mountains, the wooden chalets, the pint-sized houses, all draped with clean snow.

'I'll get in with this one,' I said. 'I shouldn't have brought her out.'

'Wait just a minute,' Peter said, holding my arm.

I wasn't sure why he wanted us all to stand there in the cold, but there was a stillness, a calmness about it all as if we were going back in time to rewrite the past.

'I remember a different time when I stood in the snow with a baby in my arms,' I told him.

He gently kissed the top of my head. 'This is a new memory for you. No need to think about that one any more.'

Sara went to Anna to help her inside, and I followed suit. It was then that I heard Peter whisper gently in my ear, 'I saw your passport in the drawer. Two stamps. Argentina.'

I felt my heart stop and wondered what he was going to say or do.

'He deserved it,' he said, and kissed the top of my head again. 'And you *both* did a wonderful job of it.'

As he closed the door, I looked to Sara, who raised her eyebrows in question at me. I shook my head gently. No need for her to know what he had said. No need for her to know that he knew what we had both done last summer. What we, Sara and I, had had to do to save us all and finally put the ghosts of the past to rest.

A LETTER FROM CARLY

Dear reader,

I want to say a huge thank you for choosing to read *The Winter Child*. If you did enjoy it, and want to keep up to date with all my latest releases, just sign up at the following link. Your email address will never be shared and you can unsubscribe at any time.

www.bookouture.com/carly-schabowski

History and fiction, and the balance between the two, has never been a more difficult thing to consider than in writing this book.

The story of Irena, in specifically, is an amalgam of stories from three women I spoke to over twelve years ago when I was researching another book. All of these women had been raped by German soldiers and each had a story to tell. All of them, too, struggled to put their trauma into words, and as one admitted, 'I never think about it, I don't let myself. If I did, I wouldn't get out of bed in the morning.'

It made me wonder how I could recount their stories in a responsible way, and in a way that was realistic. It is through Irena, through her search for the perpetrator, that she is slowly able to relive the past, one that she has locked away for a long time. To relive the event of her child being taken is one she can only fully remember once she has gone through the step-by-step investigation into what led up to this trauma.

I also wanted to bring in the little-known history of what happened in Zakopane during the war. Both the Stamary Hotel and the Palace are real places and what happened in them is true.

Finally, I wanted to investigate the moral 'grey area' concerning retribution. Irena, like others, searched for Nazi guards after the war. Whether some found closure, I do not know. But through Irena, Sara and Peter, the 'grey' area that morality operates in is hopefully shown in an authentic manner, showing the constant battle between what is right and what is wrong.

I hope you loved *The Winter Child* and if you did, I would be very grateful if you could write a review. I'd love to hear what you think, and it makes such a difference helping new readers to discover one of my books for the first time.

I love hearing from my readers – you can get in touch through X.

Thanks,

Carly Schabowski

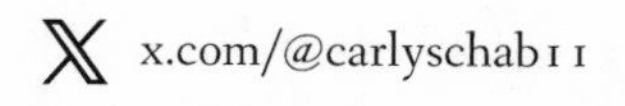

BIBLIOGRAPHY

Crane, Susan A., 'Writing the Individual Back into Collective Memory', The American Historical Review (Oxford University Press on behalf of the American Historical Association), vol. 102, no. 5 (Dec. 1997), pp. 1372–85. http://www.jstor.org/stable/2171068

Goñi, Uki, *The Real Odessa: How Perón Brought the Nazi War Criminals to Argentina* (London: Granta Books, 2022).

The Grand Hotel Stamary: History of the Hotel. https://stamary.pl/en/history-of-the-hotel-page-123823

Holocaust Education & Archive Research Team: 'Bad Rabka and Zakopane – SD Schools: "The Schools for Scoundrels"'. http://www.holocaustresearchproject.org/nazioccupation/sdschool.html

Holocaust Encyclopedia, United States Holocaust Memorial Museum, 'The Search for Perpetrators'. https://encyclopedia.ushmm.org/content/en/article/the-search-for-perpetrators

Holocaust Historical Society: 'Bad Rabka and Zakopane SIPO Schools'. https://www.holocausthistoricalsociety.org.uk/contents/naziseasternempire/badrabkaandzakopanesiposchools.html

Lang, Berel, 'Holocaust Memory and Revenge: The Presence of the Past', *Jewish Social Studies*, vol. 2, no. 2, 1996, pp. 1–20. http://www.jstor.org/stable/4467468.

Robben, A.C.G.M, 'How Traumatized Societies Remember: The Aftermath of Argentina's Dirty War', *Cultural*

Critique (University of Minnesota Press) no. 59 (Winter, 2005), pp. 120–64. http://www.jstor.org/stable/4489199

JewishGen.org, 'The Sipo SD School and Gestapo Interrogation Centre, Zakopane'. https://www.jewishgen.org/yizkor/galicia3/gal026.html

Walters, Guy, *Hunting Evil: How the Nazi War Criminals Escaped and the Hunt to Bring Them to Justice* (London: Transworld, 2010).

The Wiener Holocaust Library, 'Resistance Responses'. https://www.theholocaustexplained.org/resistance-responses-collaboration/non-conformity/refusal-to-salute

ACKNOWLEDGEMENTS

I'd like to say a HUGE thank you to my agent, Jo Bell, who has been so supportive during the writing of this book. I honestly do not think I could do it without her!

I'd also like to thank those people who shared stories with me about their experiences during the war. Although you are no longer with us, it is your story I am writing and hopefully bringing to life.

Lastly, a thank-you to my editor, Jess Whitlum-Cooper, and my friends and family, who continually encourage me and drag me out of my negative thoughts!

PUBLISHING TEAM

Turning a manuscript into a book requires the efforts of many people. The publishing team at Bookouture would like to acknowledge everyone who contributed to this publication.

Audio
Alba Proko
Sinead O'Connor
Melissa Tran

Commercial
Lauren Morrissette
Hannah Richmond
Imogen Allport

Cover design
Debbie Clement

Data and analysis
Mark Alder
Mohamed Bussuri

Editorial
Jess Whitlum-Cooper
Imogen Allport

Copyeditor
Jacqui Lewis

Proofreader
Catherine Lenderi

Marketing
Alex Crow
Melanie Price
Occy Carr
Cíara Rosney

Operations and distribution
Marina Valles
Stephanie Straub

Production
Hannah Snetsinger
Mandy Kullar
Jen Shannon

Publicity
Kim Nash
Noelle Holten
Jess Readett
Sarah Hardy

Rights and contracts
Peta Nightingale
Richard King
Saidah Graham

Made in the USA
Coppell, TX
21 May 2024